CONNIE

The Daughters of Allamont Hall
Book 3

A Regency Romance

by Mary Kingswood

Published by Sutors Publishing

ISBN: 978-1-912167-14-2 (revised paperback)

Cover design by: Shayne Rutherford of Darkmoon Graphics

A traditional Regency romance, drawing room rather than bedroom.

Connie's older sisters have managed to find husbands, but now it's her turn and she is not sure she wants to marry at all. Having only just escaped her late father's restrictive regime, she's reluctant to surrender her freedom to another man just yet. If only she could find one who would fall so adoringly in love that he would do anything for her.

The Marquess of Carrbridge has been taken in by ambitious young ladies before, and he's not about to fall for any more trickery to ensnare him. Nor will he be pushed into marriage by his hectoring grandmother. From now on, he's determined to take charge of his future and do things his own way. But not every young lady is dazzled by his title, and sometimes the best of plans may go awry.

The Daughters of Allamont Hall is a series featuring the six unmarried daughters of Mr William and Lady Sara Allamont. Each book is a complete story, but there are also background threads running from book to book as a bonus for series readers.

Book 1: Amy
Book 2: Belle
Book 3: Connie
Book 4: Dulcie
Book 4.5: Mary (a novella, free to mailing list subscribers)
Book 5: Grace
Book 6: Hope

Table of Contents

1: A Ball Is Announced

Connie was the last to step from the coach, shaking out her skirts. The Allamont travelling coach was capacious, but with five young ladies squeezed into it, she was sadly crushed. She stood for a moment, looking up at the front facade of Staynlaw House. It was a handsome building of red stone, modern and well-proportioned, and the interior fitted with every comfort. Not for the Amblesides the inconvenience of narrow stairs or rooms too dark to work in or a kitchen that produced meat half burnt or half raw, depending on which way the wind was blowing. How strange to think that she might have been mistress of it by now instead of her sister, if she had chosen differently.

There was Amy rushing down the steps, arms wide, to embrace her sisters, the ribbons of her cap flying. That was strange, too, to see Amy in her new gown and cap, a married woman, the first of the six daughters of Allamont Hall to enter matrimony.

"Connie, dear!" Amy said, wrapping her in a sisterly embrace, then breaking away to gaze into her face. "How are you? You look a little pale."

"I am perfectly well, I assure you, but we have been having a giddy time of it lately, with so many parties. I daresay I am a little tired. But let us not talk of me! We are here to congratulate the bride on her return. Welcome home, Mrs Ambleside."

Behind her, with his warm smile, stood Mr Ambleside. Connie's heart performed a little somersault at the sight of him. Only a few months ago, she had been quite sure she was desperately in love with him, and he, being an honourable man, had felt obliged to offer for her. She had quickly realised her mistake, and he had returned to Amy, his true love. Connie had no regrets, but in many ways Mr Ambleside remained her ideal of a gentleman — handsome and personable, and with a good independent fortune, which is always an advantage in a man. A little domineering, perhaps, but love tempered that facet of his character. If he had been just a few years younger, and had a title, his array of good qualities would have been complete, and perhaps she would have been tempted to hold on to him.

Amy blushed prettily, and Ambleside came to shake Connie's hand. "Welcome to Staynlaw House, Miss Connie." Then he tucked Amy's arm into his, and the bridal pair led the way into their home.

There were refreshments laid out, for the visitors were expected, but there was far too much news to impart for anyone to have the leisure to eat.

"Belle is betrothed!" Grace burst out, almost before they were properly seated. "She is to marry Mr Burford in the spring."

This news was no surprise. Amy jumped up to hug her sister. "Oh, Belle, I wish you so much joy! May you be as happy as I am."

Ambleside shook Belle's hand warmly, his smile brighter than ever. "Congratulations, Miss Allamont. Burford is a good man, and will take excellent care of you."

Miss Allamont. That was so like Ambleside, always exquisitely correct with titles. Now that Amy was married, Belle was Miss Allamont for a few months, and then it would be Connie's turn for the title, until she herself was married. And when would that be? If only she could be fortunate enough to find another Ambleside.

Belle blushed, but accepted the congratulations calmly. As she took her seat again, Amy glanced across at Hope, then quickly looked away again, but nothing was said. Poor Hope! She had been in love with Mr Burford for an age, and he with her, but then something had happened, although Connie was not very sure what, and now Belle and Mr Burford were quite in love.

"And you will never guess where they are to live," Grace said. "I was never so surprised in my life."

Mr and Mrs Ambleside agreed that they could not guess.

"Willowbye!" Grace burst out. "Cousin Henry is all to pieces, it seems, and so he is to move into the Dower House, and Belle and Mr Burford will rent Willowbye."

"Willowbye!" Amy said. "Surely Cousin Henry will not like to leave his home."

"Indeed he did not want to at all, but now that James is married to Alice Whittle and there is no hope of him bringing home an heiress with a large fortune, there is nothing else to be done. They must economise, or be ruined."

"I am sorry to hear that Mr Allamont finds himself in difficulties with money," Ambleside said. "Sorry, but not surprised. There was always an air of economy about the place, and the house left to fend for itself rather. Renting to Burford is a good solution, Miss Allamont, for then you will not be so far away from us."

"So now you know our news, you may tell us all about your tour of the lake country," Connie said. "Was it beautiful?"

"It was excessively wet," Ambleside said indignantly. "Wetter than any self-respecting place ought to be. I see now why there are so many lakes there, for it never stops raining. Next time my wife and I travel for pleasure, we will go south, I swear it. Brighton is civilised, so everyone says. We shall promenade beside the sea, and ogle the monstrous Pavilion, and perhaps, if we are extremely lucky, we may catch a glimpse of the royal personage."

"Next time we will travel in the summer," Amy said with an affectionate smile. "I cannot imagine what we were thinking to be going anywhere at this time of year. We were lucky not to be snowed up for the whole month. But come, sisters, let me show you the morning room, for Mr Ambleside arranged for it to be redone while we were away, as a surprise."

"Amy will want a pleasant room to sit in while she sews, and it was a little dark before," Ambleside said, walking down the hall ahead of them and throwing open the door. "There! Is that not a very pretty room now? The new sofas came from Bristol and the wallpaper from London. The writing desk was made by a man I found in Brinchester. The rug is the original, however, for there is plenty of wear in it yet."

They all admired the new fittings, although Connie thought the wallpaper too heavily decorated for a lady's room. Then there was some new china, a wedding gift, to be seen and the spot on the wall where Amy's portrait would hang, once a painter had been engaged. As they wandered from room to room, Connie found Ambleside next to her.

"Have you forgiven me for my ill-treatment of you?" he said, with his heart-stopping smile.

"It is all long-forgotten."

"You were always the most generous of creatures — after my dear wife, of course."

"Of course," she readily agreed. "Amy is so sweet and gentle that she deserves her happiness."

"She *is* happy, I believe," he said eagerly. "She tells me so, and gives every appearance of it."

"Every appearance of it? My dear Ambleside, she is aglow with joy, anyone might see that. Marriage suits her admirably."

He beamed with pleasure. "I am delighted to hear you say so. But what of you? Now that Miss Allamont's future is settled, it is your turn to look for a husband."

She winced. "I know, but I shall take my time in choosing. I must marry, I suppose, to fulfil the terms of Papa's will, but there is no urgency now that..." She stopped, unwilling to mention Hope by name.

Ambleside had no such scruples. "Now that Miss Hope has no suitor waiting, you mean? How has she taken the loss of Burford to Miss Allamont? She seems a little subdued to me, not her usual self."

"She is a little down-hearted, although she tries very hard not to show it."

"I am sorry for it," he said. "Perhaps a change of scene would improve her spirits? I will suggest to Mrs Ambleside that she invite her to stay with us for a while."

"Oh, how kind you are!" Connie said. "But will Amy want to share your attention with a guest just yet?"

He laughed. "My wife is used to being one of six, Miss Connie, and no matter how fond of me she might be, there is no substitute for female companionship."

Before they left Staynlaw House at the end of the morning, a firm arrangement was made for Hope to make a longer stay, if her mama approved.

"Shall you come and see us soon, Amy?" Connie said, as they waited for the coach to be brought round. "The Hall is not the same without you."

"I shall come when I can," she said, "but there is a great deal to be done here, and many people will wish to pay wedding calls. I cannot be gadding about as much as I used to. But we shall meet at dinners a great deal, and at the Assembly Rooms."

"But the next ball is an age away," Hope said. "You have just missed one. Oh, why did you not come home sooner?"

Amy just laughed, but Ambleside said, "The next ball is not so far away, Miss Hope, for we plan to have one here just as soon as it can be managed."

There was no time to elaborate on the idea, but the prospect of a private ball was so delightful that the discussion of it lasted them all the way back to Allamont Hall, and through the evening, and was not exhausted in several days of delightful anticipation.

~~~~~

Despite her protestations, it was not long before Amy visited her sisters to discuss all those small but fascinating details for the ball. The guest list was the first important point of debate.

"We must consider Connie now," Grace said. "We need to have as many eligible gentlemen as may be found. Those two brothers from High Frickham, for instance."

"That is no good," Belle said. "At this time of year, only the local families will be prepared to drive in the evening, and then only if the weather is clear."

"But all our acquaintance in the immediate neighbourhood are elderly or married or infirm," Dulcie said. "Or all three."

"That is not quite true," Grace said. "Mr Ambleside is taken, and Mr Wills is betrothed now, but Sir Osborne Hardy is still available, and what could be better than a baronet of independent fortune?"

Connie pulled a face. "I should not like to share a house with his mother. Lady Hardy is such a tyrant, and Sir Osborne is not quite appealing enough to compensate."

"Well, I do not know who else there is," Grace said. "Only Mr Drummond, who has not two pennies to his name, and Mr George Graham, who is quite wild and not at all the thing. You do not want *him*."

"There is Cousin Mark, although he is still at Oxford," Dulcie said. "And you would inherit the Hall, if you could put up with him. They are none of them very appealing, it is true, and Hugo is too young, but Mark is not so bad as James."

"Do not be in such a rush to find me a husband," Connie said. "I am not at all sure I want to marry anyone just yet. I like being free to do as I please."

"Nonsense," Dulcie said. "You must marry so that the rest of us will get our dowries in turn." Then she giggled. "What about the Marquess of Carrbridge? A title and a fortune! If his features are above passable, *I* would marry *him* at once!"

The others groaned. "He may be the Dowager Countess's great nephew and heir, but he has never in his life been to visit her," Belle said.

"But Amy is intimate with his sister," Grace said, clapping her hands in glee. "Invite Lady Harriet, Amy, and tell her to bring her brother with her."

"Well, I shall do so, but I do not suppose he will come," Amy said. "If he does not come for his great-aunt, he is hardly likely to come for me. However, Harriet may come, and I should dearly like to see her again."

"That is agreed, then," Grace said. "And for the rest, you may invite whomever you please, for they can be of no interest to Connie."

~~~~~

The day of the ball arrived. The sisters and their mother were to stay overnight at Staynlaw House, so they travelled in the morning, the two coaches proceeding in stately convoy over the rutted roads. Grace and Dulcie were in the carriage with Lady Sara, while Connie was in the lumbering old travelling coach with Belle and the maids. Hope was already at Staynlaw House, having been staying there for more than a week.

"This is so exciting!" Dulcie said. "A ball held by our own sister — what could be more perfect? I cannot wait to see the rooms with the doors all thrown wide for dancing. I do hope the musicians arrive in good time."

"I am sure everything will go off splendidly," Belle said. "Ambleside is an excellent organiser."

"When shall you hold your first ball at Willowbye?" Dulcie said. "I long to dance in the great hall, just as people must have done hundreds of years ago."

"You will have to be patient, then, for there is a great deal of work to be done first," Belle said, smiling. "However, no doubt you will get your wish, in time. I do not know how our ancestors danced, but I doubt they performed the cotillion. Those huge skirts would have made it very difficult. We do not appreciate how lucky we are to have a practical style of dress."

"What shall you wear?" Dulcie said. "I did not see what you packed."

"The white silk with the lilac trim."

"Oh, that one. You wore that at the Grahams' last ball. Why do you not wear something new? I am to wear my pink, and Connie has not yet decided."

"I wish I had brought my other gown," Connie said mournfully.

"You have packed two — or is it three — already," Belle said. "Is that not enough to choose from?"

"It is three, but now I think I should like to wear the one with the pretty gauze sleeves, with the gold under-gown."

"I like the one with the green embroidery round the neck and sleeves," Dulcie said. "It suits your complexion, I fancy. Do you not think Connie looks well in the green, Belle?"

"It is no use asking me," Belle said. "You know I have no eye for colour. I always allow Mama and Miss Purdue to decide."

"Shall you have your wedding clothes made by Miss Purdue?" Connie said. "For I do not think she has much eye for colour, either."

"She is an excellent seamstress, and not expensive," Belle said.

"Burford is so rich now you may spend as much as you choose," Connie said. "Really, Belle, you should go to London, then you would have the latest fashions and all the best colours. When I marry, I shall choose a very rich man so that I never have to worry about money."

The rest of the day passed in a froth of anticipation. Connie tried on each of her three ball gowns twice, and Dulcie's once, in case it should suit her better, and even as they descended the stairs for dinner, she fretted that she had made the wrong choice.

They found Amy alone in the drawing room, reading a journal.

"You are astonishingly calm, sister," Dulcie said. "I am sure I should collapse from nerves in your situation."

"She has been so serene, anyone would imagine this to be a regular occasion," Hope said. "The very first ball in your new home — I should be quite terrified! So many things could go wrong."

"Terrified? No, indeed," Amy said. "My dear Mr Ambleside has taken care of everything so that I need not be under any anxiety. He is so good to me."

"Well, that is too bad!" Grace declared. "Are you to have no say the arrangements for your own dinner and ball?"

"I have had a say in everything, of course, but I need not concern myself with the details. Although I confess I am a little concerned about the dining room, for we only have room for twenty four in any comfort, and I have had word today from Harriet that she is to come, and that makes twenty five. It is lucky Mr Wills is away, but even so, we shall be sadly squeezed, I fear."

"Is Lady Harriet to bring her brother?" Dulcie said, clapping her hands with glee. "It will be famous if she does. Think what a compliment it would be to you, Amy."

"I cannot tell you, for she writes so much that I cannot make it out at all. There, can you make anything of it?"

The letter was passed from hand to hand but Lady Harriet had had so much news to impart that she had crossed her lines once, and then crossed them again, rendering most of her message unintelligible.

"Where was this sent from?" Belle said. "Oh, Drummoor, I can just make it out. But look, the letter was not franked, so the Marquess could not have been there."

The sisters groaned in disappointment.

Ambleside came in, and then Lady Sara appeared, and other guests in twos and threes, almost all the principal inhabitants of the neighbourhood. Connie watched them arrive without enthusiasm. There were few single men amongst them, and those few were either too young or too poor to be of interest. She had turned her gaze on Lady Hardy, wondering whether the attractions of a fine house, a title and a large fortune that attached to Sir Osborne would overcome the disadvantage of daily intercourse with his mother, when the door was thrown open one more time. There on the threshold stood the most beautiful man Connie had ever seen. He had the face and figure of a Roman statue, his attire was in the finest of London fashions, his hair elegantly arrayed. He stood on the threshold, as if to be admired, his gaze raking the room. Every conversation died away.

"The most honourable the Marquess of Carrbridge, and the Lady Harriet Marford," the butler intoned, into the silence.

2: Of Dragons And Highwaymen

Connie spent the meal gazing at the Marquess. She had never seen such perfection of form in one man. Since he sat beside Amy and his head was mostly turned in that direction, Connie had ample time to admire his profile, with its aquiline nose and strong chin. He spoke little, and smiled not at all, but that was natural. He must be accustomed to far superior company than anything found in their paltry neighbourhood. She was sure that beneath the stiff veneer he was all amiability, for what could be greater proof of it than his very presence here?

She turned over in her mind all his numerous attractions, quite apart from his face and figure, and his elegance of person and dress. He was very wealthy, that much she knew. She was not sure of his exact income, but it must be larger than Papa's had been, and she felt certain it exceeded even Mr Burford's, and he had five thousand a year now. Then there was the estate at Drummoor. It was reputed to be a fine house — she must look it up in the guide in Papa's book room — although Amy said it was quite old-fashioned. Still, it would be an excellent project, to renovate and restyle the rooms.

Then there was the title. Connie had never dared to aspire to a title but oh, how wonderful to be a marchioness and wear ermine and be *somebody* at court. Even at the assemblies, the best seats were reserved for peeresses. How grand she would be! She would have a little carriage of her own, with the Marquess's crest on the door, and bowl around the roads waving in a dignified manner to everyone curtsying and bowing as she passed by.

She laughed inwardly at such fanciful notions. Such a man was quite out of her reach, she was well aware, and she had too much pride to chase round after a man just because of a title and a fine estate. Still, it was pleasant to imagine what might happen if he were to fall in love with her, and he was, after all, so very, very handsome that she could not help thinking about the possibility just a little.

In such happy dreaming, the meal was over almost before she was aware of it. The ladies withdrew, and as soon as they were in the drawing room, and all the doors closed, a twitter of excited chatter broke out. Lady Sara serenely took a seat, as if unaware of the babble of noise, and the other matrons smiled and shook their heads, settling near the fire. Amy hesitated for an instant, then, with a longing glance at her sisters, demurely sat next to Lady Hardy and Miss Clarissa Hardy. The youngest wife, Cousin James's bride Alice, nervously took a window seat, out of the way, and Belle went to sit beside her.

The rest of the young ladies congregated at the further end of the room in a big circle, plying Lady Harriet with questions about her brother.

"I do not know what is in his head," she said, laughing. "He has never bothered to visit Great-aunt Augusta before. He was not even at Drummoor when I left there three days ago, but he arrived in his curricle a few hours ago as if the Devil were on his tail, and he will tell me nothing, odious boy!"

"You did not mention how handsome he is," Grace said. "Why, he is like a Greek God!"

"Oh, do not say such things, and especially you must not flatter him to his face," Harriet said. "He is quite puffed up enough in his own importance as it is, and struts about like a popinjay. Ever since he came into the title he has been unbearable."

"A marquess is entitled to be a little puffed up, I believe," Connie said. "A peerage, a fine house, a large fortune — yes, he may strut all he pleases, so far as I am concerned." Especially when he looks so wonderful as he struts, she thought with a little smile.

The guests for the ball began to arrive, but as the group broke up, Grace whispered to Connie, "You should try if you cannot catch him, you know. For it would be a fine thing to have a marchioness in the family."

Connie wondered how she was supposed to catch a marquess, for he must be used to the grandest ladies of the *ton* and she was a provincial nobody. Why, she had never even visited London, still less enjoyed a season there. She had not the least notion how to begin, so she decided that she would not even try. She would enjoy his company whenever she had the chance, but in time he would go back to Drummoor, or to London, and she would see him go without regret.

Besides, her little dalliance with Ambleside had taught her to enjoy her freedom. Papa had kept all his daughters on the tightest of reins, with every hour of the day assigned its due activities, and no variance permitted. Why, they were even required to dress alike, with only the colour of a ribbon to distinguish one sister from another, with the result that half their acquaintance could not tell one of them from another. How delightful it was to choose her own style of gown, and fill her days as she wished. She had no desire to relinquish such freedom to a husband, not for a very long time.

But if she could make the Marquess fall violently in love with her — well, that would be a different matter. Adoring husbands were both pliant and amiable, as she had seen with both Ambleside and Burford. Yes, a marquess head over ears in love with her might be able to tempt her into marriage.

Not long after, the gentlemen reappeared, and with the new arrivals, the drawing room began to feel uncomfortably full. Ambleside ordered the doors to the yellow saloon thrown open, and the musicians to prepare their instruments for the ball to begin. The gallery at the back of the house had been cleared of furniture, rugs and other impedimenta, and, together with the yellow saloon at one end and the music room at the other, made a very tolerable ballroom.

The Marquess led Amy out to head the set, and Ambleside claimed Lady Harriet. As other couples joined in, Connie realised she had been so absorbed in watching the Marquess, she had not thought at all about her own partner. She was rescued from the ignominy of being a wallflower at the very first dance by Burford.

"May I have the honour, Miss Connie?"

"Oh — would you not prefer to dance the first with Belle? You may dance with her as much as you like now, you know, and no one would think it forward of you."

He laughed, but said, "I had planned to do so, but my so-called friend, Alex Drummond, got there before me."

"Then I should be delighted to dance with you, Mr Burford."

Burford was pleasant, if undemanding, company. Although he no longer blushed and stammered over every third word, he still said very little, leaving Connie free to talk or remain silent, as she chose. Mostly she talked about whatever was going on around her, but whenever the movement of the dance afforded a glimpse of the Marquess, she lapsed into silence.

Her next partner was Alex Drummond, the schoolmaster living in reduced circumstances with his sister at Lower Brinford. He was a dreadful flirt, and Connie listened to his nonsense with a smile and a few shakes of her head. But after the Marquess had gone down the set with Belle, Drummond leaned forward and said archly, "He is worth looking at, is he not? And not just his person. With a title, and ten thousand a year, one might imagine that a man of such perfection would have every young lady in London setting her cap at him."

"I am sure they do," she retorted. "It is only that no one has caught his eye yet. Oh — ten thousand? Truly?"

"That is what the estate is worth, I understand, but sadly encumbered."

"Encumbered." They moved down the set together, and when they came to rest, she said, "What does that mean, exactly — encumbered?"

"The most common form of encumbrance is heavy debt."

"Oh. Like Cousin Henry, you mean?"

"Exactly so. But the title is *not* encumbered, and a young lady of good fortune may be of the greatest aid to an encumbered peer of the realm."

And he winked at her, with his mischievous grin.

She was forced to dance with Daniel Merton next, Sir Osborne's friend, but then at last the Marquess led her onto the floor.

"You have set us quite a puzzle, Lord Carrbridge," she said, as they waited for the set to form. "Here we have been waiting year after year for you to visit our humble corner of England, only to be repeatedly disappointed. And yet now, here you are! And, delighted as we all are to make your acquaintance at last, we cannot help but wonder what momentous event drew you forth so unexpectedly. For it must have been momentous, of that I am quite convinced. Nothing short of a quaking of the earth, perhaps. Was there a quaking of the earth at Drummoor, my lord?"

"If there was, I failed to notice it," he said gravely.

He did not seem offended by her remarks, so she was encouraged to continue. "Well, perhaps it was not that. But what else could it have been? Ah, I have it! A fiery dragon descended on Drummoor, and you were forced to flee for your life — although with sufficient time to pack your box and hitch the horses to your curricle, luckily."

His lips twitched, but he said, "A poor opinion you must have of me, Miss Constance, if you imagine I would slink away from a mere dragon, even a fiery one. I have a suit of armour on the stairs at Drummoor, let me tell you, and a pair of fearsome swords. Naturally I should have slain the dragon immediately."

"Of course you would. How foolish of me to suppose otherwise. Well then, it must be that you have a secret life as a dashing highwayman, but now you are being pursued by the constabulary and must hide from the law."

This brought a smile at last, but he replied, "Now your opinion of me is sunk even lower, I perceive. First a coward, and now a thief who steals their last coins from elderly spinsters who have never harmed a soul."

There was a pause while the leading couple made their way down the set, but then she said, "I thought nothing of the kind, I assure you, my lord. Naturally you steal only from the very rich in order to give the gains to the poor. It is an act of charity."

"Ah, I see now that you intended a compliment, and if ever I look for a career, I shall be sure to consider this possibility most carefully. Should you care to guess again?"

"Very well. I think you must be running away from a wealthy heiress who is relentlessly pursuing you to persuade you into matrimony."

"Now I am intrigued, Miss Constance. I wonder why I might wish to escape from this lady, if she is indeed so wealthy?"

"Because she is exceedingly ugly."

"Hmm. I might be prepared to overlook the ugliness for sufficient wealth."

"And she has a glass eye and a wooden leg," she said triumphantly.

He laughed out loud at that. For a few minutes their conversation was suspended as they moved down the set. When they came to rest, he said, "You are most entertaining, Miss Constance, but your earlier guess came close. There is indeed a fiery dragon about to descend on Drummoor, with her three dragonet sisters, and no sword can deter them, unfortunately. My grandmama and great-aunts have decided that I am sadly ramshackle, and they must come and set me straight. And although I should like to see myself as a bold dragon-slaying knight, in truth I fear I am a coward, for I could not face them. So I ran away to hide with Great-aunt Augusta, and by happy chance arrived on this very day to find a ball in prospect, to which I was already invited, although Hatty had shamefully neglected to tell me of it. And glad I am that I came, for I have been greatly entertained. I have rarely seen such lively dancing outside town. Who is the young lady who leaps so high?"

"That is Miss Drummond, my lord. She is newly arrived in the neighbourhood from Scotland. Her brother is the village schoolmaster and she keeps house for him."

The dance ended and he led Connie to the side of the room, but showed no inclination to leave her side.

"I should not have set Miss Drummond down as a schoolmaster's sister. Her gown is of the first style."

"The Drummonds are from a long-established and respectable family," Connie said politely, although tiring rather of the subject. "Their father died, leaving the family in difficult circumstances. Mr and Miss Drummond must make their own way in the world now."

"Ah," he said. "No money, then?"

"Not a penny piece between them, beyond a hundred a year each from their mother."

"It is always unfortunate when that is the case," he said.

She had no wish to talk about Jess Drummond, so she said quickly, "Do you really have a suit of armour on the stairs?"

"Indeed I do, but I may have misled you earlier when I talked of wearing it, for such a thing would be impossible. Our ancestors were much shorter than men of the modern era, seemingly, for the armour only comes up to here." He waved a hand near his collar-bone. "Most of them are like that, although the Hepplestone one is an exception."

"Is there one at Hepplestone? I did not know."

"Have you never seen it? I would have thought your grandfather would have shown it to you."

"We have never been to Hepplestone," she said sadly. "Mama goes to stay sometimes, but Papa never went and we have never been invited, nor to Uncle Edmund's house."

"That is strange," he said. "I daresay there is a good reason for it. Ah, supper!" he added, as there was a general movement out of the room.

But before he could offer to take her in, the Drummonds arrived in a swirl of merriment, as if sharing a joke. "There you are, Miss Connie," Drummond said, beaming genially. "Are you enjoying the evening?"

Before she had done more than agree that she was, the Marquess patted her hand where it rested on his arm. "Miss Allamont, would you do me the honour of introducing me to your friends?"

And somehow, in the swirl of introductions and greetings and polite enquiries, it was Jess Drummond who was led into supper by the Marquess, and Mr Drummond who held out his arm for Connie. Without a word, she allowed him to take her through to the dining room.

3: A Visit To Willowbye

The sisters fell, happily exhausted, into their beds after the ball, so it was not until the following morning that they were at leisure to discuss the evening's events. Hope shared her room with Grace, and Belle, Connie and Dulcie shared another.

"Is he not perfect in every way?" Connie said, as they sipped their chocolate in bed. No one needed to ask which precise *'he'* she spoke of. "His appearance is all that is elegant and fashionable, and his manners! I have never seen such amiability and ease combined with such exquisite correctness."

"Who could have foreseen such a state of affairs?" Belle murmured. "After all this time, and so much anticipation that made him certain to be a veritable paragon, how could we possibly have guessed that he would in fact live up to our wildest imaginings?"

"He is quite charming," Dulcie said. "And the proof of it is this — that he stood up for every single dance. What could be stronger evidence of his good nature?"

"And such a fine dancer, too," Connie said.

"He seemed to like *you* very well, Connie," Belle said. "He appeared quite content to stay by your side, until Jess Drummond whisked him away."

"I think he liked Jess better than Connie," Dulcie said. "All the gentlemen seem to like her very much, and I do not know why, for she has no fortune."

"It may be that the Marquess feels safer with Miss Drummond," Belle said. "She is not eligible to marry a man of his rank, and so he cannot be thought to be paying court to her. He must be constantly under siege from ambitious women, so he must be very careful not to be trapped into a betrothal."

"She is very pretty," Connie conceded.

"No prettier than you," Dulcie said at once. "It is my opinion that Lord Carrbridge should be on his guard against Jess, for it seems to me that *she* is the ambitious one. She was very friendly with George Graham until Lady Graham warned her away. It would suit her very well to make the Marquess fall in love with her."

"He is too clever to be taken in by her, never fear," Belle said.

"I do believe *you* have a good chance with him, Connie dear," Dulcie said. "Anyone might see how much he enjoyed your conversation with him during the dance. What did you speak of, might I ask?"

"Dragons and highwaymen," Connie said, giggling. "I was trying to guess how it was he decided to visit his great-aunt. It was terribly silly, but perhaps I managed to amuse him. If he stays a while longer, perhaps I may try to attach him, if I can. I have no great desire for matrimony, but I must find a husband, so that my sisters may also have their chance. The Marquess will do as well as any other, I daresay."

Oh, indeed," Belle said, laughing. "And his appearance and fortune and title have nothing to do with it, I suppose."

Connie lowered her head shyly. "He *is* very attractive, it is true, and I confess, I like him very much. It would be the easiest thing in the world to fall in love with such a man, so I must be very careful not to be drawn in. If he should happen to fall violently in love with me, that would be a different matter. In such a case, I would certainly consider the match."

"Who would not?" Dulcie said. "And then, you know, you would be a marchioness and able to introduce the rest of us into superior society. He has a house in London, Lady Harriet said, and they always go there for the season. I should like of all things to go to London. You must try to make him love you, Connie, for our sakes as much as your own."

"I shall try, then, but how shall it be managed? I cannot always be talking about dragons," Connie said. "Belle, may I ask an impertinent question? How was it that Burford came to fall in love with you, when we all thought him so attached to Hope?"

Belle blushed, and stared into her chocolate for a moment. "I believe he truly *was* attached to Hope, but he found I was better suited, I think. He talked to me a great deal about books, which is not a subject that interests Hope."

"He never was able to talk to Hope at all," Dulcie said. "All that dreadful stammering — he could hardly get out a single word. I could barely keep myself from laughing. Oh, I am sorry, Belle. I am sure he is very worthy—"

"You need not be afraid of offending me, sister. He is shy, that is all, especially with young, pretty women. So fluent in the pulpit, and so inarticulate on social occasions. Foolish man," she added in fond tones. "But if you wish to know what tipped the balance, it was poetry, and in particular, love poetry. We were reading aloud and—" At this point her blushes overcame her.

The others laughed. "Never mind, we will not tease you for *all* the details," Connie said. "But which poet? Where can I find this magical poetry?"

"I will find the book for you," Belle said, laughing. "Then you may try if it works just as well on Lord Carrbridge."

~~~~~

The Marquess and his sister were the only ones at breakfast. Their great-aunt, the Dowager Countess of Humbleforth, was a very elderly lady, who never emerged from her bedchamber until well after noon, so there was the faintest hint of reproach in the two footmen at the requirement to open the dining room so early in the day. Their faces betrayed no resentment, but their steps were slower than usual, with a degree of lethargy only an inch away from insolence.

Brother and sister ate in silence for some time, before pushing their plates away with matching sighs of contentment.

"I must say, the old bird keeps a good kitchen," the Marquess said, as soon as the footmen had withdrawn. "That was an excellent repast. I must drop a crown for the cook before I leave."

"There are two, at least," Harriet said. "And three footmen. She had a pair of black pages for a while, but she found them less appealing when they grew up. She must have more than twenty servants, including the grooms, and what she needs them all for I cannot imagine. The house is not large."

"I thought she had her own chaplain, too. What happened to him?"

"He went off to be a bishop years ago, Dev. Or a deacon, I am not quite sure. Really, considering you are to inherit all this, you might take some interest in Great-aunt Augusta's affairs."

He raised his hands in surrender. "I know, I know. I have neglected the old lady shamefully. But I have written to her every week without fail, since I first went to school. And she writes back, although I have no recollection of any mention of the chaplain. She tells me all the scandal and gossip. She never stirs from this house, but she knows everything that goes on in the county. She must have a troop of spies who keep her informed."

"One spy, I believe," Harriet said, smiling. "Miss Endercott, the clergyman's sister. She is acquainted with everyone, and I suspect she is not above listening to the servants' tattling. Now, *they* know all our secrets."

"Oh, I hope not. But tell me about Miss Drummond. Ah, I can see that you do not like her."

"She is a fortune hunter, Dev. She has not a farthing to her name."

"Oh, I know, but a pretty young thing with a lively disposition — she might be an amusing diversion while I am here."

Harriet made a disapproving sound. "Really, Dev! Is it not time you gave up these diversions and settled down with a wife? Twenty six is a fine age to be setting up your nursery."

He laughed. "You need not worry, sister, I have no designs on Miss Drummond's virtue. As for the settling down, I am in no hurry. Marriage is a serious business, and I need to be sure I am choosing the right person."

"True enough. She will need to bring both breeding and a good fortune to the match, and then managing Drummoor is a great responsibility."

With a bark of laughter, he said, "No, the right person for *me*. I have servants and agents to manage Drummoor. I want to be swept off my feet, Hatty, lifted on clouds of adoration for my wife. Although, sadly, the fortune is an absolute prerequisite, too, unless one of my elderly relations sees fit to visit St Peter soon."

"As for fortune, you could do worse than Constance Allamont. She will have twenty thousand in her own disposal."

"She is very charming, to be sure, but why Constance especially? The youngest is very pretty. At least, I think she was the youngest. They are dreadfully alike, the Miss Allamonts. It was most inconsiderate of their papa to give every one of them the exact same shade of hair colour. Tell me why you would have me marry Constance?"

"They have to marry in order, under the terms of their father's will, or the dowry is lost. The two eldest are accounted for, so Constance is next."

"Of course, I remember Great-aunt Augusta mentioning something of it. So Constance must be next, eh? Interesting. Perhaps I will call at Allamont Hall today, to see if the ladies suffered no ill effects from all that delightful dancing. And the way takes me past the schoolhouse, I believe?" He flashed her a mischievous grin.

Harriet shook her head at him. "Oh, be careful, Dev. Be very careful how you proceed with that one. Remember the last time. The Drummonds are not nobody, and she has a brother."

"I will be careful," he said, and winked.

~~~~~

The Marquess showed no inclination to quit the neighbourhood, and meekly accompanied his sister on her rounds of morning visits. His person and his amiability were equally admired by all who met him, and within a week his previous neglect had been quite forgotten and he was widely acknowledged as the finest young man for twenty miles around.

He was an early visitor to Allamont Hall, and although he did not single Connie out for particular attention, she was gratified that he remembered enough of their conversation at the ball to make more than one allusion to dragons, with a knowing glance in her direction.

He was very interested in Willowbye and the work, recently begun, to repair and renovate it. "I should very much like to see what restoration you have in hand," he said to Burford. "We have a similar problem of dilapidation at Drummoor and although I cannot commit to extensive improvements just yet, I should be interested to see your plans."

"By all means, come and look around," Burford said. "I am living in the house now, so I am there most mornings."

"We should get up a party," the Marquess said. "Let us all go and inspect the work at Willowbye. Can you cope with so many, Burford?"

"Certainly, my lord, so long as you do not expect a two course dinner. If Lady Sara will allow us to use both her carriages, we shall do very well."

Lady Sara graciously assented, and Lady Harriet offered her own travelling coach, if more room were needed.

"I have my curricle, too," the Marquess said. "We may take half the village, it seems."

"Perhaps half the village might stretch the kitchens at Willowbye," Burford said. "However, I should like to invite Miss Endercott. She would enjoy such an outing, I am sure."

"Oh, certainly," the Marquess said. "What do you say to Mr and Miss Drummond, as well?"

"Mr Drummond is the schoolmaster," Dulcie said. "He cannot gad about the country like a gentleman. And Miss Drummond keeps his house and cooks the dinner."

"Well, perhaps Mr Drummond had best watch over his pupils," the Marquess said. "Miss Drummond, however, is surely entitled to a day of pleasure now and then, and her brother must live on beef broth for once."

Since he was a Marquess, no one quite liked to disagree with him, but Connie thought it reprehensible in him to take Jess away from her duties for his own amusement.

The day was fixed and all was arranged. With a little squeezing together, and some changing about, the convoy was only three carriages in the end, slowly ploughing through the mud of Lower and Higher Brinford until they reached the turnpike just outside Brinchester.

By an unfortunate chance, Connie found herself in Lady Harriet's travelling coach with the Marquess and Jess Drummond, which gave her ample opportunity to watch the lighthearted exchanges taking place between the two. Having settled in her own mind that she would try to attract the Marquess, she had begun to think of him as already her property, and it vexed her beyond measure to see Jess Drummond draw him in with her seemingly artless chatter that bordered on flirtatiousness. She wondered at the degree of ease already subsisting between them when they had met so recently.

Lady Harriet chattered inconsequentially the whole way, which Connie listened to with only half an ear. It was fortunate that Lady Harriet was perfectly capable of maintaining the conversation by herself, for Connie managed nothing but "Yes, my lady," "No, my lady," and "Indeed, my lady?" for the entire journey, so intent was she on watching Jess and the Marquess.

When they reached Willowbye, they stopped first at the Dower House, where Mary and the two younger boys, Mark and Hugo, were already settled. James and Alice, with their baby son, had set up house in the lodge cottage nearby. The work on both houses had been completed, and Connie guessed that Mary was responsible for the efficient manner in which all had been arranged. The Dower House had been furnished with items from Willowbye, and their shabby and mismatched appearance contrasted oddly with the modern wallpaper and freshly-painted wainscoting. In the lodge cottage, all was new and fashionable, paid for, no doubt, by Alice's father. Such an irony, that the farmer was better able to afford such expenses than the gentleman at the manor house.

The carriages having been sent on, they walked up the drive to the house, where a group of gardeners paused from cutting back overgrown bushes and clearing fallen tree branches to bow to them. It was cold enough for their breath to puff into clouds as they spoke, and Connie pulled her cloak closer. She was not a fast walker, and soon lagged behind the others. To her delight, as she rounded a particularly overgrown shrub, she found the Marquess waiting for her.

"May I offer you my arm, Miss Constance? My sister tells me you are not a strong walker, and might need a little assistance."

It was disappointing that the gesture had not been his own idea, but she smiled and took his arm anyway. "Thank you, my lord. Your assistance and your company are both most welcome. Gracious, I have not been here in such an age! It has quite changed. Indeed, I should not have recognised the place at all, if the drive were to be my guide. These bushes were barely as high as my waist, and the trees not much more than saplings. There had been rows of much older trees before then, very well grown, but there was so much dead wood in them, and a number had fallen altogether to leave gaps, and that looks so odd, do you not agree? In any event, Cousin Henry had them all torn up, and new planting all the way down the drive. But perhaps it is time for these to be torn up in their turn, I cannot say."

The Marquess had no interest in trees, it seemed, for he said, "How is it that Cousin Henry is your cousin, and his children are also cousins? There must be some second cousins in there somewhere, I fancy. Or perhaps cousins once or twice removed, although I am not sure quite how that works."

"Nor I!" she said, with a giggle. "Cousin Henry was — is, I suppose — cousin to Papa. Cousin Henry's father, also Henry, was brother to Papa's father, Walter. That is why we all have the same name, you see."

"Ah, yes. All is now clear to me. And Cousin Mary — she is the eldest of the children, I think?"

"Yes, from Cousin Henry's first marriage. She is said to resemble her mother in every way. Then after Cousin Elizabeth died, there was Cousin Vivienne. She is French, and James, Mark and Hugo are hers, but she went back to France a few years ago, although I do not know why."

"If Miss Mary Allamont takes after her mother, then she must have been a handsome woman indeed. It is a great shame when a pretty woman has no dowry."

Surely he must be thinking of Jess Drummond now? Yet she could not disagree with him on the point. "Certainly it is," she said, then added wistfully. "Everyone should be able to marry for love, without considerations of wealth."

"How romantic you are, Miss Allamont." His smile as he spoke was so warm that her heart gave a little somersault. Such a charming man, when his attention was not focused on Miss Drummond.

They rounded the final leaning tree to see the house before them. There on the drive to meet them was Burford, wreathed in smiles, while Cousin Henry loitered on the front step, as if unsure how to greet guests now that he was no longer master of Willowbye.

Connie paused, looking up at the house. Here at least was something unchanged since she was a child. The red brick walls and latticed windows were warm and welcoming, although perhaps the rotting window frames and missing tiles were recent developments.

It was Mary, mistress of Willowbye for more than a dozen years, who led them from room to room. Connie followed the others through the front door and into the great hall, filled with boxes of books while the library woodworm was dealt with. From the great hall, they went through a door to the north wing, and beyond that to the so-called new wing, although it was a century old, at least. Then upstairs to a warren of passageways and bedrooms.

Mary took most of the others off to survey the attics, basements and kitchens, but Connie had no interest in trailing round the butler's pantry or the linen cupboards. She began a second circuit of the principal rooms, envisaging each in her mind. This one would be gold, with Chinese wallpaper. Another would look well in a pale green, with cream cornices. The drawing room could be red, with gold decoration. She was so absorbed that she startled when Burford appeared at her side.

"I do beg your pardon," he said, jumping back. "I did not mean to alarm you. I have the book you asked for." He held out a volume bound in red leather.

"Book?"

"The Scotch poems of Robert Burns. Mrs Burford said you wished to borrow it."

"Oh. Oh, of course. Thank you, sir. You are most kind."

He waved an arm to encompass the whole room. "What do you think of it all? So much work to be done, it is difficult to know where to begin. The man I have engaged is very good on bricks and wood and glass, but not so good on paint and wallpaper. And out here…" He ushered her through to the great hall, gesturing with a rueful expression at the unplastered walls. "Look at the state of it! I do not know what is to be done. And your sister has no more idea than I do."

"Oh, but that is the interesting part," she said. "I should love to offer suggestions, if you would like that. I love putting colours together, and choosing wallpapers. Now for this room —
"

The front door flew open. A woman of about forty stood on the threshold, gazing imperiously round the hall. Connie had not much experience of the *ton*, but even so, she could tell at a glance that the stranger was dressed in the very latest fashions from London.

"May I be of service to you, madam?" Burford said.

She raked him up and down. "Who are you? And what are you doing in my house?"

He said nothing, although his mouth flapped open once or twice.

Connie looked more closely at the visitor, then gasped. "Cousin Vivienne?"

4: An Unexpected Return

A wide-eyed servant was sent off to find Cousin Henry in whatever remote part of the house he might be, and convey the news that his wife had returned after many years of absence. Connie could imagine his astonishment.

Meanwhile, Cousin Vivienne, wrinkling her nose at the brick dust and smell of mould that still hung in the air, marched around the boxes and through to the north wing. Throwing open a door, she strode through and sat herself on a sofa. She looked about her disdainfully and said, "This was a very pretty room in my day. *Henri* has let it go appallingly." Her French accent was quite noticeable now. Looking at Burford, she said, "You. Fetch me some Madeira. And have my boxes taken to my room."

"I do not imagine you still have a room after all this time," Connie said, before Burford had had time to open his mouth. "And Mr Burford is not a servant. He is the new tenant of Willowbye."

Cousin Vivienne looked at him fully for the first time. "He should still offer me refreshments, unless he is quite devoid of manners."

"I will find a servant," he said, and rushed from the room.

"Why does he not ring the bell? Is he brainless?"

"Not at all," Connie said. "He knows that it would be pointless to attempt, when the bell ropes are all rotted away. And I expect he wanted to escape from you. He is too polite to express his opinion of *your* manners."

"But you are not, I suppose? Ha! Who are you, child? You are not Mary, I am sure of that."

"I am Constance Allamont, Cousin Vivienne, and I am not a child. I am three and twenty."

"High time you were married then, *child.* I should be ashamed to be a spinster still at such an age."

Connie was tempted to reply in like manner, but she bit back her retort, for it occurred to her that Cousin Vivienne had the intent of angering her and she therefore determined to deprive her of the satisfaction. She smiled instead and sat down, although not too near the visitor.

"I trust you had a good journey from France," she said, in her most polite voice. "Were you staying in Paris?"

"France? Paris?" Cousin Vivienne hooted with laughter. "Whatever gave you the idea that I was in France? No, I have been living in Manchester, in a very poor neighbourhood, since my husband keeps me so short of money. It is a wonder I have not been forced to—" She clucked, with a shrug of one shoulder. "Well, never mind that. Ah, *Henri!* There you are!" Her gaze passed rapidly over the faces of those who accompanied him, lingering for a moment on Mary, before passing on. "Who are all these people, and why are they in my house?"

"Not your house, Viv," he said. "This has not been your house since the day you walked out of it, fifteen years ago."

"Not yours either," she shot back. "You have a *tenant* now, I hear. So where are we to live?"

"*We?*" He gave a rueful smile, and shook his head. "*We* are not living anywhere, Viv. *I* shall be living at the Dower

House, with Mary, Mark and Hugo. Remember Mark and Hugo? Your sons? And James — your *other* son — is living at the lodge cottage with his wife and son. I neither know nor care where *you* live."

"But I am your *wife!*"

There seemed to be no answer to that, and Cousin Henry wisely attempted none.

The servants had already laid out refreshments for the visitors in the dining room, and without further discussion, the party made its way there and settled down to eat. Connie had a thousand questions, and she could see the speculation in the faces around her, and hear the whispers, but neither Cousin Henry nor Cousin Vivienne said another word, to each other or to anyone else.

Not long afterwards, Ambleside deemed it appropriate to draw the visit to a close. As the carriages were being brought round, he said to Connie, "Will you ride with us, Miss Connie? Miss Allamont has already agreed to give us the pleasure of her company. Mrs Ambleside would appreciate it, I know. We will take you all the way to the Hall, so you need not have the inconvenience of changing carriages in the village."

Connie agreed with relief. At least she would not have to watch Jess Drummond flirting with the Marquess. As she was handed into Ambleside's carriage, she caught a momentary glimpse of the Marquess's displeased face watching her. Good! Let him be disappointed, if he would.

The four could talk of nothing but the return of Mrs Henry Allamont.

"Even Mary was astonished to discover that her step-mother had not been in France all these years," Amy said. "Manchester! She could have come to see her children whenever she wanted, yet she did not. How shocking!"

"But why has she returned now?" Connie said.

"Only she knows the true answer to that question," Ambleside said. "However, we could hazard a guess. Allamont must have been supporting his wife financially all this time, to the ruin of the estate. I am no judge of clothes, but that pelisse looked vastly expensive to me."

"And that sealskin muff!" Amy said. "Quite delightful, but so modish that it must have cost a great deal."

"Should you like one, my love? We must see what we can find of that style in Brinchester. Yes, she was always extravagant. I recall my mother being scandalised by the number of gowns she seemed to need. And now the supply of money has dried up, so here she is again."

"So Cousin Henry has been sending money to Cousin Vivienne?" Belle said with a frown. "But then... all these years, he must have known exactly where she was. Yet he pretended she was in France. Why would he do that?"

"Embarrassment, perhaps?" Ambleside said. "He may not have wanted the world to know his wife preferred to live alone in Manchester to being Mrs Henry Allamont of Willowbye. Telling everyone she had gone home to France suggests a benevolent husband with a care for his wife's homesickness."

"I wonder if he even knew where she resided," Belle said. "If the money he sent to her passed through a third party, he may have had no notion where she was. He seemed quite shocked to see her."

"Oh dear," Amy said. "This will be so unsettling for everyone."

And on that point they could all agree.

~~~~~

The time came for the next assembly in Brinchester. Their mother took Belle and Connie to the town at an early hour, so that they could visit the warehouses and select silks and muslin and cotton for Belle's wedding clothes, and wallpaper and paint for Willowbye. Connie had been established as the authority on colours and styles for the house, and she made rapid, confident choices which even Lady Sara approved.

"You have surprisingly good taste, Connie," she said, as they made the short drive to their hotel. "I am happy to discover that you have inherited something from me, after all."

"I wish I had looked more like you," Connie said quietly.

Lady Sara looked askance at her. "Do you really? Dark hair is much more fashionable."

"I should love to have natural curls like you, Mama."

"Ah, yes, that is a blessing, it is true. Yet you do quite well with curling papers. None of you have an appearance such as to disgrace me in public, for which I am thankful, and now that you no longer wear identical gowns — such a foolish notion! — I find you all much more presentable. And one married and one betrothed! Excellent progress. Now it is your turn, Connie. I hope you will try for the Marquess. That would be a son-in-law I could be proud of."

Belle said nothing, but Connie could not let such a slur pass. "Surely you have nothing against Ambleside or Burford, Mama? They are both respectable gentlemen of good fortune."

"Oh, I have nothing against either of them, but Ambleside's family is nothing at all, only two generations from trade, and Burford — he may be a wealthy man now, but he was merely a country curate with very poor prospects before that."

"And he was quite content to be so," Belle said, in her calm way, not at all offended. "He is not ambitious."

"Exactly," Lady Sara said. "That is precisely my point. A man of good family should always aspire to improve his position in society, by increasing his income and taking care to mix with the best company available to him, whether he has a career or not."

"Papa did not do so, did he, Mama?" Connie said, fascinated by this blunt speaking from her very proper mother.

"No, he did *not*," she said with sudden fire. "He never mixed well in *any* company, and deeply resented persons of rank, and as for increasing his income, you all know how tightly he tied his purse-strings and kept *us* on a tight rein, and all the while supporting this Barnett woman and her son in luxury."

"He left us very good dowries, however," Connie said. "*That* was generous."

"Yes, and it puzzles me exceedingly," her mother replied. "Whenever I enquired of him how much he planned to give each of you, he would say only, '*Let us see how far their faces alone will get them. Then we might see.*' So I never expected him to give you anything, frankly. As a rule, he saved his generosity for his base-born child. But I do not think even your father could have expected his by-blow to try to claim the Hall. That is beyond everything. I should have liked to see that boy in court, so that the law might have dealt with him as he deserved."

"I am sorry to disappoint you, Mama," Belle said with a smile. "Had Mr Burford known your wishes, I am sure he would never have paid Jack Barnett to drop his claim."

"Well, I am very glad he did," Connie said. "I feel much more comfortable knowing that we need never have anything to do with him again. I am sorry it cost Burford twenty thousand pounds, but I daresay he will scarce notice the loss, for he is as rich as Croesus."

They turned into the hotel's yard at that moment, and all conversation was at an end.

~~~~~

The sisters were late in arriving at the ball, for a sudden downpour of sleety rain meant that sedan chairs were in short supply, and they had to wait. Then there was only one available, which would have to run backwards and forwards to convey them all to the Assembly Rooms, and it was no simple matter to arrange the journey in such a way that all the Miss Allamonts were properly chaperoned at both ends of the journey. It was fortunate that Amy was now married and able to chaperon them, or they could not have managed.

So it came about that the Assembly Rooms were full to overflowing when they arrived, and they had to wait to be announced, with more people forming a snaking queue on the stairs behind them. At last it was their turn, their names were pronounced, and they made their way down the short flight of steps to the dance floor.

Connie always loved this moment. The floor was filled with movement and colour and shimmering silk, sparkling jewels at every throat and feathers in the dowagers' turbans. Faces flushed with the exertion of the dance beamed with happiness. Who would not be happy at a ball, and especially so at this moment, the entrance, with the whole evening stretching out like a rug at her feet. She was so light-footed as she skipped down the steps, it was almost as if she were dancing already, the music sweeping her up and propelling her forward.

But tonight it did nothing of the sort. They had barely reached the bottom of the steps when they were accosted by Cousin Vivienne, wearing the most exquisite gown Connie had ever seen. She had not realised that *modistes* in Manchester had such talents. She was so busy admiring the embroidery and delicate seed-pearl designs that she almost missed Belle's gasp of horror.

She could not, however, miss her outraged cry of, "Oh no! What is *he* doing here?"

"Who?" Connie said, but she had only to follow Belle's eyes to see the cause of her distress. A young man paused beside the master of ceremonies waiting his turn to be announced. His appearance was undistinguished and his attire gave the impression that he wished to be fashionable, and had perhaps paid a great deal to attempt it, but had not quite mastered the art. His coat was not quite the correct fit, the stockings were an odd colour and the ribbons on his shoes were tied in a most peculiar manner. As for his cravat, Connie had never seen the like.

"But who is he?" Connie whispered to Belle.

"I can scarce believe my eyes! It is that Jack Barnett, strutting about in society as if he were just as good as anyone else."

"But who are the two women with him?" Dulcie said.

The older woman, with a smirk of self-satisfaction on her face, was dressed in an expensive but unfashionable style, with an excessively ugly turban on her head. On Jack Barnett's other side, her head drooping as if to avoid notice, was a girl who looked to be no more than sixteen, dressed in the plain white of a debutante.

As they watched, the little group stepped forward, and the master of ceremonies intoned, "Mrs Algernon Barnett, Mr Jack Barnett, Miss Barnett."

Belle groaned audibly. "He has a *sister!*"

5: *Ambition*

A sister! How many more of them might be lurking at home waiting their turn to parade themselves in public, as if they had not the stain of illegitimacy about them.

Barnett's eye fell on their group, still standing in shocked silence just inside the room. His smug grin widened.

"Why, if it isn't Belle! How are you, sister? And Burford, my friend — how pleasant to meet you again! And this must be *Lady* Sara. How do you do, madam. I have heard such a great deal about you."

Lady Sara looked him up and down with aristocratic hauteur. Without a word, she spun on her heel to turn her back on him. "Come, girls," she said, walking away without haste. It was magnificent, and in that moment Connie was completely in charity with her mother. Barnett's expression darkened, but he recovered admirably, and as she followed her mother, Connie's last view of him before he was swallowed by the throng saw the smirk fully restored.

As they reached a less crowded part of the room, Lady Sara turned to her daughters. "You will none of you speak to them, or have anything at all to do with them," she said. "Amy, you will of course be guided by Ambleside, but I hope that, for my sake, you will cut them."

"Of course, Mama," Amy said. "Oh, I wish they had not come!"

"So must we all," her mother said. "However, these assemblies are public affairs, and anyone may pay to attend, even such people as that. Dressed up like their betters, they look almost respectable."

"I will go and see what I may find out about them," Ambleside said. He returned no more than ten minutes later. "It is being put about that the mother is the widow of a man in trade, which may be true for all I can tell. The son has two thousand a year, and the daughter a portion of three thousand. And there is another daughter, still in the schoolroom."

"Two thousand a year?" Burford said. "I find that unlikely. Having seen the late Mr Allamont's will and talked to Mr Plumphett, I have a very fair idea of Jack Barnett's income. I would put it at fourteen hundred at best, if he invests wisely and conserves his capital, and he does not strike me as the sort to manage either of those."

Connie tried to put the Barnetts from her mind and enjoy the evening as best she may. She found herself an object to the two brothers from High Frickham, who arrived at her side squabbling over which of them should have the right to ask her to dance first. Since they were identical twins and she had never been able to tell them apart, she had no particular interest in the outcome. Thus she was rather relieved than disappointed when Alex Drummond materialised at her side and carried her off to the dance floor while they were still arguing. The twins watched her go, open-mouthed.

From then on, Connie was in continual demand. After Mr Drummond, she danced with Sir Osborne Hardy, who was an excellent dancer, and then his friend Daniel Merton, who was less so, although not so bad as Grace for turning the wrong way. By that time, the Marquess and Lady Harriet had arrived, and Connie was gratified to be the Marquess's first choice of dancing partner.

Mindful of her plan to make him fall in love with her, she said, "Do you enjoy poetry, my lord?"

"Of course," he said. "Everyone likes poetry, I believe. I find it very soothing. The words trickle through my brain like a stream, and then trickle out again, for I never can remember them after."

"You must learn them by heart," she said. "My father always insisted that we learn a new poem every week, and recite it to him on Saturday morning."

"Really?" the Marquess said. "How extraordinary! Although, now that I consider the matter, I recall being asked to do something similar at school. One of the masters was quite keen on the idea. Not that I ever did, of course."

"You never did? Do you mean that your schoolmaster set you work to do, and you refused to do it? And were you not punished for such disobedience?"

"I was the Earl of Deveron, nobody dared to punish me," he said loftily. "Now history — that I enjoyed, especially a good battle, or a whole series of them. The Peloponnesian Wars were wonderful. And the middle ages — the Hundred Years' War! Can you imagine, Miss Constance, how delightful it must have been to be always fighting, so that one might gallop from one battle directly to another. Such fun! I should have liked to be a knight in those days, defending the Kingdom and saving fair maidens in distress."

"I do not think it was quite as romantic as that," she said faintly. "Besides, even in the Hundred Years' War, there were long gaps between the battles."

"Really? Well, what is the point of that?" he said in disgust.

"So the poets could commemorate the last battle, of course," she said quickly, trying to get him back to the point. "There must be a proper celebration for each glorious victory."

"You are quite right, of course. The poets — and the painters. The victors would want to have their portraits painted, showing them triumphant, and their enemies ground into the dust, their entrails scattered for the crows."

She pulled a face.

"Oh, I do beg your pardon, Miss Constance," he said. "Oh, look, there is Miss Drummond. How high she leaps! She is as light-footed as... as a bird, do you not agree?"

Connie gave it up, and resigned herself to listening to a recital of all Jess Drummond's virtues, which were manifold, it seemed. The Marquess took her into supper, and regaled her with the many exploits of his ancestors, who had all had the good fortune to be born into an age when wars were to be had at frequent intervals.

"I wonder you do not join the army, my lord, if you enjoy war so much," she said in exasperation. "You could perhaps knock some sense into the French. All Europe would be grateful to you, I am sure."

"Not my place," he said firmly. "I am the eldest — responsibilities, you know, Miss Constance, responsibilities and duties. Cannot be shirked. No, the army is for Reggie, although he seems reluctant, for some reason. Personally, I think it would suit Gil better, but there you are. I have not the least notion what we are to do with *him*. Nothing but trouble, but I daresay he will settle, in time. Even so — not the church, I think. Now Humphrey..."

She sighed, and smiled. She supposed that in the unlikely event that she found herself the Marchioness of Carrbridge it would be helpful to know something of her husband's brothers, so she listened and nodded from time to time and tried to get them straight in her head, but it was no good. There were just too many of them.

A group of diners moving away just then, Connie and the Marquess were joined by Cousin Henry and Mary, who was escorted by Daniel Merton.

"Where is Cousin Vivienne?" Connie asked.

Cousin Henry made a noise in his throat, his face darkening, but Mary answered calmly, "She is about somewhere. She still has a few friends in the neighbourhood."

"She is making mischief," Cousin Henry said, his anger barely restrained. "It was always her greatest delight to cause trouble. She is engaged in spreading the word that certain people here are kin to the Allamonts."

Mr Merton paused, the plate he was about to offer to Mary suspended in mid-air. "I heard that rumour, too, to my great surprise. Do you say that it is untrue, or is it a matter best left unsaid?"

Cousin Henry seemed on the point of apoplexy, so Mary said, "There is a distant relationship, but not of a kind we would wish to acknowledge."

"Ah." His eyes glittered with interest as he digested this information. "In that case, the persons in question were ill-advised to come here at all. They know no one, and the daughter has not danced a step. She is a pitiable sight! I had considered asking for her hand myself, if no other partner offered, as an act of charity. However, I shall not do so now, out of respect for the feelings of those I have the good fortune to consider friends."

"Your sensibility does you the greatest credit, sir," Mary said warmly. "I applaud you for your compassion. Yet I fear that not everyone will share your delicacy. Where there is money, there will always be those willing to overcome their scruples as to rank and circumstance. The Barnetts will add to their acquaintance soon enough."

"For myself, I cannot express my distaste for such ambition strongly enough," Merton said. "Where is the respect for rank if everyone with a little money to his name is to be allowed to ape his betters and walk about as if he is as good as the next man? There is more to being a gentleman than having an independent income — a man's breeding shows in every word he speaks, in his manner of dress, in his treatment of others and his knowledge of the world. One cannot disguise one's true rank."

"You think it reprehensible in a man to have the ambition to rise?" Cousin Henry said. "Surely you approve of *some* flexibility in our stratified society."

Merton gave a little bow. "Your point is well made, sir, and naturally there must be some who rise and others who fall. But even so, there must be limits or society would crumble. One cannot dress the ploughman in fine clothes and pretend he is the equal of a duke, nor can the duke ever be other than noble, even if he were ploughing a field. Breeding is innate, and can be neither disguised nor feigned."

"That is too deep for me," the Marquess said cheerfully. "But then I am only a marquess, not a duke. Miss Constance, I hear the musicians warming up again. Shall I return you to your mama?"

As Connie rose and took his arm, Mary leaned forward intently to continue the discussion.

"Mr Merton is a deep thinker," Connie said as they descended the steps from the supper room. "I do not understand a quarter of anything he says."

"Merton likes to think he is clever," the Marquess said. "As far as ambition is concerned, I should think he speaks with some authority. He has certainly beguiled Sir Osborne Hardy, or so my great-aunt says. Ah, here is Lady Sara. Thank you for the pleasure of your company, Miss Constance."

He bowed, and almost before she had made her curtsy he was gone. She was not unhappy with her progress, however. So long as he lingered in the neighbourhood, more opportunities would arise where he just might happen to fall in love with her. She passed the rest of the evening with very favourable thoughts of the Marquess. With every meeting she became more convinced that they would suit each other admirably.

~~~~~

The furore over Jack Barnett, his mother and sister did not die down quickly. All the Allamonts' friends were scandalised. It was not the mere fact that the late Mr William Allamont had had a mistress and several illegitimate children that offended, for such happenings were all too common. Rather, it was the ostentatious public display that so affronted sensibilities. Mistresses and their children were expected to understand their place in the world and keep out of the sight of respectable people.

Connie was surprised to discover, however, that the existence of this particular mistress had been widely known for years. The absurd pretence of the home for foundling children, Mr Allamont's supposed charitable establishment, had not deceived anyone, apart from his own children. But there was not much to be done about it. The prospect of meeting the Barnetts in public was a distressing one, but if they were determined to enter society now that they could afford it, they could not be deterred.

About the other scandalous development, the return of Cousin Vivienne, there was also very little to be done. Cousin Henry had never taken the final step of official separation or divorce, and so she was as much his wife as she ever was.

"He is very upset about it, as you may imagine," Belle told her sisters after a visit to Willowbye. "She is determined to stay and make a nuisance of herself. She will not move into the Dower House, either, and neither Cousin Henry nor Mr Burford seems able to force her to do so. But I can, so Mr Burford and I will be married just as soon as the banns can be read."

"How is it that *you* can persuade her to move out, if her husband cannot?" Hope said, eyes wide.

"Because I shall be mistress of the house, the servants will answer to me and Cousin Vivienne must give way." She paused, her mouth set into a determined line. "And if she still will not go, I shall have all her things packed up and forcibly removed. Willowbye is mine, and she will just have to get used to that."

But Connie thought it sounded like a difficult start to married life, all the same.

6: Lord Reginald

Connie had to wait some time for the perfect opportunity to introduce the Marquess to the pleasures of Scotch poetry. She had looked through the book herself, and not understood much of it. Scotch seemed to be a queer language, like a mangled form of English with some foreign words added in to confuse her. However, it had worked its charm on Mr Burford, so she was optimistic it would have the same effect on Lord Carrbridge.

Her moment came one day when Amy and Ambleside were to visit, and by happy chance had brought Lady Harriet and the Marquess with them. It was not a day when other callers might be expected, so Connie had reasonable hopes of the Marquess's undivided attention. At first, it seemed that all was going well, and she found herself sitting beside him, a little apart from the others, who were gathered around the worktable. Not wanting to waste the opportunity, she began, "You told me once that you like poetry, my lord?"

"Indeed I do," he said. "I find it very soporific. Like sermons."

"Oh." Connie had no idea what that meant, but it sounded hopeful. "I have a book of poems that I have been trying to read, but I find the words difficult. I wonder if you would be so good as to help me understand them?"

"No use asking me, dear lady," he said cheerfully. "If you can make nothing of it, then I am sure I shall not do any better. Not in Greek, are they, these poems?"

"No, no. Only in Scotch, which is much like English, only some words are difficult. Will you not have a look?"

"Well, if you would like it. No wish to be disobliging."

Eagerly, she jumped up and fetched the book of poems. "There! It is very kind in you."

"Which poem is the troublesome one? Oh, I see what you mean, Miss Connie. These are very odd indeed. *"Fair fa' your honest, sonsie face, Great chieftain o' the pudding-race!"* Pudding? Is the man writing a poem about a pudding?"

He burst out laughing, which was not at all the effect she had hoped for.

And then, the very worst thing that could have happened — the door opened and Young announced Mr and Miss Drummond.

"The very persons we need," the Marquess declared. "I say, Drummond, you are Scotch, are you not? And Miss Drummond, too. Will you not come over here and help us out, for these poems are too difficult for Miss Constance to understand, and I cannot help, you know."

"What are you reading?" Mr Drummond said, taking the book from the Marquess's hand. "Oh, Robert Burns. Good Lord, what are you doing with this nonsense? Here, listen to this one, for it is quite my favourite."

He struck a pose, and recited a verse in a loud voice.

"To A Mouse, On Turning Her Up In Her Nest With The Plough
Wee, sleekit, cow'rin, tim'rous beastie,
O, what a panic's in thy breastie!
Thou need na start awa sae hasty,

Wi' bickering brattle!
I wad be laith to rin an' chase thee,
Wi' murd'ring pattle!"

He roared with laughter. "A mouse! Imagine writing a poem about a mouse! The fellow's a fool."

"Alex, read the one about the louse on the bonnet," Jess Drummond said. "That one is quite my favourite."

She sat herself down beside the Marquess, and the three of them spent the next hour reciting choice nonsense from the book, and laughing at the absurdity of it all.

Connie knew there was no hope of reclaiming the Marquess's attention, so she quietly joined the group at the worktable.

Belle smiled at her and whispered, "Wrong poems, Connie dear. Those are amusing, but not terribly romantic."

Connie laughed. "No, indeed! But I do not think Lord Carrbridge really likes poetry after all. I shall have to think of a different approach. Amy, how did Mr Ambleside come to fall in love with you?"

Amy blushed. "Oh, he *said* that he had been in love with me for ever, since I first came out. So I do not know what made him do so."

"Your sweet nature, I expect," Belle said, smiling at her, so that she blushed even more. "But it was a long time before *you* were in love with *him*, was it not?"

"Yes, although I always liked him very much, but I did not know I was in love with him until he so admired one of my flowers in the new shrubbery. He knelt down to hold the blossom in his hand. Flowers are *so* much more romantic than poems, I think."

"Flowers," Connie said thoughtfully. "That has possibilities."

~~~~~

The following day brought an unexpected caller — the Marquess returned, and this time he brought one of his brothers with him. Lord Reginald Marford was three years younger than the Marquess, and had none of his brother's aristocratic good looks, nor his flamboyant style of dress. However, he was very personable, and since he spent the entire visit in conversation with Connie, and was very cross when told it was time to leave, she decided she liked him very much.

He was so amiable that she felt she had known him for years instead of a single half hour visit. So it was that she ventured to say, as the brothers prepared to depart, "Are you escaping from the dragons, too?"

He roared with laughter, and bent down to whisper, "Yes, I am, but do not tell everyone how cowardly I am, to be afraid of two dowagers and a pair of elderly spinsters."

"Ah, but that is the most formidable kind of dragon, I believe," she whispered back. "I do not blame you one bit."

He laughed again, and raised her hand to his lips. "I am quite delighted to make your acquaintance, Miss Constance. I hope to see you again very soon."

And with that he was gone, leaving Connie in a very pleasant frame of mind.

~~~~~

The Marquess and Lord Reginald rode home in silence, each brother deep in his own thoughts. When they arrived at Great-aunt Augusta's house, they found Harriet just descending from her own carriage after a visit to Staynlaw House.

"Reggie? Oh, it *is* you! Of all things, this is the most charming — quite a family reunion we have here. All is well at Drummoor, I take it?"

"As well as you might imagine, with Grandmama and her three cronies at large in the house," Reggie said gloomily. "There is only so much berating a man can take."

"What a feeble pair you are, to be afraid of a few old ladies," Harriet said. "Is this the spirit of English heroism that won the day at Agincourt?"

"I would a thousand times rather face the French than Grandmama on the rampage," Reggie said indignantly. "It is all very well for you, Hatty, since she thinks the sun shines out of you, but we get the worst of it, you know."

"That is only because I behave myself, whereas you boys are always in some scrape or other. And what are you up to now, I wonder? One of you running to hide behind Great-aunt Augusta's skirts I might just about accept, but two of you? No, you are up to some scheme or other, I am certain of it."

"I think it very shabby of you, sis, to be always suspecting us in this way," Reggie said in aggrieved tones. "Surely Grandmama is reason enough for us to want a change of scenery?"

"If it is the usual — that you are a pair of rapscallions, who ought to settle down with a nice heiress apiece and start breeding little lords and ladies — then I should think you know well enough how to fob her off, for you have grown very skilled in the art these past five years."

"Well, it *is* that, it is true, but this time she has the heiresses all marked out, and is planning to invite them to London. There is no escaping it this time, and you might be more sympathetic, Hatty. Our days of freedom are numbered."

"No, you are not convincing me, Reggie. You are up to something, the pair of you."

The Marquess smiled benignly at her, and said nothing.

~~~~~

News arrived that Mr Wills was returning to Lower Brinford. As one of the very few eligible bachelors of the district, he had at one time been thought a possible suitor for Amy, until Mr Ambleside had dispatched the rival for her hand by the simple expedient of buying up all his debts. Thus freed from the immediate threat of penury, Mr Wills had set about fully restoring his fortune with determination. He had gone to Bath, where his fine estate and not inconsiderable person might attract a wealthy heiress or, failing that, a rich widow.

Now Mr Wills was returning in triumph from Bath with his bride. The whole neighbourhood was wild to see the former Miss Harris of Hartlepool, sole daughter of the owner of a fishing fleet, and possessor of fifty thousand pounds. Since Hartlepool was a great distance from Bath, there was much speculation that the lady had taken herself there for a very similar purpose to Mr Wills. How fortunate, then, that they had happened to meet and, in less than a fortnight, to find themselves quite in love.

Lady Sara and the Miss Allamonts had paid the customary wedding visit, which enabled them to determine that Mrs Wills was even stouter than her husband, with prominent teeth and an unfortunate liking for excessive amounts of lace. Before Mrs Wills could repay the courtesy with a visit to Allamont Hall, Sir Matthew and Lady Graham decided to hold one of their generous dinners to welcome the bride to the neighbourhood. Since the dining table at Graham House, when fully extended, could seat fifty guests in comfort and as many as sixty-four if they could contrive to eat without moving their elbows, the evening promised to be a lively one.

Almost as soon as Connie entered the crowded drawing room, she saw Lord Reginald's smiling face. He waved to her from the far side of the room, then ploughed his way in a determined manner through the crush to join her.

"Miss Constance, how are you? Looking enchanting, as always. Is this not delightful? Such a large party, and several faces new to me. You must tell me who everyone is. Who is the gentleman in the extraordinary waistcoat over there?"

"That, my lord, is Sir Osborne Hardy, of Brinford Manor. The lady in purple is his mother, and the lady in blue is his sister, Miss Clarissa Hardy. There is another sister lives at the Manor, but Miss Hardy is very frail now and never ventures out. The gentleman talking to Mr Ambleside is Mr Merton, Sir Osborne's particular friend."

"Ah, I see. And the striking lady in the green and gold over there?"

"That is my cousin, Mrs Henry Allamont…"

And in this way, the time before dinner passed rapidly, Lord Reginald asking about this person or that, Connie giving names and details, her hand comfortably resting on his arm. It was only when she saw the Marquess going into dinner with Jess Drummond on his arm that she realised that she had spoken to no one but Lord Reginald. Naturally, he also sat beside her at dinner, and when the rugs were lifted in the saloon for dancing, he earnestly besought the honour of her hand.

She liked him very well, but his attentions were quite marked, and he was distracting her from her scheme of getting the Marquess to fall in love with her. Fortunately, propriety was her friend, preventing Lord Reginald from standing up with her again immediately. Her next partner was Mr Drummond, who flirted outrageously, as always, and then Sir Osborne, who said little, but was so attractively attired that he set Connie's new gown off to perfection. She had no wish to become Lady Hardy, but she could not but feel that they made a most handsome couple. Then Daniel Merton claimed her, and finally, to her relief, for she had begun to fear she would not exchange a single word with him all evening, the Marquess.

Yet his first words to her beyond the commonplace courtesies were, "So how do you like my brother, Miss Constance? Is he not charming?"

"He is a very pleasant fellow," she said.

"A pleasant fellow? Is that all you have to say of him? For he is the finest brother in the world, I would have you know. He is not so handsome as I am, of course, and his style of dress is sadly plain, do you not think? Not a bit of colour about him, but he is always impeccably turned out."

"Oh yes," she replied. "I will grant you that he is excessively well-dressed, but I do not judge a man's character by the quality of his tailor and valet, my lord."

"By jove, no, I should think not. But his horse — now there is a far better means to determine the soundness of a man. His choice of horse, his manner of driving and perhaps how well he dances. Yes, now that I give the matter proper consideration, I believe that only the most complete gentleman will be able to excel in all those areas."

Connie tried not to laugh, not altogether successfully.

"Oh, you do not agree with my assessment?" he said, not at all offended.

"By no means."

"Then pray tell me, what encompasses your ideal of a gentleman?"

Connie knew the answer to that at once, for he was presently watching the dancing with his wife. Mr Ambleside was her ideal made flesh, but she could hardly say so. After a moment's thought, therefore, she replied, "A gentleman is defined by his manners, Lord Carrbridge, and by the way he treats others. I expect honesty and openness, and he must be everything that is honourable. If he is kind and generous and thoughtful, his aim only to please, *that* is a man I should think well of, whatever manner of horse he rides."

His expression became thoughtful. "Honesty, eh? Honourable — of course, honourable, or so I should hope. But his aim only to please? That is asking a great deal, Miss Connie. A man, particularly a man of some standing in society, may surely have some expectation that *others* would wish to please *him*, do you not agree?"

"Oh, certainly. Everyone of breeding should aspire to the same ideal, but in a gentleman, perhaps something more may be expected, by the unequal nature of the sexes. A man must always have power over a woman, my lord. He may order her life as he chooses, and therefore it is imperative that he treat her kindly, otherwise her life would be quite miserable."

Now she was thinking of her father, and his strict regime that had kept his daughters in subjection and, if she were honest, not a little fear. She fell into abstraction, reflecting on her narrow escape from matrimony with Mr Ambleside. She had so nearly stumbled from the clutches of one autocratic man to another, and although Amy was happy to have her life ordered for her, and all decisions made by her husband, Connie hoped for something more equal for herself.

She looked at the Marquess, aristocratic hauteur infusing even his dance steps, and wondered. It would be as well, she told herself, not to be fooled by his pleasant manner. She would need him made very docile by love before she could consider him as a husband. And then she thought again of the younger brother, less handsome, but charmingly eager to please, and wondered.

7: An Invitation

Two days later, Connie and Belle went to stay at Willowbye to oversee the beginnings of the decoration phase, now that most of the building work had been completed. Lady Sara had gone on one of her mysterious journeys again, although where she was going and what she planned to do there she would not say.

This created a dilemma in Connie's mind, for it would not be possible to take their usual chaperon for outings, Miss Bellows, their former governess.

"Miss Bellows must stay here with Dulcie, Grace and Hope," Connie said fretfully. "Is it quite proper for us to stay at Willowbye without her, do you think? I know you and Mr Burford are as good as married, but even so..."

Belle laughed. "Oh, we shall be thoroughly chaperoned, sister, for Cousin Vivienne is still in residence at Willowbye."

"Oh. She has not moved into the Dower House yet?"

"No, and still refuses to do so. It is beneath her dignity, apparently."

Connie gasped in outrage. "That is monstrous! The house is yours — well, Mr Burford's at present, but the lease is signed and everything legal, is it not?"

"And the rent paid for a full year in advance, so that Cousin Henry may defray the cost of repairs to the Dower House. He very kindly stays on too and tries to stop his wife interfering, but I fear we shall have to be hard-hearted soon and ask them to leave."

"Indeed you must! There cannot be two mistresses in one house."

"Quite so," said Belle.

Their arrival at Willowbye was rather different from Connie's previous visit, when only Mr Burford and Cousin Henry had emerged to greet them. The two men were both there again, loitering timidly in the doorway, while the steps in front of them were occupied by Cousin Vivienne, Mary, and James's young wife, Alice. A whole troop of footmen and grooms also appeared to hand the visitors out of their carriage, unload their boxes and take care of the horses. These were augmented by the butler and housekeeper, issuing terse instructions.

"How very pleasant this is," Belle said, stepping forward to greet the ladies and shake hands with Cousin Henry. "Such a reception! We could not have expected it."

"Do come in," Cousin Vivienne said, for all the world as if she were the mistress of the house.

Belle made no response, instead placing her hand on Burford's arm with a warm smile that he answered with one of his own. For an instant, Connie felt a pang of some emotion that was not quite jealousy, but rather a wish that she too had a man who looked at her in just that way. As Ambleside looked at Amy, too. The sooner she could make the Marquess fall in love with her, the better. Or Lord Reginald, perhaps. But the moment passed, and they all proceeded into the great hall. The boxes of books had been cleared away, and the walls were plastered but still unpainted.

Several maids in neat uniforms waited to relieve them of coats and bonnets and gloves. Amongst them was an older woman with a severe face, her clothes well-cut but plain.

"Ah, Beecham," Belle said. "You have arrived safely, I see. Are you settling in well?"

"Very well, thank you, madam."

"Connie, Beecham is the lady's maid I have engaged. You will not mind attending my sister during her stay, Beecham? We shall be sharing the rose bedroom in the new wing."

"It would be a pleasure, madam, but I believe it is to be a different room."

"I have chosen the green room for you, Belle," Cousin Vivienne said. "It is a more convenient location, and I have arranged the room personally with every comfort."

"Thank you, cousin, that was very thoughtful," Belle said smoothly. "However, I believe we will keep to the original plan. The green room is likely to be chilly in this east wind. Phillips, will you prepare the rose bedroom."

"It is already done, madam," said the housekeeper. "You will not find any deficiency."

"You disobeyed my orders!" Cousin Vivienne said, her face darkening.

"Not at all, madam. I thought it best to prepare both rooms, just in case."

Cousin Vivienne would have said something more, but Belle said in her quiet way, "I am delighted to be met with such attentions from both of you. I am sure my sister and I will enjoy our stay immensely, with such unparallelled devotion to our comfort. Come, Connie, let me show you to our room. You will want to refresh yourself after the journey, and then Mr Burford will show us all that has been done to the house since we were last here."

Connie meekly followed her sister through twisting corridors and up a flight of stairs. The various parts of the house had seemingly been added on in a higgledy-piggledy fashion, so there were oddly-shaped doors, mismatched windows and changes of level as they moved from one wing to another. Connie wondered if she would ever be able to find her way about.

"You have remembered the way remarkably well, sister," she said, as they ducked under a low beam, and went through a narrow door into yet another part of the house.

Belle laughed. "I asked Mr Burford to draw me a plan, so that I might not get lost, for I cannot always be calling on Mary or Cousin Vivienne or one of the servants to show me the way. Here we are. If I have it correctly, this is the rose bedroom."

It was as different as could be imagined from Connie's room at Allamont Hall, with its high ceiling, pale walls and light, elegant furniture. Here, dark wood covered the walls completely, and heavy, old-fashioned furnishings stood, solid and sturdy as oxen, in the corners. The massive bed with its maroon velvet drapes was set almost in the middle of the room. Only the deep pink of the ceiling suggested the most tenuous of connections to the name of the room. But a fire burned brightly, there were pressed flowers in frames on the walls and large casement windows revealed a pleasant view over the gardens, with trees and farmland beyond.

The rest of the day passed in a whirl of discussions with the man engaged to oversee the renovations, to explain Connie's ideas for the principal rooms, and to discuss the possibilities for the great hall and some of the bedrooms. Then there was an hour of efficient ministrations by Beecham, who rendered Connie's hair in a new and wonderfully fashionable way. She found herself peeking into every mirror they passed on their way to the dining room, just to reassure herself that this stylish creature really existed.

Dinner was fashionably late, and was rather a large affair, for in addition to Cousins Henry and Vivienne, they were joined by Mary, James and Alice, as well as Alice's parents, Mr and Mrs

Whittle. It was odd company indeed, and all the odder because Henry and Vivienne took their places at the head and foot of the table, exactly as if they were still master and mistress. Cousin Henry looked uncomfortable about it, but Vivienne played the role of gracious hostess with perfect composure.

When they retired to their room that night, Connie burst out, "Oh, Belle, how can you stand it! That woman treats you abominably. I could scarce hold my tongue."

"I hope you will do so, however," Belle said seriously. "I am sorry to say such a thing of a relative, but Cousin Vivienne delights in being vexatious, and much of her pleasure comes from discomposing one or other of us, or setting the servants wrong. She *will* order the servants about as though they are her own, without reference to Mr Burford's wishes in the matter. And he does not quite like to countermand her."

Connie said nothing, for it was not her place to criticise, but she could not help considering whether the virtues of amiability and malleability in a husband might not be outweighed by a little more firmness in the matter of dealing with troublesome relatives. Amy's husband was a little too domineering, but perhaps Belle's was a little too lacking in forthrightness. It was very difficult.

"But there we are," Belle went on, heaving a sigh. "None of us have a say in the family we happen to be born into. And sometimes," she added, half to herself, "we think we have dealt quite successfully with a particularly troublesome individual, and there he is again, quite unwilling to vanish, as one might like."

"You are thinking of Jack Barnett," Connie said.

"Indeed I am. I will not deny, his appearance at the Assembly Rooms was most unsettling."

"It removed all the pleasure from the occasion," Connie said heatedly.

Belle smiled at her vehemence. "Not quite *all*, I hope. There must surely be compensations to someone who finds herself courted by two members of the nobility."

Connie flushed uncomfortably. "You mean, I suppose, the Marquess of Carrbridge and Lord Reginald, but you are quite mistaken, sister. They have both been very amiable, but I do not presume to regard their behaviour as courtship. They have shown no evidence of any attachment stronger than the friendship arising as a natural result of Amy's intimacy with Lady Harriet."

"And what of you, Connie?" Belle said with an affectionate smile. "Either of them would be quite a conquest, and you are on the easiest of terms with both. A little attachment would be quite natural."

"Oh... well, I am not sure..." Connie lowered her head bashfully. "I *do* like them, I must confess. A little *tendre,* perhaps. The Marquess in particular — so handsome! And his brother is very amiable, too. If one of them should fall in love with *me*, then I should be quite happy... although I do not wish to rush into it, you know. There are a great many gentlemen in the world, and I should like to look around me a little before tumbling into matrimony. I was too hasty with Mr Ambleside, but now that I have realised my mistake, it will be better to take my time."

"I heartily approve of *that*," Belle said, adding gently, "And perhaps you should be especially cautious with the Marquess, since it seems to me unlikely that he would consider marrying anyone without a title. Nor is he in need of your fortune."

"Mr Drummond said the estate may be en... en..."

"Encumbered? Even so, he will look for a wife from his own rank, and very likely his brother will too. I should not like you to be disappointed."

"I understand you, and I shall try very hard not to be in love with either of them if I can possibly help it," Connie said, laughing.

Belle laughed too. "I am pleased to hear it. In which case, perhaps you would like to come to London with us in the spring? We are to take a house with the Amblesides, and it needs only Mama's approval to invite you, if you should wish to go. If you were on the point of a betrothal, of course, you would not want to be away from home, but otherwise, think how delightful it would be!"

Connie agreed with this sentiment so whole-heartedly that she cried with joy for an hour at least, and even when she was finally persuaded to climb into the vast bed and the curtains were drawn, she could think of nothing else. Oh, the balls and parties and routs and entertainments that awaited her! And somewhere in London she was sure to meet the perfect man, handsome and charming and strong, full of adoration for her, and richer even than Ambleside or Burford.

~~~~~

This happy plan fell to pieces within an hour of Connie's return to Allamont Hall. Lady Sara had just that day returned from wherever it was that she had been to, but the visit had not mellowed her quite enough.

"Go to London? What nonsense is this?" Lady Sara said in her sternest tones.

"Amy and Belle are to go, Mama, and they have very kindly offered to take me with them. Just think how much my prospects will improve in London society! It is everything of the most delightful, and I would *so* much like to go. May I, Mama? Please may I?"

"Connie, your prospects, as you put it, could hardly be improved upon. You have two sons of a Marquess dancing attendance upon you, and at the last two assemblies you were never without a partner. You will have an offer very soon, I am certain of it. There is no need to go to London."

"But I may get a *better* offer in London, Mama," Connie said.

Her mother looked at her quizzically. "One offer is much the same as another, Connie. One *man* is much the same as another."

"Oh no, surely not!"

"Indeed it is true. Just because your sisters fancy themselves in love is no reason for you to make the same mistake. Love is a poor guide to happiness, and I hope you would never refuse a sensible offer for some foolish romantic notion. A respectable gentleman with a good income — that is all that is required, and you can find that here just as easily as in London. Indeed, the distractions of London are like to bring you home still single. Concentrate on the Marquess and his brother, or, since that is aiming a little high, one of those two young men from High Frickham. They are both very keen, and you may have your pick of them, you know, if you feel you *must* have a choice."

This was no consolation to Connie, who could not tell one from the other. She wept until her eyes were red, and pleaded until her throat was sore, but to no avail. Lady Sara was implacable.

Dulcie was almost as distressed by this refusal as Connie herself, for if there was anything almost as glorious as a season in London, it was her dearest sister enjoying such pleasure in her stead. The two retired to their bedroom at night to weep in each other's arms until they slept in sheer exhaustion.

The lassitude and headache brought on by this despair kept them at home for several days until one morning brought the Marquess and Lord Reginald to call, bearing flowers from their great-aunt's hot-houses.

"We missed you yesterday, for you always call on Great-aunt Augusta, you know," Lord Reginald said. "So we made enquiries and discovered the dreadful news — that Miss Constance is indisposed, and Miss Dulcie stays home to take care of her. But look — we have brought you a few blooms to cheer you up. There! That smile is more like yourself."

"You are too kind, my lord. I thank you — both of you — for your concern for my welfare. I am not ill, truly, but... well, I was at Willowbye and perhaps I over-exerted myself."

"Ah, yes, that would do it, for you are so generous, Miss Constance. Really, you should think of yourself more, for we cannot have you suffer any malady as a result of your efforts for others. But perhaps a short walk in the garden would do you some good? It is mild today, and that dreadful wind has finally blown itself out. I almost feel we are in spring at last."

Connie and Dulcie dutifully fetched cloaks and bonnets, and showed the two lords the way to the garden door. Such attention cheered Connie immensely, especially as Grace and Hope had gone to the village and they could stroll about the paths as two pairs, in a manner that was most comfortable. Connie was moved to explain to Lord Reginald, on whose arm her hand presently rested, the whole sorry tale of her raised hopes, Mama's intransigence and the consequent lowering of her spirits.

"Good Lord, Miss Constance, no wonder you are out of sorts, after such a disappointment! London is of all things the most charming place to be, and I should be upset myself to be deprived of the pleasure of the season. Indeed, we *were*, only last year, for dear Mama died at last, poor soul, and we were kicking our heels at home for the whole season and very dull it was too. So you have all my sympathy. Hey, Dev! Did you hear? Miss Constance has been invited to London for the season, but her Mama will not hear of it."

And in the discussion of the invitation and refusal, and a general milling about, somehow Connie ended up on the Marquess's arm instead. He was just as full of indignation on her behalf, beguiling her with many little tales of the eccentricities of the London season and the pitfalls for the unwary, which made her rather glad she had been spared the ordeals of Court presentation and Almacks and the very modish, but critical, residents of the capital. In this pleasant way, they had walked round half the garden without Connie much noticing her surroundings. She was not a fast walker, however, so gradually Lord Reginald and Dulcie had drawn ahead and disappeared from view.

Connie became aware that she was now quite alone with the Marquess. If she were ever to inspire love in him, she must seize the moment. Poetry had not answered, but there was still Amy's romantic suggestion of flowers. What could be more apt, since Lord Reginald had brought hot-house flowers, for the Marquess to find her some wild flowers?

Consequently, she looked about her for any signs of early blooms. She was not much of an expert on garden plants, and the shrubs around her bore no more than buds as yet. But surely there must be something flowering, even so early in the year?

They had climbed up from the lake and entered the old shrubbery, where bushes as high as trees towered over them and beyond the path lay a tangle of dried stalks, brambles and odd shoots of green. But then, through the undergrowth, she caught a flash of something yellow.

"Oh, look, my lord!" she cried. "Is that a flower, so early in the year? It must be, surely it must be! What a brave sight, after all the winter rain. I should dearly like a closer look at it, but I fear for my gown."

He was very gallant, she had to give him that credit. He immediately plunged into the morass of brambles, to the great risk of his coat, and scrabbled about enthusiastically. But when he returned, covered in leaves and bits of twig, his face was rueful.

"I am sorry to disappoint you, Miss Constance, but you may not be so enchanted with your flowers when you see them."

And he held out a handful of spindly yellow mushrooms.

Connie sighed a little over this second failed attempt to win the Marquess's heart, but he seemed amused and teased her gently about it for the rest of the visit. The following day brought one of the now regular dinners at Allamont Hall, but the first to which the Marquess and his brother had been invited. And no Jess Drummond, to Connie's great satisfaction, which ensured her a pleasant evening with nothing to distract the Marquess. It was a little disappointing that it was Lord Reginald who clung, limpet-like, to her side, but she was reassured by the Marquess's continuing presence in the neighbourhood. Surely he would not stay unless he felt some attraction for her?

But the following day put an end to all such hopes. News came from the village that the Marquess of Carrbridge was engaged to marry Jess Drummond.

8: A Secret Betrothal

"No, no, no! This cannot be," Dulcie exclaimed. "He is in love with Connie, I am quite sure of it."

Belle shook her head. "I never saw any sign of love in him, not for Connie, and not for Jess Drummond, either, although he certainly paid her a great deal of attention. But they are most definitely engaged, or at least there is an understanding, for Miss Endercott had it direct from the housekeeper at the White House, who was told it by Lady Humbleforth's maid. It was all settled between them yesterday, although it is to remain secret for the moment, because of her father's recent death. He told his great-aunt this morning. She is not pleased, apparently."

"I should think not!" Dulcie said. "She should disinherit him at once! That is what I should do, for being so disobliging. Who is Jess Drummond to be marrying a Marquess, I should like to know? She has not a farthing to her name, and although her family may be respectable in Scotland, she is nobody here. I never liked her, never. Did I not say there was something sly about her?"

"Poor Connie," said Hope, wrapping her sister in a warm hug. "Now you will have to start all over again."

"There is always Lord Reginald," Grace said. "Would that answer, do you suppose?"

"What, and have Miss Constance Allamont of Allamont Hall give precedence to the likes of Jess Drummond?" Dulcie said hotly. "Never!"

"Well, it is done," Belle said. "So we must all learn to curtsy to Jess Drummond now."

Lady Harriet arrived very soon afterwards, all indignation and outrage. "I despair of Dev, truly I do," she said, eyes sparkling with anger. "Such a fool, to be taken in by a pretty face and winning ways, when he could have had—" She glanced at Connie, but clamped her lips tightly shut.

"Connie does not want him, I am sure," Dulcie said stoutly.

"Oh. Is that so? That is good, for I had supposed..." Again she trailed off, eyeing Connie speculatively.

"It is quite all right, my lady," Connie said quietly. "There was no attachment on my side." It was not quite true, and now that all possibility of the match was lost, she felt sure that the Marquess would have suited her admirably. Still, if he was so devoid of taste that he preferred Jess Drummond to herself, there was no hope for him, and she would not repine. There was still Lord Reginald, after all, and had she not liked him right from the start? Yes, upon reflection, she was sure that she had felt an attraction from the first moment she had seen him. Such a pleasant man, and so thoughtful.

"Thank goodness!" Lady Harriet said. "For I was worried... Well, no harm done, then. But still, it is *not* a sensible match, however one looks at it, and Great-aunt Augusta was very displeased to be woken to such news. Smelling salts were called for, I hear, and she was positively shouting at Dev, and Great-aunt never raises her voice. She whisked him away to her sitting room, and he had been closeted away with her for an hour or more when I came away. The house was in uproar, as you may imagine."

She rattled on in like manner for some time, requiring no response, for which Connie was very thankful. Although she was quite certain that she was not broken-hearted, yet, in some way she could not quite explain, the idea of the Marquess married to someone else caused her surprising pain. She had begun to consider him as her rightful property, and that had been foolish of her, she could now see. After all, he had been drawn to Jess from the very first, and although his manner to Connie herself had been all that was charming and amiable, he had never distinguished her in any particular way. Latterly, she had spent more time with Lord Reginald, if truth be told.

She could not decide whether it was the loss of the Marquess himself that distressed her, or whether it were merely the idea of Jess Drummond stealing him from under her nose. Eventually, she settled in her own mind that it was the humiliation that hurt her the most. Even though there had been nothing between her and the Marquess, there had been speculation surrounding them. The coincidence of his arrival just at the point when she might be expected to be looking for a husband was bound to attract comment. It was a natural pairing, after all, and even Lady Harriet had wondered about it. Now that the possibility had been lost, she was exposed to the scrutiny of the world as a woman who had been... not jilted, that was too strong a term, but unsuccessful in securing him. Yes, she would be thought to have failed, indeed, she must consider herself to have failed, for had she not set out to entice him to fall in love with her? She had one comfort, that her behaviour had never been such as to court reproof.

But no matter how much she told herself that her heart was still whole, the tears were unaccountably close to the surface, and she was glad when Lady Harriet left, and she could creep away to her room and weep in earnest in Dulcie's sympathetic arms.

The following morning brought Lady Harriet again, and Lord Reginald too. Lady Sara had taken Belle to Brinchester for fittings for her wedding clothes, and Grace and Hope had gone to the village with Miss Bellows, so only Connie and Dulcie were in the winter parlour when the visitors arrived.

"Ah, excellent," said Lady Harriet, surveying the two of them as they bobbed their curtsies. "Dulcie, dear, I wonder if you would be so good as to leave us for a moment, for we wish to talk to Constance alone."

Dulcie's eyes were huge with speculation, but she hastily did as she was bid.

"Now then, dear," Lady Harriet said, sitting down on a sofa and waving Connie to the seat beside her, "let us talk seriously about this business."

Connie could not pretend to misunderstand her meaning, although she was not sure what remained to be said about it, since the Marquess seemed to have concluded the matter most decisively.

"Reggie and I have been considering the situation, and really, it will not do. Miss Drummond is all very well in her way, but she is hardly a suitable Marchioness of Carrbridge. We are both agreed that *you* would be a far more appropriate choice."

"Surely it is a little late for that?" Connie burst out.

Lady Harriet and Lord Reginald laughed. "You may think so, but we know what Dev is like. He plans to whisk Jess off to Drummoor to present her to Grandmama and the great-aunts, and you may be sure he will receive no warmer reception than he obtained from Great-aunt Augusta. Naturally, they will point out to him all the disastrous aspects of this proposed marriage, and he will begin to waver. Now, so long as Jess is there, in sole possession of the field, so to speak, she will keep hold of him, you may be sure. However, if we can present him — and Grandmama — with a far more suitable alternative, we may be able to prise him out of Jess Drummond's grasp."

"I do not think…" Connie began, her voice tremulous. Then, taking a deep breath, she went on, "I believe the Marquess has made his choice. I do not wish to… to *prise* him from the woman he loves."

"Ah, but is it love?" Lord Reginald said. "Infatuation, more like. Dev has been dazzled by this woman, but he will come to realise that he has made a dreadful mistake. All that is required of you, Miss Constance, is to be there when he begins to understand his error."

"But I do not see—" Connie began. "Are you inviting me to Drummoor, my lady?"

"In a manner of speaking," Lady Harriet said. "Now, if you just come for a visit, that would look too particular, as if you were chasing after him, you know, and that would never do. But Reggie and I have come up with a very clever trick. Dev and Jess are secretly betrothed, so why should not you and Reggie be secretly betrothed, too? We will pretend there is an understanding between you, and then you may come to Drummoor as Reggie's soon-to-be betrothed, and that would be quite unexceptional. No one could possibly object to that. "

Connie thought it very likely that a number of people could object, namely the Marquess himself, who would see at once what she was about, not to mention the dragons. It was an outrageous idea.

"I do not much like the idea of pretending," she said quietly. "It all seems dreadfully complicated and… a little dishonest."

"Ah, your scruples do you credit," Lord Reginald said. "How admirable! But there is nothing dishonest about it in the slightest. Hatty, do explain it to Miss Constance."

"All perfectly above reproach," Lady Harriet said firmly. "You will come to Drummoor as my friend, which is no less than the truth. Naturally, everyone will *assume* that there is an understanding between you and Reggie, but there will be no need for it to be said openly. If anyone is so impolite as to ask directly, you need only blush, I shall look knowing and Reggie will deny the existence of a betrothal in the strongest terms. That will fix the idea, yet not a single untruth will be told. People believe what they want to believe. I shall write a letter to your mama inviting you to Drummoor, with just a hint about Reggie. She will get the point, I am sure."

Connie was not comfortable with the plan, but they sounded so certain of it, and who should be better placed to judge the propriety of an action than the son and daughter of a marquess? And Mama would forbid it if she saw anything in the least irregular about the scheme. She hesitated, torn. A visit to Drummoor would be everything that was delightful, although she had no intention of trying to *prise* the Marquess away from Jess Drummond, not the least idea in the world. If he should happen to tire of her, Connie would be there on the spot, but she would not interfere. Oh, but a visit to Drummoor! How enticing a prospect it was!

"Besides," Lord Reginald went on smoothly, "if we are secretly betrothed, you will have to come to London with us and stay at Marford House, and think how much fun that will be, eh? We shall take you about, and you must realise, Miss Constance, Hatty and Dev and I are very good *ton*, received everywhere. We can get you vouchers for Almacks, you know. But you will have to have a great many new gowns and such like. Hatty can take care of all that for you. What do you say?"

Connie could not say a word. If she opened her mouth, even a little, she felt that she would burst into raptures and be quite unable to stop. Her mama could not possibly object to such a plan if she believed there was a betrothal involved, and a pretend, secret betrothal would do just as well for the purpose.

But here her conscience prickled a little at the thought of deceiving her mother. That was not right, surely? And yet, where was the deception? Mama would know exactly where she was and with whom, and there was nothing underhand about her purpose in going to London. She had already given up any thought of detaching the Marquess from Jess Drummond, nor was she interested in securing a husband for herself. It would be good for her to mix in the upper echelons of the *ton* for a few weeks to gain a little town polish, and there was no more to it than that.

So she nodded vigorously enough to leave them in no doubt of her acceptance. Lady Harriet clapped her hands in delight, and Lord Reginald beamed at her, raising her hand to his lips.

And thus it was that Connie found herself secretly not-quite-betrothed to Lord Reginald Marford, and packing her boxes to leave for Drummoor.

~~~~~

There was a short delay while a chaperon was obtained for the journey. Lady Harriet was rather cross that the Marquess had summoned her first choice in order to chaperon Jess, but she seemed to know an array of ladies suited to the purpose and willing to rush about the country at a moment's notice. Within a few days all was arranged and they could set off.

The journey to Drummoor lasted three days, but nothing could have been more comfortable. Connie sat beside Lady Harriet in that lady's luxurious carriage, with Lord Reginald opposite, while the two of them chattered endlessly about Drummoor and their vast web of relations and acquaintance, and told any number of entertaining, not to say scandalous, stories of the *ton*. Her companions were delighted to discover that she had never been away from home before, and regaled her with every detail of the roads, the towns and villages they passed through, and the rivers and rocky hills they spied, until her head was spinning.

The chaperon was a timid soul who said scarcely a word the entire time, merely nodding and smiling whenever anyone else spoke. If asked a question directly, she answered as briefly as possible, nodding the whole time, but since Lady Harriet and Lord Reginald seldom addressed a word to her, she remained mostly silent.

"She is terribly quiet," Connie murmured to Lady Harriet on one occasion. "Is she quite well, do you suppose?"

"There is nothing more trying than a talkative chaperon," Lady Harriet said, eyes twinkling. "She is well paid to be silent, I assure you."

One of the grooms rode ahead on Lord Reginald's horse, so that every time they stopped at an inn, there was a private parlour already secured with a fire burning merrily, a hot meal appeared within minutes, and at night there was hot water and a comfortable bedchamber, with none of the filthy sheets or nasty insects or pungent odours Connie had been led to expect of inns.

At last they came to Drummoor. The carriage swept through a turreted archway, and then along a winding drive bordered by oaks and lesser trees, so arranged that occasional gaps afforded a partial view of the house on a distant hill. With a final twist, the trees were left behind and there was the house in all its glory, its mellow golden stone warm in the spring sunshine, and the battlemented roof making it seem quaintly medieval.

Connie cried out in delight. "Oh, you live in a *castle!*"

Her two companions were vastly amused by this epithet. "Just because it has a crenellated roof does not make it a castle," Lord Reginald said.

"Well, that is disappointing," Connie said. "I should like to imagine archers lurking behind those battlements."

"Ah, how romantic you are," he said. "Sadly, there is no moat, either, nor a portcullis, nor any crevice for the deposit of boiling oil on enemies. There are two secret passages, however, and a priest hole."

Connie's eyes widened. "How exciting!"

"But not very accurate," Lady Harriet said with her ready smile. "Reggie, do not tease so! The house was built long after the era of priest holes, and what Reggie is amused to describe as such is probably no more than a closet which has been boarded over. And the secret passages are stairs for the servants. Here we are at last. Are you ready, Constance?"

A troop of servants streamed out of the house to receive them, bustling about the carriage and the less luxurious coach behind them which conveyed Lady Harriet's maid, Lord Reginald's valet and all their many boxes. Connie stepped down onto the drive, looking about her with interest. From a distance, she had noticed only the impressive size and splendour of the house. Now that she was so close, she could see weeds growing through the gravel, faded paint on doors and windows, and the patched uniforms of the servants. It now struck her how worn was the velvet upholstery in the carriage. There was no deficiency in the attire of Lady Harriet or her brothers, but elsewhere there were noticeable signs of neglect.

Lady Harriet tucked Connie arm into hers. "I know you would rather rest, but Grandmama will want to meet you at once. Do you mind terribly?"

"Of course not," Connie said, shocked at the very idea of refusing a Dowager Marchioness anything she might wish for.

The four dragons, as she still thought of them, were seated in the red saloon, an overpowering room decorated and gilded and embellished in every conceivable way. Massive portraits of previous occupants stared haughtily down from the walls. Four bewigged and powdered footmen stood as rigid as soldiers in the corners of the room, and an imperious butler watched everything hawk-eyed.

"Ah, Miss Allamont! Do come in," boomed a large lady in purple filling a chair at the far end of the room.

"Grandmama," whispered Lady Harriet.

Connie made her obeisances to the Dowager. On a sofa nearby sat the other three dragons in a row, the stout Lady Christopher Marford, the more slender Lady Ruth Marford, and the wafer-thin and very frail Lady Hester Marford. Connie wondered whether they deliberately chose to arrange themselves both by size and by age for effect, or whether it was entirely a matter of chance.

The dragons were not the only occupants of the room. Connie was very thankful for the hours of instruction received on the journey, for otherwise the array of companions, cousins and other distant relatives would have left her sadly confused. But there were two she recognised immediately — the Marquess and Jess Drummond, the latter sitting smilingly beside the Dowager. Connie was given a seat on the Dowager's other side, and nothing could have been more gracious than that lady's manner, all welcoming smiles and gentle questions and not in the least intimidating. And as the others beamed at her benevolently, she felt, in some extraordinary way, quite at home.

9: Tambray Hall

Connie passed ten days at Drummoor, and reckoned them amongst the happiest of her life. It was a little awkward to be the recipient of so many hinted good wishes for a betrothal she knew to be a sham, but Lord Reginald was always there to respond, so she never had to say a word. Her blushes were taken as the natural bashfulness of a woman soon to be a bride, and before too long she began to be quite easy about it. Then there were the pleasures of being a guest at Drummoor. She had her own bedroom for the first time in her life, and was assigned a maid who lasted precisely five minutes before unbending towards her and regaling her with all the below-stairs gossip.

Lord Reginald and Harriet took it upon themselves to show her every room and passage and closet in the building, and introduce her to everyone from the butler down to the blushing scullerymaid, rigid with fear at actually meeting members of the family. The Marquess and Jess were usually of the party, too, and there was so much teasing between the sister and brothers that the five of them got along merrily. Connie soon lost any trace of shyness and chattered away as if she had known them all her life. Even Jess was friendly, and since she was every bit as frivolous here as at Lower Brinford, treating life as one huge joke, and not in the least presumptuous or stuffy about her betrothal, Connie began to like her despite her best endeavours not to.

One day they all went up to the roof, which was much the same as any other roof, to Connie's intense disappointment. However, the two brothers were grinning with glee.

"We have a surprise for you," Lord Reginald whispered to Connie. "We are going to transport you back to the middle ages."

With cries of triumph, they produced two rusty old swords from a corner where they had hidden them, and began bashing away at each other with great metallic clashes and shouts of delight, while the three ladies squealed and urged them on.

"Is this not the greatest amusement?" the Marquess said to Connie, when the two broke apart momentarily to catch their breath. "We are knights, you see, fighting for the hand of the fair maiden."

"I was under the impression you had already won the hand of your fair maiden, my lord," she said sharply.

"Oh — oh yes, of course." He threw a quick glance towards Jess, then gave a little laugh. "It is just a pretence, of course. This is all in pretence, Miss Allamont."

Then, with shouts of glee, the battle started up again. They went on until Lord Reginald clouted his brother on the ear, drawing blood.

Connie gasped with alarm, but the Marquess was laughing too hard for her to sustain any fears for his safety. "Ow, ow, ow! What are you about, brother? Look, I am bleeding! Supposed to be blunt," he gasped, between bursts of laughter. "Good Lord, Reggie, were you trying to have my head off? A pretty scheme for the second son, eh?" And he went off into more peals of laughter.

"Is this not fun?" Lady Harriet said, slipping an arm through Connie's. "They are idiots, of course, but very amusing."

"Yes, very amusing," Connie said, then added, half to herself, "Papa would not have approved."

It pleased Connie greatly to find that the Marquess treated her exactly the same as before. He showed Jess no special attention, and was just as likely to sit beside Connie at dinner or while playing cards. Since the plan concocted by Lady Harriet and Lord Reginald was simply for Connie to provide an alternative to Jess, and wait for the Marquess to see the error of his precipitous betrothal, she need do nothing but enjoy his company, something she found all too easy to do. Nothing could have been more pleasant.

Even the dragons were far less fearsome than she had been led to believe. The Dowager Marquess could be a little stiff, it was true, but her three sisters-in-law were most amiable, and Connie enjoyed talking to them, and asking what Drummoor was like in the past.

"Ah, the glory days!" Lady Christopher sighed. "The masked balls! You never saw the like, my dear. And the fashions so much more robust than nowadays. These flimsy muslins have no substance to them, and no one dreams of wearing a woollen cloak any more, something heavy enough to deter a shower and defeat the wind. No, they must needs wear these silly little spencers, and then are astonished when they take a chill. I hope you are more sensible, my dear."

"Oh, yes, I—"

"A woollen chemise all year round," the Dowager said. "That is the way to avoid chills."

"And a hot brick in the bed," Lady Ruth said.

"Yes, very true," the Dowager said. "For myself, I take a purgative every week, without fail, and a posset before bed. No malady can prevail against such a regime."

Connie looked at the Dowager's robust appearance, and suspected that no chill or fever would dare to inflict itself upon her.

Yet Lady Hester, the eldest of the dragons, looked as if a puff of wind would be too much for her to endure. She walked only with support on either side, wheezing as she went, and ate almost nothing. Connie wondered that she had made the effort to travel to Drummoor at all.

She got very confused, sometimes, too. "When you are married to Francis..." she would say.

Then Connie would gently pat her arm. "No, my lady, the Marquess is to marry Miss Drummond, remember?"

"Oh. Miss Drummond. Yes. I see." But she would frown, as if she could not quite grasp the concept, and sometimes she would say, "Not you, Miss Allamont?" in a querulous tone.

Lady Hester's companion was almost as old and infirm as she was, so Connie delighted in running little errands for them both, and indeed for all the dragons. She had never known her own grandparents or great-aunts, or the pleasures of a vast array of distant relations, and it pleased her beyond measure to be part of the Marquess's extensive family.

Some mornings there were callers to receive, and on other days the ladies summoned the carriage to make their own duty calls around the neighbourhood. It was necessary for Jess and Connie to be a part of these expeditions, and Lady Harriet was quite shameless in hinting at their status as the future brides of Drummoor. Connie blushed and blushed again at the devious way it was managed without a single untruth, relieved beyond measure that she had no need to broach the subject herself. Still, she had agreed to the situation, so it was foolish to have reservations now, and in all other respects she enjoyed these outings immensely.

One such visit was of particular interest. Drummoor's estate was bounded to the north by the land belonging to Tambray Hall, where Lady Sara's brother lived.

"We really ought to pay a call at Tambray," Lady Harriet said one day at breakfast. "We have not seen them for an age. Either they are away or we are, so we keep missing each other. But I had word yesterday that they are home again for a while. Should you like to visit them?"

"Oh, I should like it of all things!" Connie cried, clapping her hands together. "For I have never met my uncle and aunt at all."

There were twelve people sat around the table, and they all turned to stare at Connie. One of the cousins raised a lorgnette to her eye.

"Never met them?" Lady Harriet said. "What, never?"

"Not once. They have never visited us at Allamont Hall and I have never been to Tambray Hall. Or to Hepplestone. Mama goes occasionally, but my sisters and I have never been invited."

"That is extraordinary," the Marquess said.

"Families are odd in a multitude of ways," Lord Reginald said easily. "I daresay there is a good reason for it. Hatty, may I trouble you for the bread bowl?"

So to Tambray Hall they were to go, Connie, Jess and Lady Harriet in the carriage, and the two men on horseback. Connie could not quite disentangle her feelings in the matter. Naturally, she had a great deal of curiosity to see the house and meet her uncle and aunt, but at the same time, she had to agree with the Marquess that there might be some very good reason why she had never been invited there, and why her relations had never come to Allamont Hall. And none of them ever had, not from Mama's side of the family, and not from Papa's either. So many aunts and uncles and cousins and grandparents, but she could not picture them or their houses. They were just names.

Tambray Hall was a plain little house, very modern, built of the same yellow stone as Drummoor, but without any of the grandeur or style that epitomised the older residence. Nor were the grounds extensive. There were no sweeping vistas, follies or tumbling streams, just neatly trimmed low hedges arranged in squares, with a larger bush, trimmed to a perfect sphere, on every corner. There was no colour, no wilderness, not a leaf out of place.

They were shown into a square room with dark wainscoting, the upper walls covered in a dull blue silk. The ceiling was painted a paler blue. Connie felt quite nauseous, as if she were under water. Chairs and sofas, upholstered in the same blue as the walls, were arranged in a perfect square. How much these people liked squares! And how Connie longed to refit the room in paler colours, with more elegant furnishings.

Viscount and Viscountess Melthwaite rose to greet them, polite smiles on their faces. They glanced briefly at Jess and Connie, but were too well-bred to show any surprise. Connie watched them as Harriet curtsied and made her greetings, and then her two brothers. Her aunt and uncle! Such a strange way to meet them, and how astonishing to be faced with a man who had Mama's mouth and nose and wavy blond hair. Even the eyes were the same, although where Mama's were almost unlined, Uncle Edmund's crinkled a little at the corners, as if he smiled a great deal. Or frowned, perhaps.

Jess was introduced first, and then Harriet turned to Connie. "And this is a lady you have never met before, I understand — your niece, Miss Constance Allamont."

The squeals of delight were all that Connie could have hoped for. She found herself wrapped in a tight embrace from her aunt, who shed tears of joy over her.

"My dear, dear Constance! You cannot imagine how much we have longed to see you — indeed, all of you! Such a joy! Let me look at you! Oh, Edmund, is she not pretty? And you are staying at Drummoor! Such delight! Oh, my dear, this is a wonderful surprise. Your poor mother told us nothing about it, nothing at all."

Connie laughed and cried, too, as much in relief as for any other reason. It struck her as odd, however, that they should have wanted to see the sisters so badly, and yet not contrived a meeting in twenty five years, especially when Mama had stayed at Tambray Hall on a number of occasions over the years. It was not as if there were an unbridgeable breach between the two sides of the family.

After a few minutes of these raptures, her uncle coughed in a meaningful way. Aunt Emma's eyes immediately lowered demurely.

"Do please be seated," she murmured. "How was your journey today? Are the roads tolerable?"

Lady Harriet responded in the same manner, and for several minutes the conversation was stilted and formal. But then Aunt Emma burst out, "Oh, my dear niece, how delightful this is!" And away she went again, in excited twitterings.

They stayed for two hours, Aunt Emma talking with barely a pause the entire time. Every once in a while, Uncle Edmund coughed and Aunt Emma subsided into polite nothings for a few moments before becoming animated again. Although she asked innumerable questions, she barely listened to the answers, and would ask exactly the same thing a few minutes later. Connie did not mind in the least. She set it down to excitement, and made allowances accordingly. She was almost as excited herself. Finally, she had met some of her family!

Still, it was odd how little her aunt and uncle knew of affairs at Allamont Hall. The Viscount and Viscountess had seen Lady Sara when they had stayed at Hepplestone just after Christmas, but they knew nothing of Amy's marriage or Belle's betrothal, and when Connie mentioned her brothers Ernest and Frank, Aunt Emma said casually, "They must be well grown by now, but even so, it will be daunting for them, taking on the responsibility of the Hall, and being head of the family. I have always been thankful that Edmund has not yet been called upon to shoulder that burden. The poor, dear boys! How are they coping?"

Connie hardly knew what to say. In the end, she could think of no gentle way to break the news. "They know nothing of it. They ran away from home seven years ago, and not a word has been heard from them since."

Lady Melthwaite made a little mewing sound of distress, her hands covering her mouth.

The Viscount frowned. "Ran away? Seven years ago?"

"Yes, my lord."

"But why? Why?" Lady Melthwaite wailed.

"We have no notion why they would do such a thing," Connie said. "It is a mystery."

"No, no! I meant to say, why would Sara not tell us about it? Why has she told us nothing at all about any of you?"

It was not a question Connie could answer, so she kept silent, although she clutched her reticule rather tightly.

Lord Melthwaite put a calming hand on his wife's arm. "Sara was always a deep one, my love. She keeps her own counsel, and even as a child one never knew what was in her head. No doubt she has her reasons for her silence."

"One cannot imagine what they might be," Lady Melthwaite said indignantly. "We have never had any *real* quarrel with her, always corresponded, never cut her even when—"

Her husband coughed, and squeezed her arm, and she lowered her eyes at once. "Let us talk of pleasanter matters," he said. "Do tell us more of your family, Miss Drummond. So you are neighbours to the Earl of Strathmorran?"

Jess jumped in quickly, and the conversation moved into calmer waters, but Connie took no more part in it. So confusing! Why would her mother visit her relations regularly, and yet say nothing about her own family? She could not understand it in the least.

Then, just as they were preparing to leave at last, her aunt said brightly, "You must give our regards to your poor mama, Constance. How I wish we could see her more often! I suppose there is no hope of her being in London this season?"

"I cannot say," Connie answered.

"No, for she never goes there."

"Oh, indeed, she does. She has been there several times since Papa died."

"Really?" Her aunt looked at her quizzically. "She went to London, yet never stayed at Heatherington House? Never even left her card? Well, that is too bad, to put up at a hotel like the merest nobody." Her voice rose querulously, but again a touch from her husband calmed her.

"I daresay it was a very brief visit for business reasons," Lord Melthwaite said, frowning at his wife. "There must have been many matters to settle, papers to sign, and so forth. Perhaps the house was shut up and she did not wish to open it up for a short time. An hotel is more practical in such cases, and some of them are quite tolerable, so I believe."

"Oh no, she did not stay at an hotel," Connie said brightly. "Mama stayed with Aunt Tilly."

This time, Lady Melthwaite's scream was loud enough to turn all heads towards her. Then she fell back unconscious into her husband's arms.

10: A Wedding

The three ladies sat in silence in the carriage as it swayed over the ruts and splashed through puddles. Through the window, Connie caught an occasional glimpse of the rump of Lord Reginald's horse trotting along ahead of them. It was difficult to see much else, for her eyes would keep filling with tears.

They were more than half way back to Drummoor when Lady Harriet gave a low chuckle. "Well, I must say, Connie, your family is most intriguing. I have the liveliest wish to know more of Aunt Tilly. You must find out all you can about her, in order to satisfy my curiosity, for I warn you, I shall not be satisfied until every secret—" She made a clucking noise. "Oh dear, do not cry. There is nothing to dismay one in having disreputable relatives, you know. We all have them. Emma is such an excitable creature, and so stuffy that ten to one you will find that Aunt Tilly married someone in trade, and there is no more to it than that. There, there, do not take on so!"

"I am very sorry," Connie said through her sobs, in a whisper.

"For myself, I should be more interested to know why Lady Sara tells her own brother so little about her family," Jess said. "That seems very queer to me."

"I am sure Mama had very good reasons for that," Connie said with some heat. "Indeed, why should she talk about domestic matters when she is a guest elsewhere? Parties at

Tambray and Hepplestone are so gay that I daresay she never had a moment to think about us."

Jess arched her eyebrows. "Hepplestone, perhaps, but nothing gay ever happened at Tambray, I would wager. I am sorry to speak ill of your relatives, Connie, but your aunt and uncle are dry old sticks. That is to say, your uncle is, and your aunt is very much under his thumb. I am not sure they even know how to enjoy themselves."

This piece of spite was all the more irritating to Connie because it was precisely in agreement with her own opinion. She chose to be offended, however, and stared in silent vexation out of the window for the rest of the journey, the only happy aspect being that her annoyance with Jess had quite dried up her tears.

The subject could not be forgotten, however, for the Dowager Marchioness insisted on hearing all about the visit, and so the whole story came tumbling out. Lady Harriet chose her words carefully but there was no disguising their import.

"The Lady Matilda?" Lady Carrbridge said. "Oh, yes, I remember the scandal. A viscount, it might have been, and then there was a whisper about a member of the royal family, although I never did discover who. But what of it? Such things happen in the best-ordered of families, and it is not so terrible that one would bother to fall into the vapours. But Emma always was dreadfully silly. Dear me, Lady Matilda! I have not heard a word about her in an age. And so she lives in London still, and your mama goes to visit her? Well, well."

~~~~~

Connie was already in bed that evening, and rereading the last letter from Belle before the candle was quite burnt down, when there was a scratching at the door, followed almost instantly by its opening and Jess Drummond's head appearing round it.

"May I come in for a minute?"

"Oh — of course, if you wish."

Jess slipped into the room, and closed the door softly behind her. Setting her candle down beside Connie's, she perched on the side of the bed, pulling her wrap closer around her.

"I wanted to apologise to you, Miss Allamont," she said quietly, all her usual ebullience quite gone. "I was very rude about your uncle and aunt, and I fear I offended you. Sometimes my tongue runs away with me, and... no, that is no excuse. I should know better. I am ashamed of myself. Can you ever forgive me?"

"What did you say that was untrue?" Connie said, smiling wryly. "They *are* dry old sticks. And that house! Not a curve or so much as a candle-snuffer out of place. Symmetry is over-rated, I feel."

Jess laughed. "It *was* very rigid, was it not? So many straight lines! That bend in the staircase must irritate them so much. I had to bite my tongue to prevent myself from asking why they do not have the whole stair ripped out and replaced with straight flights. Right angles, Miss Allamont, every house must be constructed entirely in right angles."

That made Connie giggle. "Now *this* house is very symmetrical, but it is a pleasing symmetry, and not at all dull. Every room in perfect proportion, every wing placed in such a way as to enhance the whole."

"Yes, it is lovely." Jess heaved a sigh. "If only I could stay."

"But you can! You will be living here after you are married. My dear Miss Drummond, it will be your house."

Jess was silent for a while, then she said quietly, "I cannot see it happening. It is like a dream... You have no idea, Miss Allamont, how delightful it is to find myself living in comfort once more. Do not mistake me, for Alex and I are exceedingly grateful for the offer of employment and the schoolhouse at

Lower Brinford. Truly I do not know what would have become of us without it, but the house is so *small*. I felt so cramped there, as if I were living in a hen house. And then I came here, to discover that the old ladies have one wing and the young ladies another, and the brothers yet another, and there are still innumerable rooms to spare. It is too perfect for words, but I dare not depend on it. I shall have my season in London and then... who knows what will become of me?"

"Why, you will marry the Marquess and be very rich and very grand," Connie said, in surprise. "What else?"

But Jess shook her head, with another sigh. "He could find himself a far more suitable wife, and as soon as he reaches London, that is exactly what he will do, I am certain."

Connie hugged her tight. "The change in your situation is excessive, I agree, and it is no wonder you are unsettled at the suddenness of it all, but you must trust the Marquess's judgement on the matter. He is the one who knows what qualities in a wife would best suit him, after all."

Jess's face lit up. "Yes! You are very wise."

Connie shook her head. "Not wise, no, but I do think that men are capable of deciding on a wife for themselves. I am sure the Marquess is."

"I believe you are right, Miss Allamont."

"Surely we know each other well enough to be on first name terms?"

"Oh — thank you! And now, I must go back to bed, or I shall be yawning tomorrow and the old ladies will glare at me, and make disapproving tutting noises. Goodnight, Connie."

"Sleep well, Jess."

This conversation gave Connie a much better opinion of Jess, for all her sympathies were aroused by her difficulties, and she could see that Jess was not at all mercenary in her dealings with the Marquess. But still, she was betrothed to him, there was no getting around that point, even if it must be kept secret for now, and Connie was determined not to interfere. Of course, there was still Lord Reginald...

~~~~~

The date set for Belle's wedding to Mr Burford was fast approaching, and Connie wished to return to Allamont Hall in time for this event. Lady Harriet, her two brothers and Jess obligingly made the journey too, which was identical in nature to the previous one. They were several times struck by sudden showers of freezing rain, or even sleet, but the weather was never so severe as to delay them or make the roads impassable.

Connie was delighted to be home, and happy to answer her sisters' excited questions. There was so much to tell, and every little detail was of the utmost interest to the Miss Allamonts, most of whom had never travelled beyond the confines of the local villages and Brinchester. Amy and Belle had enjoyed a month in London when they first came out, under the auspices of Aunt Lucy who had come down from Liverpool to bring them out, and Amy had herself been to Drummoor briefly some months ago, but the younger sisters had never travelled at all. So there was a keen interest in all that Connie could tell, made all the more fascinating by the supposed double betrothal of the two lords, and the delicious secrecy involved, which appealed to their romantic instincts.

Yet Connie shivered as she spoke, for sooner or later she must reach the disagreeable parts of her tale — Tambray Hall, and the matter of Aunt Tilly. What could she say that would not sound melodramatic? How to explain that the mere mention of Aunt Tilly had induced Aunt Emma to faint clean away? And, most of all, what would Mama say? But it could not be avoided.

Lady Sara said nothing at all. Connie glanced repeatedly at her mother's face, but it was as serene as always, giving no hint of disapprobation. After a while, she left the room altogether, leaving the sisters alone. But later, when Connie was in her room with Dulcie, overseeing the unpacking of her boxes, a knock on the door heralded the housekeeper.

"Beg pardon for interrupting you, Miss Connie, but her ladyship would like a word. She is in her sitting room."

"Whatever can Mama want?" Dulcie said, but then answered her own question. "Oh, it will be about your clothes for London, I expect. That will be it."

Connie thought it unlikely to be anything so mundane. Meekly she crossed the landing to Lady Sara's new sitting room, walking on her toes as if that way her arrival might be so silent as to pass unnoticed. The room had been a bedroom for guests originally, but it had been so seldom used for that purpose that, after Papa's death, it had been refurbished to become her mother's private retreat. Connie had never been inside it before. Knocking timidly on the door, when her mother answered she opened it just enough to peer into the room.

"Do not loiter on the threshold like a housemaid, Connie," Lady Sara said. "Come in, do."

Obediently, she stepped inside and carefully closed the door.

"You wished to see me, Mama?" she said, as she made her curtsy.

Her mother stood beside the fire, one arm resting on the mantlepiece, her fingers running over the decorative swirls on an ornate clock.

"I wish to know why you think it necessary to tell the whole world our business."

Connie hung her head, feeling tears very close. "I beg your pardon, Mama. I did not know…"

"What did you not know?"

"That… that I should not talk about… certain things."

"Certain things?" Her mother uttered a ripple of laughter. "You mean Aunt Tilly? No, I suppose you would not know that she is excluded from all good society. How could you, indeed?"

"Is she?" Connie said, lifting her head abruptly. "How is that possible, when *you* visit her, Mama?"

That brought gusts of laughter from Lady Sara. "Oh yes, I am such good *ton* that I bestow consequence and respectability on everyone I encounter. Oh, Connie, you are such an innocent. Sit, child, and let me explain it to you."

Lady Sara settled on a silk-covered chaise longue, and Connie perched on a matching chair. They were very elegant pieces, she decided, and the yellow Chinese wallpaper was the perfect foil for them. Her mother had excellent taste.

"I know you see me only as your mama," Lady Sara said. "When I am here, that is, of course, exactly what I am. That is *all* I am. But I am also the Lady Sara Heatherington of Hepplestone, daughter of the Earl of Harkwood, and when I go there, or to Tambray, that is exactly who I wish to be. My life is divided into little boxes, Connie, and when I am in one box, nothing else exists. When I go to London, well, that is another box. When I go into Shropshire... you understand what I am saying, I am sure."

"I think so, Mama," Connie said, although it was all terribly confusing. "So I may not mention Aunt Tilly to anyone?"

"It would perhaps be better to maintain a discreet silence on that subject. As for Ernest and Frank, and your sisters' marital arrangements — these are of no concern to anyone outside our immediate family, I am sure. People do like to gossip, and I have the greatest dislike of being the subject of gossip. You did not mention Mr Eddington, I hope?"

"No, Mama."

"Good. Do not do so. Your Aunt Emma is a very worthy person, no doubt, but she always thinks the worst of people.

She would be bound to put an erroneous interpretation on my friendship with Mr Eddington, and we would not want to throw her into more paroxysms of hysteria, would we?" She laughed again, quite merrily, as if Aunt Emma's hysteria were a great joke.

Connie could think of no sensible response, so she lowered her head again, hands neatly folded in her lap.

"Well, so you are to go to London after all," Lady Sara went on. "That was a sly piece of work, to take up with Lord Reginald in that devious manner, but you were always so good at manipulating people to get your own way. You will do very well in London, I make no doubt, and I am pleased that there need be no expense or inconvenience to me. I just hope you do not fall into error. London is so seductive, it is very easy to be led astray, so take care, child. Now off you go, and close the door behind you."

~~~~~

Amy's wedding had been a pleasantly quiet affair, for Mr Ambleside had no close relatives still living, and only a pair of cousins made the journey. As Connie now knew, none of Amy's relations had even been informed of the occasion.

Belle's wedding, however, was very different. Mr Burford was amply provided with brothers and aunts and cousins, he had notified them all well in advance of the wedding, and a great many of them liked him well enough to travel from Yorkshire. Or perhaps the attraction was his sudden very large inheritance, a change in circumstance which tends to attract even the most reticent and distant of kin. Whatever the reason, they filled all the guest bedrooms at the Hall, spilled over into the parsonage at Lower Brinford and squeezed into every available inn in Lower and Higher Brinford.

Mr Burford's father and three brothers were staying at the Hall, as well as a couple of the more important cousins. The days were filled with excursions and bustle, and each evening brought more visitors for dinner, filling the house with chattering voices and music and merriment. Such evenings were a delight to Connie, with card tables brought out, or the furniture moved aside for impromptu dancing, and so many new sources of conversation that she hardly knew where to turn. She had never known such a lively time at the Hall.

On the last night before the wedding, when the gentlemen rejoined the ladies after dinner, Mr Luke Burford came to sit beside her.

"Miss Connie, is it not? Ah, I am beginning to recognise each one of you at last, for I have to tell you that, to a stranger such as myself, you and your sisters look very much alike."

"So I have been told, sir, and indeed, when poor Papa was alive, the difficulty was even greater, for he insisted we all dress alike. Only a coloured ribbon was allowed to distinguish one from another. Green was my colour, and I did not mind that, for it is quite a favourite of mine, but poor Belle had to wear pink which is *not* flattering to her at all, and Hope was in worse case, for her colour was black. Do you not think it a strange notion? Oh, Mrs Luke is to sing for us. She has the most charming voice, do you not agree?"

"Yes, indeed, and—"

"And her mastery of Italian is excellent. I know a little of the language, but not enough to sing in it without stumbling."

"Perhaps we should listen to the singing?" he suggested gently.

"Oh. Oh, certainly."

Mrs Luke sang quite well, but her voice was not strong and Connie's attention soon wandered. Gazing around the room, her eye fell on Amy, Mr Ambleside next to her, as always. Such a devoted husband, and especially now, in her delicate condition. He was fussing around with a screen, trying to shield her from some imaginary draught, Connie supposed. To think that she might have been the one to suffer such excessive attentions. She was glad to have escaped that trap!

Not far away, Belle and Burford sat, whispering with their heads bent together. They were smiling contentedly, and there was no doubting their mutual affection, but what an awkward beginning they would have to their married life, with Willowbye still full of men with ladders and paintbrushes, and Cousin Vivienne interfering and upsetting the servants. They seemed not to mind, but Connie could not contemplate such an unromantic arrangement.

As her gaze roamed, she caught sight of Lord Reginald watching her. He stood on the far side of the room behind the instrument, leaning casually against the wall, arms folded, as if merely enjoying the music. But when he caught Connie's eye, his smile deepened and one hand fluttered in the smallest of waves.

Immediately she was overwhelmed with guilt, for in all the excitement of the wedding and the endless comings and goings, she was inclined to forget for hours at a time that she was supposedly engaged to marry Lord Reginald. It was all a great secret, but nevertheless, she ought to pay him some attention. Even when she was with him, she thought very little about him. Her reflections tended still towards his older brother, with his so-beautiful features and his incomparable style. Beside the Marquess, Lord Reginald did not appear to advantage, very much second best in her opinion.

But now, seeing that smile, so like the smiles she saw on Ambleside and Burford as they gazed at their loves, it occurred to her for the first time to wonder whether Lord Reginald was really as indifferent as he pretended to be? Was there, perhaps, a little more warmth in that smile — the same charming Marford smile as his older brother — than might be expected in a pretend lover? Her heart gave a little lurch.

"Miss Connie?" said Mr Luke, and Connie had the feeling that it was not the first time he had addressed her. The song had ended, and there was an opportunity for conversation again.

"I beg your pardon, sir, I was wool-gathering, I fear."

"Ah, but you have no need at all to apologise, madam, for I observed the direction of your thoughts very clearly, and a very handsome personage he is indeed." Connie could only blush, and hope that he could not, in fact, read her thoughts. "I shall not tease you with speculation on the precise state of your connection to that gentleman, for although I have heard certain rumours, I understand your reticence very well. In such an exalted family as the Marfords, the legal arrangements can be considerable and take some time to untangle to the satisfaction of all parties. You are wise not to rush headlong into... well, you understand me, I am sure."

Connie was too embarrassed to utter a word, her cheeks aflame.

"But however elevated the gentleman may be, you need not be ashamed of your own contribution. In fact, delay is very much to your advantage." He laughed suddenly. "I daresay I should not tell you this, Miss Connie, for it is rather a confidential matter, but I know from all John has told me that you are aware of the situation. The longer you wait before you marry, the larger the dowry you will have."

Connie stared at him. "You know something of that?"

"I do. My partner — and also my wife's father, as it happens — has the management of the fund which is to provide your dowries."

"Oh! Then you must know why it increases!"

"I know *how* it increases, Miss Connie, but not why. The account is held at a local bank in Market Clunbury, where I live. Each Monday, a man arrives at the bank and pays in a sum of money to that account, always in coins, never notes. Two or three hundred each week goes into that account, nothing is ever withdrawn, apart from the dowries for Mrs Ambleside and Miss Belle, and nobody has the least idea who he is or why he does that. It is a great mystery, and I should dearly like to know the answer."

11: To London

The wedding took place, the sun made a brave effort to shine, and half the village drove down the lane or walked through the woods to Allamont Hall for the wedding breakfast. At noon, the smiling couple stepped into their new carriage and departed for Willowbye.

Two days later, with most of the visitors departed, Lady Sara deemed it appropriate to visit her daughter in her new establishment. Lord Reginald, who showed no sign of leaving the neighbourhood, borrowed his sister's carriage for the occasion, offering to take Connie and whichever of her sisters she chose. It was agreed that it would be Dulcie, but whether from mischief or accident, Dulcie happened to enter her mother's carriage instead, and Connie found herself quite alone with Lord Reginald.

It was beginning to prey on her mind rather that he was unusually attentive for a man who was only pretending to be in love. She could not help but prefer the Marquess, but would Lord Reginald make an acceptable alternative? He was pleasant and unassuming, without the streak of arrogance which characterised his older brother, and she did not mind the lesser title, she told herself firmly. But she was not quite sure what income he might have on his own account, and although she would not judge a man's eligibility by fortune alone, she did not feel that it would be comfortable living in poverty, or dependent on his older brother for support.

And then he had not quite the style of his brother. The Marquess was blessed with handsome features, a shapely form and an admirably fashionable mode of dress. Whenever Connie had danced with him, heads had turned to watch them and she knew they made a splendid couple. Not, she chided herself, that such a matter should affect her judgement, but it was very pleasant to stroll about a room on the Marquess's arm, knowing how well they looked together. And he was not yet married to Jess, or even officially betrothed.

As a consequence, Connie was not pleased to find herself alone in the carriage with Lord Reginald, and fell into embarrassed silence. Nothing, however, could have been more proper than his behaviour. Very far from making violent love to her, as she had half feared, he chatted as calmly as if they sat in the drawing room, talking innocuously about the Hall and the houses they passed and the streets of Brinchester they drove through. In this way, he beguiled away the journey, putting her quite at her ease.

There was only one awkward moment. "I hope you are not too upset by Lady Melthwaite's overwrought behaviour," he said, his tone quite placid, as if he were discussing the weather. "She is not typical of her rank."

Connie blushed, and hung her head. She was mindful of her mother's instructions not to speak about her family, but even without that stricture, she could not have uttered a word.

Lord Reginald laughed gently. "It is quite all right, Miss Allamont. All families have their scandals, and those that do not are too dull for words. I assure you that I do not regard it in the least. And nor does Dev," he added, almost as an afterthought. "It will not be… an obstacle."

His meaning was perfectly clear, but she clutched her reticule tightly, keeping her head lowered, and after a moment he said, "Look, Miss Allamont, have you ever seen so many lambs in one field? What a prosperous farm that must be. Are we on Willowbye land yet?"

Belle and Burford were at the front door to greet them as they arrived, smiling, hugging, ushering them inside. The smell of fresh paint was rather overwhelming, and Connie could barely wait for the exchange of well-wishes before asking, "And how is the work coming on? Is the Chinese saloon finished yet?"

Belle laughed. "Almost, but I need your advice about the dining room. Mama, you will not mind if I steal Connie away for a moment? Mr Burford will tell you all about the departure of Cousin Vivienne."

As they left the room, Belle linked arms with her sister. "I have had the painters splash some colours onto the wall for us to choose from, but I shall not decide until I have had your opinion."

"Of course. And is she really gone? Did you have to throw her out bodily? For Mr Burford is very well able to do so. I recall him dealing with those dreadful men who applied for the post of schoolmaster."

"I remember! He was quite masterful, was he not? He is such a gentle soul as a rule, but when the occasion calls for it, he can be very determined. There was an occasion last month when..."

Connie tried not to look impatient at yet another recitation of Mr Burford's perfections, especially since she had heard this particular tale several times already. However, Belle was in the throes of newly-wed ardour, so allowances must be made. Fortunately, they arrived at the dining room in time to put an end to the story, and for some time the conversation was all of paint and wallpaper and decorative plasterwork.

When all was settled, Belle said, "It is very pleasant to have the house to ourselves at last."

"Then Cousin Vivienne went willingly in the end?"

"Not her! She was still here when we arrived from the Hall, and the servants all in agitation, for she swore she would not leave without taking the cook and butler and housekeeper with her, and two footmen, if you please, even though only one of them was here before, and we engaged the other ourselves."

Connie gasped at the audacity of it. "So what did you do?"

"I told her that this was no longer her house, that she was welcome to call on at home days like anyone else, but I must ask her to leave, and if she did not, Mr Burford would carry her out." She giggled, hand over mouth. "You cannot imagine the thunderous expression on her face!"

"Oh, how brave you are! I should never have dared. And what did she say to that?"

"She said again that she wanted all the senior servants, so I had them all brought into the great hall, and asked them to say whether they wished to stay or go. And they all chose to stay, of course, as I knew they would, for they had told me so several times already. Besides, Mr Burford is to pay them more than they had before."

"I am sure their loyalty is due to the way you have dealt with them, rather than money," Connie said indignantly.

"Well, I hope I will earn their loyalty, in time, but they do not know me at all, and most of them do not remember Cousin Vivienne, either. Mary has been mistress here for years, and I did think some of them might wish to stay with her. Poor Mary! She will have a difficult time of it, I fancy, cooped up in that house with Cousin Vivienne, when she has been used to managing her own life."

"Perhaps Cousin Henry can afford to provide her with a dowry now," Connie said optimistically.

Belle shook her head. "I do not think there is much money to spare, even now. Not enough for that, anyway. I feel very sorry for her. I have suggested that she might come to London with us, but Cousin Vivienne will not permit it, and there is nothing we can do about that. But I am so happy that *you* are to be there. Such a pity that Dulcie, Grace and Hope cannot be of the party, but still, we shall have the most delightful time of it, you and me and Amy."

"And Jess Drummond," Connie said gloomily.

Belle laughed. "You must not begrudge Jess her time in the sunshine, Connie dear. Her life has been hard enough, lately. She is entitled to a little happiness."

Connie would be willing enough to allow her that happiness, if only she had not snatched the Marquess away to accomplish it.

~~~~~

The time for Connie's departure to London was fast approaching. One day Lady Sara invited Connie into her bedroom, and allowed her to choose several pieces of jewellery from her collection. Most were old-fashioned, for Mama had had no new pieces for a long time, and indeed seldom wore what she had, but Connie chose several delicate necklaces, a couple of jewelled combs, a silver circlet and a ruby bracelet which she felt was too ostentatious for all but the grandest gathering, but she loved the colour.

Lady Sara and her maid exchanged glances. "You see, Peters? She has excellent taste."

"Indeed she does, mi'lady."

"I do believe that she will not disgrace me in the society she is now entering."

"Oh no, mi'lady. She will be the handsomest young lady in town, and so much admired, just as you were, mi'lady."

Lady Sara laughed indulgently. "Well now, that was a very long time ago, Peters. A very long time." She sighed. "Now,

Connie, has Lord Reginald made any provision for a lady's maid for you?"

"No, Mama, he has not mentioned such an idea."

"Then you had better take Annie with you. What is her surname, Peters?"

"Smith," said Peters.

"Smith, yes. You must call her Smith now, Connie, and Peters will show her a few tricks before you go. Dulcie can have Janet, now that Amy and Belle have gone. If you look in that drawer in my dressing table, Connie — no, no, the left-hand one — yes, there, you will find a small purse. I daresay you have spent most of your allowance, and you will need to have enough money to buy a few small items, and leave tips for the servants. Well, well. If this comes off with Lord Reginald, I shall have three daughters married before too long, and Dulcie may start to look about her for a husband. She need not aspire to a lord, though. She has not your looks, dear, and there is a spiteful streak to her nature than I have never managed to eradicate, but perhaps she will find someone suitable. One of those brothers from High Frickham would suit her very well. Off you go, child, and take good care of those jewels."

"Yes, Mama. Thank you very much, Mama." Connie bobbed her curtsy and dashed off to show Dulcie her new treasures.

~~~~~

The journey to London was tedious but the roads were mostly good, and travel was still such a new experience that even the discomforts of the road did nothing to diminish Connie's excitement. The Marquess drove his own curricle, while Connie, Lady Harriet, Lord Reginald and Jess Drummond shared the carriage, squeezed in with another of Lady Harriet's tame chaperons.

"Why do you travel with the ladies, my lord?" Jess said to Lord Reginald, as they waited for fresh horses at an inn on the first day. "Would you not be more comfortable in the curricle with your brother? Or do you prefer to be close to your *betrothed*?" And for some unfathomable reason, this sent her into gusts of laughter.

"And why should I not travel with Miss Allamont?" Lord Reginald said testily. "Perhaps *you* would be more comfortable in the curricle with *your* betrothed, Miss Drummond."

But that only made her laugh all the harder. Connie shook her head at Jess's behaviour, not even trying to discover the source of her amusement.

Marford House was a great mausoleum of a place. All the principal rooms were gloomy, filled with vast pillars and statuary, the ceilings painted with fat nymphs and a variety of unidentifiable creatures, and an array of furniture dating back to the middle of the previous century. Connie followed Lord Reginald from room to room, her spirits lowering with every step. The housekeeper who showed them around knew the prices paid for every single item, and Connie would look at a bloated, over-decorated sideboard or an oil painting of a sea battle covering half a wall, and despair. For once, even Jess was subdued, although whether the overwrought decoration depressed or overawed her was hard to fathom.

"What do you think?" Lord Reginald whispered.

"I am exceedingly glad I do not have to live here for the whole year," Connie said, without bothering to lower her voice. That just made him laugh.

"You do not like it?" the Marquess said, turning to her in surprise.

"Not much, no. The artwork is excellent, as far as I am any judge, but the colours and the ornate furniture render it all dreadfully overpowering."

"How would you change it?" the Marquess said.

She smiled at that. "Change any part of Marford House? It is hardly my place to suggest alterations, my lord. Surely the grandeur is part of the desired effect?"

"But suppose I were to ask. It is my house, after all. Suppose I were to decide that indeed, it is all dreadfully gloomy and dismal, and I want some alterations made? If I were to ask your opinion, what would you suggest?"

"Why, pale colours, for one thing. Lighter, more elegant furniture, such as that made by Mr Hepplewhite or Mr Sheraton. Plain walls or simple patterns, delicate draperies, vases instead of these heavy statues, mirrors everywhere to reflect light."

"Oh! That sounds delightful," he said, his handsome face lighting up. "How charming you make it sound, Miss Allamont."

He smiled down at her, so exquisitely beautiful, so amiable, so perfect in every way, inspiring in her a pang of real regret. At such times, he seemed almost within her reach. She had to remind herself sternly that he was immovably in love with Jess. Sooner or later, the betrothal would be announced, a date would be set for the wedding, and all that would remain for Connie would be the humiliation of admitting to the world that she was not, after all, to marry Lord Reginald Marford.

At least she would have a season in London, she reminded herself, and that was a consolation indeed. Nor was this the shabby month-long affair that Amy and Belle had enjoyed, but a full season in the company of one of the foremost families of England, with connections everywhere. Not for the Marfords the embarrassment of sitting unregarded at the perimeter of events, hoping for notice, or the long wait for vouchers for Almacks, or driving through Hyde Park without exchanging greetings with anyone.

So she would enjoy herself, and store up memories to take back to Lower Brinford, pleasant remembrances to sustain her through countless dull evenings at home, or when fending off the attentions of the brothers from High Frickham at assemblies. And if there was a little knot of unhappiness deep inside whenever she looked at the Marquess or Jess, she was determined to pretend it did not exist.

12: Cards And Fans

Even before her death, Lady Harriet's mother had not been well enough to travel to London for many years, so the role of chaperon and mistress of Marford House for the season had fallen to one or other of the late Marquess's sisters. This year it was the turn of the Dowager Viscountess Moorfield, a large lady with a booming voice, who wrapped Connie, Jess and Lady Harriet in perfumed embraces in a rustle of bombazine and crepe.

"How adorable this will be! Two debutantes to introduce, although I have heard just a whisper that my matchmaking skills will not be required. As for you, Harriet, I am sure we shall find someone to your taste this year. I almost had a match five years ago, did I not, Harriet? But somehow he slipped through my fingers and married that wretched Stowercroft girl. Ha! A merry dance she is leading him, too, so he has got what he deserved. But since then, we have had no luck at all. Not that I would expect anything from Patience, she is a little goose and has not an ounce of common sense where matchmaking is concerned. It is an art requiring the utmost delicacy, I must tell you, and not a matter for blundering about. But I did think that Theodosia or Beatrice might have managed to get you safely wed. Now you are almost an old maid, I declare. Never mind, for I am here to take care of you this season, and I have one or two prospects in view, my dear, you may depend upon it."

"I beg you will not concern yourself over me, Aunt," Lady Harriet said, laughing. "I am perfectly happy as I am."

Lady Moorfield took not the slightest notice. "Now, the Earl of Limpole's eldest is to be in town this year, back from his grand tour at last, and that business at Brighton all forgotten, I am sure. That would be a good match. Or the Duke of Cherton's son. Only a third son, but he stands to inherit a fine estate in Norfolk from his uncle, and a handsome fellow, by all I have heard. A little younger than you, but you cannot be *too* choosy at your age. Or that boy from Westmorland — so rich, my dear, you cannot imagine."

She rattled on in the same vein for some time, to Connie's amusement. Lady Moorfield seemed to know everybody who was worth knowing, and although they were merely names to Connie now, she hoped to meet all of them, so she listened and tried to learn them and work out how they were all related. It was difficult, but years of her father's strict teaching methods had left her well able to memorise details. With a few judicious questions to Lady Moorfield, she soon began to untangle the web of family links that connected the highest levels of society.

The responsibility for introducing Connie and Jess into society was one to which Lady Moorfield accorded the utmost seriousness. The first day at Marford House was entirely taken up with inspecting every gown, bonnet, brooch, hair comb, pair of gloves or stockings, necklace or fan they had brought with them, every item to be tried on and approved. Connie's clothes brought forth a tilt of the head to one side, and a "Hmm, that will do for now", whereas all Jess received was a tilt of the head in the opposite direction, and a "Hmm, we could do something with that, perhaps", in a dubious tone.

Lady Harriet had brought boxes of her old gowns from a season or two ago, which could be altered to fit and brought up to date, so there was an enormous amount of pushing and tugging and measuring and pinning. Two seamstresses were brought in to ensure all was made ready before the season's round of engagements was underway.

With these important preparations in hand, the next step was to drive to the houses of all the Marfords' acquaintance leaving their cards, to tell the world that they were in town. Jess knew nobody, but there was the matter of Lady Sara's family to be considered. Lady Moorfield insisted on leaving their cards at Heatherington House.

"We are only on nodding acquaintance with the Earl and Countess, but we know the Melthwaites well, of course."

"I do not believe they are very pleased with me after I visited them at Tambray," Connie said. "Perhaps we should not—"

"Nonsense! Emma may or may not be pleased with you, but what does that signify? She knows perfectly well what is due to you as a relative, and one moreover a guest of the Marquess. She is a stickler for protocol, so you need not worry that she will cut you, or anything of that nature. She will be all complaisance, you may be sure."

So cards were duly left at Heatherington House. Connie sat in the carriage watching the butler accept them, his face revealing no emotion, and wondered how the Viscountess would react. They were bound to meet at social occasions, so perhaps she would consider it prudent not to make a fuss. Still, her reaction at the mention of Aunt Tilly suggested that she would want nothing to do with the daughter of a woman who stayed with such a person.

When the delivery of cards palled, there were shops to be visited. Connie had no wish to spend her limited funds on frivolities, and she was now very well provided with clothes and the like, but there was still much to enjoy on these expeditions. When she tired of looking at the displays within the shop, she could watch the fashionable passers-by through the window.

The Marquess and Lord Reginald generally accompanied them on these outings. Somehow the presence of the two men made shopping a more serious and important occupation, and since Connie was now established as the artistic arbiter, her advice was frequently sought on the matter of a snuff box or a cravat pin. When she decreed that one was superior to another, the Marquess or his brother would buy the chosen item instantly. It was immensely flattering.

Lady Harriet and her aunt seldom asked for advice, and even when they did, took no notice of Connie's opinion. They thought nothing of requiring the assistant to spread half the shop's wares on the counter, discussing the merits of each item in disparaging terms and then, after an hour, when the assistant's smile was beginning to fray, deciding there was nothing at all that they liked. Occasionally, however, they would spend vast sums of money on something Connie thought hideous.

Jess was unusually quiet on these occasions. She had no money of her own to spend, and seemed uninterested even in examining the goods on offer, sitting demurely on a chair near the door. Once or twice, when a prospective customer entered and looked around seemingly at a loss, Jess jumped up and offered him assistance, guiding him to the required display or counter. Once she entered into a lengthy conversation with a gentleman, before he was caught up in the business at hand, and she slipped back to her seat. Connie wondered at it, for it almost seemed as if she were putting herself forward to be noticed by these gentlemen, yet how could that be so? Yet the Marquess made no protest, and made not the least effort to keep Jess by his side, as one might expect.

Connie preferred to look at all the pretty trinkets and baubles laid out for examination. In one shop, a lacquered fan caught her eye, and she kept returning to it, admiring the workmanship in the design, which was of the finest execution.

"Do you like it, madam?" the assistant said.

"Oh, indeed! I have never seen one so beautiful."

"Try it," said the Marquess, appearing at her side just then.

"Oh — may I?" she said to the assistant.

"Of course, madam. It is a lovely piece, is it not? And light enough to be not in the least tiring to use."

Gently she lifted it up, turning it over in her hands. Her only fan was an old one of Mama's, given to her when she first came out, and she liked it well enough. But this was exquisitely made, displaying quite superior artistry. Flicking it open, she fanned herself, smiling for the pleasure of holding such a magnificent ornament.

"Do you like it?" the Marquess said.

"How could I not? And the colour! It would be perfect to carry when I wear my ruby bracelet."

"Oh, yes, madam!" the assistant cried, sensing a sale. "Nothing could be more perfect. You have such an eye for colour, if I may say so."

"You may," said the Marquess, "for it is quite true. Miss Allamont is going to redesign my house for me."

"Oh, no, I do not think—"

"You may wrap the fan."

"Oh, no, my lord," Connie said, paling. "I cannot afford anything so lovely. I am sure it is too expensive."

"Then I shall make you a gift of it, for I insist that you have it."

"No, no! That would be most inappropriate."

"But why should I not—?" He stopped abruptly, catching sight of his brother glowering at him.

"It is for *me* to buy gifts for my *betrothed*, Dev," Lord Reginald said.

"Oh. I suppose so, yes."

"You may buy something for *Miss Drummond*, if you wish."

For a moment, the two brothers glared at each other, in the most unsettling way. Then the Marquess nodded once, curtly, and strode off to join Jess at her chair near the door, while Lord Reginald paid for the fan, which was indeed very expensive. Connie blushed and stammered her thanks awkwardly. She could not quite decide on the propriety of the matter, for although it was certainly proper for a man to buy gifts for his future bride, she was only too conscious that she was no such thing. But it was such a delightful fan, and she wanted it quite badly, so she made no protest, and only her stumbling words betrayed her confusion.

As for the Marquess, he never did buy anything for Jess, not on that day, or any other, as far as Connie could tell.

~~~~~

The cards scattered so industriously in all the better parts of London began to bear fruit. A little stream of interesting cards were left in return on the polished table in the entrance hall of Marford House, and before too long they began to make and receive morning calls. The cards were succeeded by invitations and within a very few days of her arrival in London, Connie attended her first ball. It was not, Lady Moorfield, informed her in disapproving tones, one of the more superior occasions, such as she might expect to see later in the season.

"However, it will be a good place to begin," she said. "There are not so many families here just yet, so you will show to advantage. Connie, you may wear the pale green with the gold trim, and one of your Mama's little necklaces. Jess, the lemon silk with the silver overskirt, if it is finished, and nothing round your neck. It is not your best feature, so let us not draw attention to it. We will do something striking with your hair, I think, for that is where you are blessed. Such lovely curls! I will have Marte trim the front a little."

Evening engagements could be quite chancy affairs in the country, whatever the time of year, for rain or snow could make the roads impassable, and then there was the anxious business of hoping for a clear night to provide moonlight. In London, Connie found, the difficulties were quite different. The roads provided no obstacle, and street lamps lit the way, but the crowds and noise and smells that assaulted her senses, and the press of traffic that slowed the carriage to a snail's pace were frightening.

"Do not look so fearful, Miss Allamont," Lord Reginald said. "The coachman has been with us for ten years, and has managed not to overturn us once. Not yet, anyway," he added cheerfully, thus adding to the list of worrying possibilities for Connie to fret over.

Eventually, they arrived, and bewigged footmen stepped forward to open the carriage door, let down the steps and assist the ladies to alight. Lady Moorfield descended first, and then Lord Reginald, who turned to offer his hand to Connie. She stepped onto carpet laid between lines of torches. In the gloom outside the circle of flickering light they cast, white faces gazed impassively at her.

"Who are these people?" she whispered.

"Poor people," he said with a shrug. "They come to see the upper class at play. Ignore them. Ah, here is Dev's carriage now."

The Marquess leapt down almost before the wheels had stopped moving, helping his sister and Jess to alight. There was another lady, too, a mousy creature whose name Connie had forgotten, a cousin or aunt of some sort. It seemed the Marquess had forgotten her very existence, for he turned away before she descended, and she had to wait for a footman to assist her.

Connie smiled at her. "There you are," she said brightly. "Now we shall all go in together."

"Oh, no, no!" the mouse said in dismay. "All in the proper order. The Marquess and Miss Drummond, then the Dowager and Lady Harriet, then you must enter with Lord Reginald, you see, and I go last. The proper order, Miss Allamont."

The next carriage was arriving, so Connie was obliged to move onwards — in the proper order, naturally — without making any response, but she stowed the exchange away in her mind to consider at a later time, when she might have the leisure for philosophy. Something jangled in her brain, but she could not quite work out what it was.

They followed the carpet up broad steps and into a pillared hall filled with displays of white flowers, their heady perfume erasing all the noxious smells of the street. The hall was lit by hundreds, perhaps thousands, of candles, and as they processed at a stately pace through the house, every room was just as bright, although the flowers were different colours — one room yellow, another pink, and one red. Ahead of them, the stream of guests was marked by a line of waving turban-feathers, with more following on behind. Then the ballroom appeared, and the stream stopped, inching forwards as each party was announced. Their turn came, their names were called out, they moved forwards into the room.

The dazzling array of lights and shimmering chandeliers, the gilt decoration and jewels, and the soft glimmer of flowing silk in frighteningly fashionable styles made Connie gasp with astonishment. Despite the earliness of the season, the room was crowded to overflowing, and the heat rose up to engulf her. Music played, dancers leapt and twirled, onlookers watched impassively.

And she knew not a single person, and no friendly smiles greeted her. Eyes turned to stare haughtily at her, lorgnettes were raised and strangers looked her up and down with penetrating calculation. She felt as naked as if she had just stepped out of the bath under the disdainful gaze of the *ton*. For a moment, it was overwhelming and she clung tightly to Lord Reginald's arm, almost in tears. How had she ever thought that she, an ignorant provincial nobody, could mix with the cream of society?

13: Brook Street

"Shall we stroll about for a while?" Lord Reginald said, not noticing Connie's distress. "Or should you like to dance at once?"

She could not speak, could not even raise her head and felt as if she might faint away, had she not his arm to cling to.

He turned to her in surprise when she made no reply. "Miss Allamont?"

But then, she hardly knew how, the Marquess was there, calmly detaching her hand from Lord Reginald and tucking it comfortably into his. "Reggie, Miss Drummond is wild to dance. Do you take her onto the floor, while I find Miss Allamont a quiet seat so that she might catch her breath."

"Dev, I do not think—"

"Miss Drummond, Reggie," he said firmly, and with a curt nod, Lord Reginald disappeared.

Holding her hand in a firm grip, the Marquess steered Connie through the throng. Once or twice he exchanged greetings with someone, but Connie being still too overcome to lift her head, she saw nothing. She wondered what these grand people must think of her, too inept even to move about a ballroom without support.

She found herself in a many-windowed room with a tiled floor, divided into quiet corners by palms with huge fronds. Lord

Carrbridge led her to a bench and by some black art produced two glasses of champagne.

"Here we are, Miss Allamont, a quiet spot for us to have a drink. Just a sip, mind you, for it will go straight to your head if you imbibe too quickly. There! Is that not better?"

When she dared to look up, his head was tipped to one side, with that smile that made her stomach jump about. "Th-thank you. You are... too kind."

"Not at all, Miss Allamont. It is all very different from what you are used to, I daresay. It is not surprising that you find it a tad overwhelming. I remember my first season, when I thought I was all the crack, you know, a real out and outer, but I quickly discovered my mistake. But you will soon get into the way of it, and then you will be perfectly comfortable."

"Thank you," she said again, but his sympathy brought the tears close again and she found it impossible to say more.

He seemed not to mind, sitting quietly by her side, sipping his champagne and occasionally pointing out this or that personage who passed into view.

After a while, she felt strong enough to say timidly, "Do not let me detain you, my lord. You must want to meet your friends or... or stroll about or something of that nature, rather than hiding in the conservatory with me."

He smiled at her over the rim of his champagne glass. "Now why on earth should I want to do anything of the sort? I am perfectly happy here with you, I assure you."

She blushed at this, but went on, "Lady Moorfield says we must... move slowly around the room. It is important to be seen, she says."

"I like Aunt Juliana well enough, but she spouts some nonsense at times. Debutantes on the lookout for a husband might need to be seen, but not the Marquess of Carrbridge. I may hide in the conservatory with a beautiful young lady if I choose."

She blushed again, hanging her head, and wondering what Jess would say if she heard him talking so. The impropriety of it struck her forcibly, for they were both supposedly betrothed to other people, and their retreat was quite secluded. Even if her own betrothal was a sham, his was not and he should not be talking to her in such terms. She would have been less than human if she had not basked in his attention. So kind, so handsome, so amiable! If only he were hers, and not in love with Jess Drummond! But he was, and it was not at all proper for her to be alone with him, in such a well-hidden spot.

"Nevertheless, I think perhaps we might return to the ballroom, my lord."

"Of course, if you feel strong enough."

"I... I believe so."

He stood up and offered her his arm again. "Deep breath, Miss Allamont. Remember that nothing can daunt you, for you are a Marford of Drummoor. Or nearly, at any rate."

She thought she was not very near at all, but could not say so. Instead she said, "Nothing can daunt me because I am a daughter of Allamont Hall, my lord."

He smiled at her, eyes twinkling, and escorted her back to the ballroom.

In the end, the evening was far from being a disaster. She stood up to dance first with Lord Reginald, and then with the Marquess, and after that she had no lack of partners. A friend of the King's smiled benignly on her, dowagers nodded with something close to approval, and any number of bucks presented themselves to entreat her hand for the dance, or to enquire if she might be attending this or that rout or ball or party of some kind. Almost before she was ready, she was swept away to their waiting carriage and back to Marford House.

"There now, that is the first ball out of the way," Lady Moorfield said briskly as the carriage rattled over the cobbles. "You did well, my dear, very well indeed, and it will be easier now, you will see."

Then she closed her eyes and was asleep almost instantly.

Lord Reginald leaned closer to whisper in her ear, "Did you enjoy the evening?"

"Oh yes! Very much! Although... I am sorry I was so... so *missish* at the start. I felt so... *provincial*."

She felt, rather than saw, his smile. "You need have no concerns on that head. There was not the slightest deficiency in your dress or manner or deportment. You were a great success."

She glowed inside at the praise. "You are very kind to say so, my lord. I was so afraid of... of letting you down, but Lord Carrbridge was so kind to me and made me feel quite at ease."

He leaned back on the squabs abruptly. "Oh yes, Dev is very kind indeed, the kindest fellow in the kingdom."

And not another word did he utter for the rest of the journey.

~~~~~

The following morning brought happy news — a letter from Belle announcing their safe arrival in London.

"May I go to see them?" Connie asked Lady Moorfield as soon as that lady surfaced from her bed. "Not, of course, if you need me—"

"No, no, my dear, by all means go. We are at home all day, you know, so if you go early, you will be back in time for any late callers, and then we are at the opera this evening. You would not wish to miss *that*, I am sure. Where are they staying, your sisters?"

"They have taken a house in Brook Street."

"Brook Street — oh." Lady Moorfield's eyebrows rose a fraction. "That is most respectable, and only two streets away. If the rain holds off, you might walk there. I cannot spare the time to accompany you myself, and the gentlemen are off with their male pursuits today, but Mrs March will chaperon you. That would be quite unexceptional."

"Oh, certainly, very happy to!" the mousy lady said. "Very happy. Such a fine day for walking."

It was not, in fact, a fine day at all, for a bitter wind whipped Connie's new pelisse about and tore at her bonnet, but the walk was mercifully short. The Brook Street house turned out to be one of the larger ones on the street, with an attractive frontage. They were admitted by a neatly-uniformed maid. Inside, the furnishings were not of the first quality, but serviceable.

Belle was alone in the drawing room when Connie was shown in, and the two sisters fell on each other as if they had not met for a year instead of a mere two weeks. Mrs March was introduced, and the maid dispatched to find the rest of the household.

"Although I do not think Amy will be dressed yet," Belle said. "She keeps to her room until noon at least these days, and the journey taxed her considerably."

"Travel is so arduous," Mrs March said. "You have come such a distance, too. I know one or two remedies that might be of use to poor Mrs Ambleside, if you feel it might be in the least helpful."

"Time is the only cure for what ails Amy, I fear," Belle said, smiling.

"Oh, indeed, time is a great healer," Mrs March said brightly.

"Very much so, in this case. She expects to be confined in the autumn."

"Oh!" Mrs March giggled, hand covering her mouth. "Oh, I see! Such a blessing! Such happy news!"

When they had exhausted the possibilities of Amy's health, the state of the roads and inns, news from Willowbye and Allamont Hall, and Connie's many engagements, conversation faltered somewhat. Connie wanted very much to talk to Belle about the Marquess, but could hardly do so in front of Mrs March. She guessed that Belle felt the same constraint, for she made no mention of the Marquess or Lord Reginald.

After a while, Belle said, "Mrs March, you mentioned some remedies for travel fatigue. I wonder if—"

"Oh, indeed, Mrs Burford! Quite delighted to oblige. You take a pint of water—"

"I wonder if I might trouble you to tell the cook of your receipts? Since she will have the making of them, it would be as well for her to understand the exact method. It would not do to make a mistake in the quantities, would it?"

"Oh, indeed! Certainly!" She jumped up, Belle rang for a servant and a maid led Mrs March off to the kitchens.

The two sisters sighed with relief.

"She is a dear soul," Connie said. "I am glad she is gone for a while, however. That was clever of you, Belle."

"I am getting used to managing people, thanks to Cousin Vivienne," Belle said, with a wry smile. "Now, tell me all about—"

But Burford and Ambleside arrived just then, with many smiles for Connie, and so the same topics had to be gone over again. But they soon returned to the one of most interest to Connie.

"It sounds as though the Marfords are taking good care of you, Miss Allamont," Ambleside said. "One always worries a little with these great families, for they are not always as careful with the proprieties as might be wished."

"I have not noticed any carelessness in that way," Connie said.

"But this betrothal between the Marquess and Jess Drummond," Ambleside said. "It is very eccentric of him."

"She is very pretty and lively," Burford murmured. "Sometimes a man might be dazzled by such attractions and look no further."

Ambleside laughed. "Very true!" They all smiled, remembering Burford's own infatuation with Hope. "Nevertheless, it is hardly appropriate for a man of his station to take a wife without fortune or rank. Miss Drummond has nothing but her own charms to recommend her, and it is not enough, no matter how considerable those charms may be. A peer of the realm is expected to be ruled by his head, not his heart. He cannot — *should* not — marry according to his own whims. Miss Allamont would be a much better match for him. Is there any sign of him realising his mistake with Miss Drummond?"

How much Connie longed to answer in the affirmative! Yet honesty compelled her to say, "Not the least bit. He is the same as ever towards her."

"But is he affectionate with her?" Ambleside said. "He never seemed to me to be a man in love. Indeed, he always seemed most attentive to *you*, Miss Allamont. I confess, I have found his behaviour confusing. A gentleman should always make his intentions clear."

"He is certainly very kind to me," Connie said, remembering the chivalrous way he had intervened the previous night when she had been quite overcome. "I do not think he treats me any differently from before, however. I am just a friend to him, his brother's future wife, so he believes. As to his intentions, those are clear enough, surely?"

"And yet I wonder," Ambleside said. "There has been no notice of the engagement in the papers."

"The betrothal is a great secret," Connie said. "It is too soon after the death of Jess's father, I understand."

"That was more than a year ago. It does not seem to me that his heart is entirely lost to Miss Drummond. Living under his roof, there must be opportunities to draw him into a closer attachment to you, Miss Allamont."

"A man cannot be manipulated into marrying if his heart is not in it," Burford said in mild reproof. "Nor should he be."

"Perhaps, but he might be manipulated *out* of an inadvisable marriage," Ambleside said.

"Oh, no!" Connie said, rather shocked. "Manipulation? No, that would be quite wrong." Once again she was relieved to have escaped marriage to Ambleside, a man who thought nothing of manoeuvring others to get what he wanted, as he had with Amy.

"*Any* sort of manipulation is abhorrent to me," Belle said firmly. "A man must make up his own mind, without interference. A woman may hope to show herself off to advantage in front of him, to beguile him, perhaps, to put him into a romantic frame of mind..." She smiled knowingly at Connie here. "But marriage is too serious a business to be subjected to scheming by those whose interests may not coincide with those of the parties concerned."

"I hope we all have Lord Carrbridge's best interests at heart," Ambleside said. "Are we not all agreed that Miss Allamont would be a more suitable wife for him?"

It was a sentiment that Connie herself had thoughtlessly espoused, but now that she had had some little experience of London society, she could no longer sustain the idea. The previous evening had proved to her just how unsuited she was for life in the *haut ton*, while Jess had stepped into the role as if born to it.

"I do not believe Miss Drummond is at all unsuitable," Connie said with some heat. "She is far more at ease in London society than I am, and if the Marquess truly loves her..." She trailed off, miserably aware that she was acknowledging the end of all her hopes. Then, straightening her back, she went on, "It was foolish of me to suppose that I could ever entice a Marquess, and I have quite given up the idea. Jess is a much better match."

"I am not well acquainted with Miss Drummond," Burford said calmly, "but I know her brother well, and the family is very long-established in Scotland, even if they have fallen into a degree of poverty of late. It is perhaps not the best match Lord Carrbridge could have made, but there is nothing to be said against the lady, nothing at all."

"Then it appears to be an excellent match and I wish them both joy," Ambleside said, with his ready smile. "Let love take its course with no intervention, as far as I am concerned."

At that moment, Mrs March returned from the kitchens, and, all private conversation being at an end, Connie soon after prepared to leave.

"But you will come often to see us, I hope," Belle said wistfully.

"Of course, and you will call at Marford House, but we will meet a great deal in company, I am sure."

"I doubt it!" Belle said, laughing. "You move in very exalted circles now, sister dear. We have so few acquaintance in London that we will not receive many invitations. Perhaps we may meet at the theatre sometimes."

As she walked back to Marford House, Mrs March walking two paces behind her like a maid, Connie was thoughtful. The idea that London society was stratified was not a new one, but the realisation that she and sisters fell into different levels of it was shocking to her. At home, there was no distinction between a nobleman and a respectable gentleman. The nobility were accorded their due deference, of course, but every rank dined and mingled with every other. But here, rank was everything. It made her uncomfortable, she had to admit, and she missed the freedom of country life.

For the first time, she began to wonder if she really wished to be a Marchioness at all, even if he could be turned away from Jess. The Marquess had seemed to be the perfect husband, his title and estates dazzling her, and how could she help being attracted to him, as delightful as he was? But if the price of such a match was to lose her sisters, then she determined that she would not marry at all, and Jess was welcome to him.

14: A Drive In The Park

The Marfords were to hold a ball of their own, which was, Connie deduced, to be a splendid affair to which all the *haut ton* were to be invited, and which would be the talk of every salon in town. Connie had no involvement in the preparations, for her experience of arranging little dinner parties at Allamont Hall was not in any way comparable to the organisation involved in a ball during the London season. She imagined that entire wars must have been managed with less preparation than Lady Moorfield and her helpers thought necessary.

The helpers consisted of her three daughters, all stout and all blessed with lisps or buck teeth or twitching eyelids, or some combination thereof. Lady Harriet's advice was also called upon at frequent intervals, but she rarely expressed an opinion.

"It is best to keep one's head below the parapet on these occasions," she whispered to Connie. "If I say that the flowers should be pink, Aunt Juliana will be sure to decide immediately on yellow, and if I say yellow, she will instantly favour pink. So I keep out of it, and I advise you to do the same."

"I shall," Connie said. "Although I should prefer white flowers, myself, in silver vases."

"Oh. That does sound elegant. But still, she will not listen, so it is best to say nothing and stay out of the way."

The gentlemen had much the same idea, expressing their feelings quite openly.

"We shall be the first into the ballroom on the night, and the last to leave it," the Marquess said firmly. "More than that cannot be expected of us."

"You are so clever about arranging these affairs, Aunt Juliana," said Lord Reginald. "If we try to interfere, we should only slow you down."

Jess, too, managed to absent herself during the planning sessions, disappearing for hours at a time with Mrs March to chaperon her. Connie had no notion what she got up to, for she returned with no parcels, and appeared not to be making calls. When asked, she talked vaguely about parks and galleries. It was very odd.

Connie had not the least desire to wander about London. Shopping held no appeal since she had little money to spend, and she had few acquaintance of her own to call on. Nor was it in her nature to sit quietly with a book or a piece of needlework. She liked to be in the centre of things, with chatter all round her. So as often as not she would find herself drawn into the preparations for the ball, writing lists of guests, or flowers, or food items, or extra servants to be hired, or orders for the chandler or vintner.

When the guest list was being drawn up, Lady Moorfield said, "Now, Connie dear, who do *you* know that will be in town? We shall invite the Melthwaites, naturally, and you may add his papa to the list, too, although the Earl seldom goes into company these days, and the Countess never leaves Hepplestone. What about your papa's side of the family? I do not recall any Allamonts for many years. Your grandpapa, now, he was a very lively soul, and an excellent dancer, as I recall, and his brother Henry, too." She sighed, and paused momentarily, lost in some reminiscence. "Ah, well, they are long dead. So many of them are dead now. But since Mr Walter Allamont's time, I cannot think of anyone."

Connie said timidly, "Might I be allowed to invite my sisters, Lady Moorfield?"

"Your sisters, eh? Remind me, what are their married names?"

"One is Mrs Ambleside of Staynlaw House, Higher Brinford, and the other is Mrs John Burford, of Willowbye, Brafton West."

"I do not know of any Amblesides or Burtons," Lady Moorfield said, wrinkling her nose.

"Burford. His family lives near York."

"Never heard of them. Are they acquainted with anyone of importance?"

"I... do not believe so, no. Not that I have ever heard. Just a few old school friends. But since this ball is to be my official come-out, it would be pleasant to have someone from my own family present." And someone she knew, with familiar, welcoming smiles, rather than the endless haughty stares she was becoming used to from the higher ranks. London was filled with strangers.

"We shall keep them in mind, my dear, if we do not have as many acceptances as we expect, but we must concentrate on those who have the most influence, and can add to your consequence. You must not cling to your old connections, you know. Once you are married to Reggie, your object will be a very different set of acquaintance, and you will not have time for your sisters."

"I hope I shall always have time for my sisters, Lady Moorfield," Connie said with dignity. "Are you quite settled on Lady Hartshill, or shall I cross her off the list again?"

Lady Hartshill epitomised an aspect of high society that Connie found very difficult to deal with. The nuances of rank she understood very well, but there were subtle differences that she felt she would never be at ease with. In the course of their evening engagements, Connie was often introduced to this earl or that baronet, yet Lady Moorfield would whisper confusing instructions — "Just nod and move on" regarding a duchess, while an untitled lady might elicit the comment, "Your deepest curtsy". Some quite grand-sounding persons she was told to cut entirely. A few of the respected ones, like the patronesses of Almack's, she knew about but others seemed incomprehensible, and Lady Hartshill fell into the latter category.

Every week, Lady Hartshill held a small, select card party. Not for her the ostentatious balls or routs or masquerades or grand dinners that others revelled in, and she never attended such occasions, either, nor was she well-connected or particularly wealthy. She seemed, on meeting, to be no more than a rather shy, slightly frumpy matron. Yet her card parties were held as a sign of acceptance in good society. The Marfords had been invited to the very first one, just three days after their arrival but never since, and Lady Moorfield fretted about it rather. Had they made some unknown *faux pas* and been eliminated from the list of desirables? And if so, how could they work their way back into Lady Hartshill's good graces?

"You had better leave her on the list, Connie dear," the Viscountess said. "She will not come, of course, and she is not one of those who cares about receiving more invitations than anyone else, but it will do no harm. At least... one hopes it will not. Oh dear, it is very difficult. No, I am quite decided, leave her name. But there again..."

Connie wiped her pen and waited patiently.

~~~~~

One day when they were all at breakfast and the letters were brought in, there was one for Connie. She read it with a smile on her face.

"Do you need me today, my lady?" she said to Lady Moorfield.

"Ah! Do I detect an invitation?" that lady said with a knowing smile. "Who is it from, my dear? You were on very close terms with the Duke of Rockall's daughters the other night, so it might be from them. Or Lady Gillingham took a liking to you."

"It is from my sisters. They have rented a barouche for the season and, the weather being so settled at the moment, they propose an outing today, to Hyde Park, Belle says. Please may I go? They will call for me at noon, and I shall be brought back by four at the latest. May I?"

"If you want to tool round Hyde Park, I can take you," Lord Reginald said, setting down his knife and fork with a clatter. "You had only to ask, you know. Always happy to oblige a lady. We have a barouche somewhere about, if that is your fancy, or I might borrow Dev's curricle."

"No, that is not—"

"Borrow my curricle? I should rather think not!"

"Well, it will have to be the barouche, then. Or the phaeton! That would be just the ticket. But you do not want to go so early, Miss Allamont. Five o'clock, that is the fashionable hour."

"But—"

"Not the phaeton, Reggie, for Mrs March must go too," Lady Moorfield said. "You must wear your green pelisse with the new bonnet, my dear. That will be perfect, and everyone will take notice of you. There, that is all settled."

"Oh." Connie looked from one to another in dismay. "So may I not go out with my sisters after all?"

"You would be better advised to go with Reggie, my dear," Lady Moorfield said.

"Do you not want to go driving with me, Miss Allamont?" said Lord Reginald in hurt tones.

"Of course, but... perhaps some other time. Today I should very much like to go with my sisters."

"Better with Reggie," Lady Moorfield said crisply. "*Your* expedition will add nothing to your consequence, my dear."

"What does that signify?" Connie cried. "I should like to see my sisters, and *consequence* has nothing to do with it!"

Lady Moorfield frowned and was about to speak, but the Marquess lowered the newspaper he was reading and waved a hand languidly. "Of course you must go driving with your sisters, Miss Allamont. Such family affection is most touching."

"Dev..." Lord Reginald began, glowering at his brother.

"You may take Miss Allamont another day, Reggie," the Marquess said. "We shall get up a party, eh? You may accompany Miss Allamont in the barouche with Mrs March, and I shall take Miss Drummond in my curricle, and perhaps the ladies may change places after a while, so that Miss Allamont may enjoy the curricle too."

"Really, Francis, you are dreadfully high-handed," Lady Moorfield said petulantly. "I am trying to establish Miss Allamont in society, and you are not helping."

"Aunt Juliana, when Miss Allamont is married, she will have all the consequence she needs from her husband. I would not have her turned into one of your snooty society matrons who shun their less exalted relations. Besides, I like her sisters."

And with that he retreated behind his newspaper again, and the breakfast table fell into silence.

~~~~~

Connie enjoyed her outing enormously. It was rather a squeeze with five of them in a barouche designed for four, but none of the ladies were large and their pleasure in the occasion far outweighed any minor discomforts. Ambleside had provided hot bricks and rugs in case of any chill in the air, but the sun shone, the conversation was merry and a delightful morning was had by all.

True to his word, the Marquess arranged a drive through Hyde Park, too, at the fashionable hour. His curricle and the Marford barouche inched their way through the press of walkers, riders and carriages, everyone displaying themselves in their finest clothes. Lady Moorfield having decided to accompany them, she pointed out this or that important person to Connie, whose face ached from smiling. Half way round the park, the Marquess drew aside and insisted on an exchange — Jess got into the barouche and Connie climbed into the curricle beside the Marquess.

"Really, Dev, is this necessary?" Lord Reginald grumbled.

"Got to be fair, Reggie," the Marquess replied with his charming smile. "Must give the ladies equal enjoyment, you know."

It was indeed much more pleasant to sit high up beside the Marquess, looking down on everyone passing by, as he contrived to bowl along at a surprising pace.

"We have quite left the others behind, I fear," Connie said anxiously, but the Marquess only laughed. He nodded to one or two of his acquaintance, but otherwise took no notice of the crowds thronging the paths. When they left the park, they rattled through the streets at a merry clip and drew up outside Marford House all too soon.

Laughter bubbled up in Connie's throat. "Oh, this has been the greatest fun," she cried. "Thank you so much, my lord."

He turned his charming smile on her. "The pleasure was all mine, Miss Allamont."

Handing the reins to his tiger, he assisted her to alight, tucking her arm in his as they walked up the steps together. In the hall, he bowed and lifted her hand to his lips. "We must do this again some time," he murmured, leaving her in such a warm glow that she could do nothing but blush.

It was so *difficult*, she decided. She was determined to leave him to Jess and not to regret him, and he, it seemed, was equally determined to charm and enchant her. If only he would leave her alone! And yet a small voice inside her objected violently to that idea.

~~~~~

The drives became a regular arrangement, both with the Marquess and his brother, and with the Amblesides and Burfords. Connie enjoyed them all, although those with her sisters were more relaxing than the frenetic drives through Hyde Park. It was more pleasant to sit comfortably watching the scenery go by than to be constantly on the alert for important members of the *haut ton* who must be greeted correctly or risk the opprobrium of society. Connie had not yet received vouchers for Almacks and was in constant terror of offending one of the patronesses and finding herself forever excluded.

It was strange to her, however, to move in two such separate circles, with no overlap. Night after night her engagements brought her into the same exclusive company, people she scarcely knew and who had little interest in her, except in her relationship to the Marquess and his family, all vying for position in the constant swirl of rising and falling consequence. It was exhausting, especially when she had nothing in common with such people. It would have been the greatest relief to see the familiar faces of her sisters in a crowd.

Nor did she see anything of the more distant branches of her family.

"Have you seen Viscount Melthwaite yet, Connie?" Amy asked every time they met, but Connie was never able to answer in the affirmative.

"We have not seen them anywhere, nor have they called, but Uncle Edmund and Aunt Emma have both left their cards," Connie said. "I daresay I shall meet them at one or other engagement, for they go everywhere."

"We left our cards, but have heard nothing," Belle said, as the barouche rattled through the streets. "We cannot do more, for the approach must come from them. But it makes me sad, for they are Mama's family and I should like to get to know them. It is so strange to have a whole branch of the family of whom we know virtually nothing. Mama's sister in Scotland is another matter, for it is such a long journey, but Hepplestone is not so far away. Why do they never visit?"

"I do find it odd that you know so little about your own uncles and aunts," Burford said. "Even your grandparents are a mystery to you. It is most unusual."

"Not so unusual, I feel," Ambleside said. "In my own family, there are several branches that have no contact with each other. You have a large and very close family, Burford, whereas I have no parents or grandparents yet living, no brothers or sisters, not even a cousin to my name. The only people I was able to inform of Mrs Ambleside's condition were two cousins, and one aunt living in Ireland, and she is ninety three."

"That is very sad," Connie said. "How dreadful to have nobody with whom one may be completely at ease, and never have to watch what one says or does."

"Ah, but I no longer have nobody," Ambleside said, with a smile at his wife of such sweetness that Connie found herself smiling too.

As they came to Marford House, and Connie prepared to step down from the barouche, she said, "There is nothing we can do about the Earl of Harkness, or Viscount and Viscountess Melthwaite, but there is one relative that I believe we *might* approach, for I would dearly love to meet her — Aunt Tilly."

15: The Saloon

Connie's evenings were very busy now. The family usually dined at home before sallying forth in their best attire to a ball or rout or some other splendid event, each more extravagant than the last. Although she loved to dance, and was never short of partners, the constant swirl of social events began to pall after a while. Sometimes she longed for a quiet evening at home, or a gentle card party amongst friends.

On one occasion, the ballroom was draped with coloured silk like an Arabian tent, with ostrich feathers dyed in violent colours hanging everywhere. It made the atmosphere very close.

When Lord Reginald came to claim her for the next dance, she said, "Would you mind very much if we do not dance? It is excessively hot in here. Perhaps we might find a cooler spot, and... and just talk? Is that acceptable, do you think?"

He smiled, the slightly lop-sided smile that was almost like his brother's but not quite. "Perfectly acceptable. And since we are rumoured to be secretly betrothed, we may withdraw a little way into the saloon with perfect propriety. Not so far that we cannot be seen, but just far enough to escape by one or two degrees the crowds in the ballroom."

The saloon was only marginally less crowded, but it was beyond the confines of the tent arrangement and the brilliance of hundreds of chandeliers, so it immediately felt cooler.

"Ah, that is much better," she said. "I declare, I was quite worn out from so much dancing."

"Poor Miss Allamont," he said, lifting her gloved hand to his lips and bestowing a quick kiss upon it, although his manner was too playful for her to be offended. "Are you not enjoying your first season in London?"

"Oh, yes!" she cried. "I like it of all things! Only I should find it a little less tiring if we had not to go out every night, and sometimes two or three engagements in one night. One has only just become settled and one is whisked off somewhere else. Look, like Viscount Preston and his sisters there. They arrived just before the start of the last dance, and now they are leaving already. And see, the Duchess of Elmsleigh is only just arriving this minute, and it must be close to midnight."

"The Duchess of what?"

"Elmsleigh. The one with the dreadful diamond tiara."

"Oh, her. I never knew her name. How clever you are, to know all this, and you have only been in town five minutes."

She blushed at the compliment, not quite knowing how to answer. He was still holding her hand, and now he began to run his fingers all the way up her arm, right to the point where her glove ended and bare skin began. For an instant, she was too shocked to move. Was he daring to make love to her? Or merely amusing himself with a woman gullible enough to agree to pretend to be betrothed to him? She could not tell, but she knew it would be advisable to steer him back into the ballroom as soon as possible.

Just then, a group of gentlemen came past, talking in over-loud voices, and rather the worse for drink. One of them staggered, and would have crashed straight into Connie, had not Lord Reginald pulled her aside at the last moment. She found herself crushed against him, his arm around her waist, his face inches from hers and a light in his eyes there was no mistaking.

"Connie…" he murmured, bending towards her.

"Lord Reginald!" she hissed, leaning away from him as far as she was able, although he held her fast.

His face dropped and he released her abruptly. "I beg your pardon, Miss Allamont. I… I…"

"Reggie? What are you doing with Miss Allamont?" The Marquess's imperious tones were loud enough to turn heads.

"Sshh! Nothing at all, I do assure you. Although… what business it is of yours, I do not know."

"What business—? Good Lord, Reggie, the bats have got into your head. You know perfectly well what business it is of mine."

"No, as it happens, I do not."

"What the—? Well, really, you are the very devil, Reggie, do you know that? She is living under my roof as my guest, and is therefore under my protection. There, will that do?"

Lord Reginald hissed, "But she is betrothed to *me*, Dev, so you can go back to your *own* future wife, and leave Miss Allamont to *me*."

The Marquess glared at him and Lord Reginald glared back, his fists clenched into angry balls. For a dreadful moment, Connie was afraid they would come to blows, in the middle of one of the grandest balls of the season, and then what a scandal there would be. And the worst of it was, it was all her fault. If only she had stayed in the ballroom, they could have been dancing in perfect respectability, not embroiled in this horrid quarrel. She felt almost ready to faint.

"Please…" she whispered, and the two men turned to her, bemused, as if they had forgotten her presence.

But then the Marquess nodded curtly, spun on his heel and strode off. Connie dared to breathe again, but all her enjoyment in the evening was gone. When Lord Reginald took her back to Lady Moorfield, she took one look at Connie's face and declared, "Oh, you poor dear! How you are suffering in this heat! Do you know, I have a mind to take you straight home and tuck you into bed."

This was such a tempting prospect that Connie felt tears pricking at her eyes. "Oh — indeed I should be very glad to go home, my lady, if it would not be a terrible inconvenience."

"Well, I confess I should be glad to escape this crush myself. A great success, of course, but not at all comfortable. Reggie, do you go and arrange for the carriage to be brought round. Where is Jess? But I daresay *she* will not want to leave yet. Francis will bring her home later with Mrs March. There now, my dear, let us go and wait in the hall. It might be a trifle cooler there. Indeed, it could hardly be any warmer. Do you have the headache? Too much heat always gives me the headache. Summer is such a torment to me, you cannot imagine."

Connie was relieved that Lady Moorfield asked no awkward questions, and saw nothing untoward in her sudden indisposition. Lord Reginald handed her gently into the carriage, but then Lady Moorfield shooed him away, the door was shut and they lurched off into the night. The short journey back to Marford House passed in silence, then there was just the climb up the stairs, a half hour of fussing from Annie, Lady Moorfield's maid and Lady Moorfield herself, and then blessed peace.

As soon as the door was closed, Connie slipped out of bed again and lit a candle. Wrapping herself in a shawl, she hid behind the curtain covering the window, and sat, arms around her knees, gazing out. Her room overlooked the back yard, the outhouses and buttery, and beyond those, the dark outline of the coach house, silhouetted by a single lamp. Her room at Allamont Hall was smaller, but had fine views over the gardens, with trees and the scent of roses and damp grass in the summer, and rustling leaves in the autumn. She ached for that view, for everything that was familiar. London was enjoyable, in its way, and everyone had been so kind to her, but she felt very small and insignificant and uncertain and overwhelmed. And alone. The Marfords were not and never would be her family.

For a little while, she allowed the tears to fall unchecked, but then she saw movement down by the coach house, as the carriage was shut away. Then soft steps on the landing outside her room, and a nearby door opening and closing — Jess returning.

Jess. Connie sighed. She had set out to dislike Jess for stealing the Marquess away, but it was hard to dislike someone who enjoyed life so much and had such a lively personality. In addition, she made nothing of her betrothal to the Marquess. Whenever anyone hinted at the possibility, she would laugh and say there was no betrothal and besides, she was in no hurry. She never clung to him, as some fiancees did. She would stand up with him for the first dance, and was then quite content, it seemed, to let him go off to the card room, or dance with any other lady who took his eye. As often as not, he danced more with Connie than with Jess. It was all rather strange.

But she could not think about Jess, not tonight. Her mind was full of Lord Reginald, and that moment when he had held her tightly against him and seemed on the point of kissing her. And such a look in his eye as she had never seen in a man before! The look of love, surely. What else could it be? Was he in love with her? Or was it, perhaps, just a momentary feeling, brought about by her sudden nearness?

When she had gone over all these questions a dozen times, she could no longer avoid the most important one — was she in love with him? She tried to remember what she had felt when she had fancied herself in love with Mr Ambleside — the fluttering of her heart when he came into the room, the thrill of delight when he smiled at her or spoke to her, the longing to see him when he was not there and the joy every time he called. She could not say that she felt any of that for Lord Reginald. If anything, it was the Marquess who set her heart thumping and caused her to blush and blush again.

But no, she told herself sternly. The Marquess was not for her. He was spoken for, and Jess would suit him very well. She must steer her thoughts in a different direction and look to Lord Reginald, or else go home a failure, unmarried still, reduced to choosing between the brothers from High Frickham. That would never do! The second son of a Marquess was still quite a catch, and she liked him well enough. Surely love could not be far behind liking? She set herself the task of enumerating all Lord Reginald's good qualities, which were plentiful, she was sure. And yet... she could not quite see herself as Lady Reginald, condemned to suffer the sight of the marital happiness of Jess and her Marquess for the rest of her life. It was all too confusing, and her thoughts lurched from one brother to the other, and back again, for hours, yet she was no nearer to knowing her own heart.

The first grey light of dawn was touching the sky when she heard heavy footsteps on the stairs and male voices, gradually drawing further away, as the Marquess and Lord Reginald made their way upstairs. Their voices could be heard for some time, rising and dropping. Then a slammed door and all was quiet again.

Connie crept back into bed, and tried to sleep.

~~~~~

The two brothers were not at breakfast the next morning, but the ladies all fussed round Connie as if she were an invalid.

"A hot posset, that is what you need to restore you," Lady Moorfield declared.

"I know several excellent remedies, Miss Allamont," Mrs March said.

"That is true," Lady Moorfield said. "Jane knows a remedy for every ill you can imagine."

"Can she cure the lovesick?" Jess said. "Or better yet, cure the *lack* of love, for there are far too many men in the world who stubbornly refuse to fall in love when they are expected to. A simple potion, and they would be halfway to the altar in no time."

Mrs March tittered, but Lady Moorfield looked at Jess quizzically. "You are a shade too frivolous, sometimes, Jess, dear. A little more decorum might not go amiss if you hope to be a Marchioness."

"I beg your pardon, my lady," Jess said demurely, but she had difficulty suppressing her smile.

Connie refused all offers of possets and remedies, and since her appetite was unimpaired, she was deemed to be sufficiently recovered not to need them.

"Even so, you should stay quietly at home today," Lady Moorfield said. "We cannot have you overset, not at this important point in the season. You must be at your best for our own ball, you know."

"I am sure I shall be perfectly well," Connie said. "Indeed, I am well now. The heat overcame me, just a little, I think, but it was no more than that. I beg you will not be anxious about me, for I am quite recovered now."

"You are still a trifle pale," Lady Moorfield said. "Plenty of rest, and perhaps a bowl of beef broth — that should do it. That will set you up for the theatre tonight, and then the rout at Melbury House, and perhaps the ball at Berkeley Square — everything to be in gold, so I hear, and one of the royal dukes will be there."

Connie sighed inwardly, and drank her coffee.

Gradually, the house emptied and grew quiet. There was still no sign of the gentlemen, but Connie was not sorry for it. She could not quite determine her own feelings for either of them to her own satisfaction, and so she chose not to think about them at all. She spent a pleasant hour with Annie, sorting through gowns and bonnets, finding a tear here or a wrongly placed ribbon there. Then she wrote a very full letter to Dulcie, and a rather shorter one to Mama. After that, she settled down to dismantle a bonnet that she was not quite pleased with, refashioning it with different trimming to match a new gown, and then changing her mind and starting over.

She was thus engrossed when she became aware of someone else in the room. Turning, she saw Lord Reginald idly sifting through the pile of newspapers and journals on a table.

"Oh — good morning, my lord."

Lifting his head abruptly, he said, "I did not see you there, Miss Allamont. Good morning."

His tone was so stiff and cold that she cried out, "Pray what have I done to offend you!"

"Why, not the least thing in the world," he said in surprise, and now that he was fully facing her, she saw that he had a long gash over one eye, and a bruise around the other.

"Oh, whatever happened to you?" She jumped up and ran towards him, but to her consternation he jumped backwards, as if to evade her. She stopped. "Were you set upon by footpads?"

That earned her a lop-sided smile. "No such thing, I assure you. Just... a little boxing, that is all."

"Boxing? For sport? But why did you allow your opponent to hurt you so? It must give you great pain."

A slightly broader smile. "My pride is injured more than my face, Miss Allamont."

"Will you not let me attend to it for you? A little raw steak—"

"No, no, you must not trouble yourself. I shall do very well, I assure you." Again he backed away, leaving Connie quite bemused.

Just then, the door opened and the Marquess strode in, his gaze sweeping over the two of them. "You here!" he said in stentorian tones to Lord Reginald, for all the world as if he were a stranger, and not his own brother who had every right to be there.

"Yes, yes, I am going," Lord Reginald said crossly, hands raised in mock surrender.

The Marquess held the door open for him, his brother sauntered out, and the Marquess shut the door again rather more forcefully than Connie thought strictly necessary.

"There, that is far better," he said in satisfaction.

"You cannot expect me to agree with you, my lord," Connie said indignantly. "Do you have no sympathy for Lord Reginald, who has been grievously injured by some wicked person?"

To her astonishment, the Marquess laughed. "Oh, very wicked, Miss Connie. You have a tender heart, but do not waste your compassion on my worthless brother. He deserved every bruise, and more."

"Worthless? You forget yourself, sir! The man you describe as your worthless brother is my future husband."

But he just laughed all the more. "Nonsense! Let us have no more of this tomfoolery. Your betrothal is all a sham, and we shall hear no more of it, if you please. You are not to marry Reggie—"

"But—"

"—because you are going to marry *me*."

16: A Glass of Brandy

Connie's head was spinning. What could he possibly mean? "But what about Jess?"

"Oh, Jess and I — that is all a sham, too. You see, I wanted to be absolutely sure before committing myself. There was a young lady—" He threw himself into a chair, legs stretched out. "Well, that was a few years ago, but it has made me excessively cautious. I needed to be certain that you would *do* before rushing to the altar, do you see? This way, I could get to know you, and watch how you went on in company and at Drummoor and so forth, without any awkwardness."

"Without awkwardness," she said faintly.

"Without any *expectations* on your part. If you believed me already betrothed, then you would be entirely yourself and I could judge your character without any falsity on your part."

"Judge my character," she repeated in disbelief. "Falsity..."

"Exactly so!" He smirked in a self-satisfied way. "Is it not a clever scheme? It was all my own idea, you know — well, mostly, for Reggie may have had a hand in it, just a little. He played his part very well, do you not agree? Until the end, at least — he did get a trifle out of line there, and I had to take him down a few pegs, you know. But the bruises will heal soon enough."

"Bruises..."

"What, did you think he walked into a door?" He chuckled. "No, he walked into my fists."

"I thought he had been set upon by footpads," she said indignantly.

He laughed uproariously, as if she had made some great joke. "I shall tease him about that, you may be sure. Footpads! Ha! Poor Reggie. No such thing. Your sympathy is quite misplaced."

"I do not agree," she said hotly. "He has been severely injured, and at his own brother's hands! It is quite monstrous, sir!"

"Oh, monstrous, is it?" he said, sitting a little more upright. "Well, it is not surprising if you have grown to like Reggie, since you have been thrown together rather, and you may continue to do so, you know, after we are married."

"It would serve you right after all your scheming if I had fallen in love with him, and he with me!"

"But you have not," he said smugly. "You love *me*, for why else would you try to seduce me with poetry, and wild flowers, eh?"

She flushed uncomfortably. "How would you know anything about that?"

"Ah, because Miss Dulcie told me. Trying to be helpful and throw us together, I dare say, but she put me quite on my guard, so I knew exactly what you were about. It was most entertaining to watch your efforts to attract me. It was largely because of your little tricks that I felt obliged to protect myself, you know. But it did not make me think worse of you, so you need have no fear that I shall reproach you on that score when we are married."

"When we—!" She was so angry that she could barely catch her breath.

"So that is all settled. I shall put the notice in the Gazette next week."

"No, you shall not!" she hissed.

"What? Why ever not? Oh, you want me to ask your mama first, is that it?"

"No, that is *not* it! Never in my *life* have I met such an arrogant, high-handed...*obnoxious* man as you are, my lord! Notice in the Gazette, indeed! Such presumption!"

"There is no need to take that tone with me, madam! What is the matter with you? Here I am offering to marry you, and all you can do is hurl abuse at my head like a washer-woman. You had better be careful, or I shall decide not to marry you after all. It will hardly enhance my comfort to have you shout at me over the breakfast table."

"Enhance your—!" She paused, too stupefied to order her thoughts for a moment. "You are dreadful, quite dreadful! It is of no possible interest to me what you may decide to do. Please go away."

"Go away? In my own house? Now you are being foolish."

"Then I shall go."

He stood up, his face suffused with anger. "Now, this has gone far enough! I have no notion what bee is buzzing in your bonnet, but it will not do. You will calm down, like a good girl, or I shall be forced to withdraw my offer."

"You have not *made* me an offer, my lord. You have told me that I must marry you, but you have said nothing of love or respect or honour or... or any of the proper things, and you have not once asked me what *I* want."

"Good God, Connie, of course I love you and all the rest of it. That is what this is about, after all. And I already know you want to marry me so—"

"I do *not*. Why should I want to marry anyone as horrid as you?"

"Because I am a Marquess, you goose."

"You could be the King himself, and I would not marry you!"

"Really, Connie—"

She stamped her foot in frustration. "Do not *dare* to call me that. You have no *right*. Oh — you are *impossible*! I am leaving at once."

Her anger carried her out of the room, onto the landing and down the stairs. In the entrance hall, she stopped, uncertain. A footman turned in surprise, and then bowed.

The Marquess galloped down the stairs after her. "And just where are you planning to go, without a coat or hat, in the rain?"

She had not yet thought that far, but the answer rose into her mind without effort. "I shall go to my sisters," she said with as much dignity as she could muster, although she shook from head to toe. "Milford, pray tell Annie to fetch my brown pelisse and bonnet, and to bring her own cloak and bonnet."

"Yes, madam." The footman bowed deeply, face impassive, and disappeared down the service stairs.

"Connie... Miss Allamont, this is not necessary. You are making a great piece of work about nothing."

"I shall send for my boxes later. Pray thank your aunt for all her kindness."

"Pfft. This is ridiculous."

And with that he stamped back up the stairs, leaving her standing alone in the hall, shaking, fighting back tears and waiting for Annie to appear.

~~~~~

"Dev? What was all the shouting about?" Reggie's battered face peeked out from the library door.

"What is it to you?" the Marquess snapped. As if it was not bad enough to have Connie getting uppity with him, now he supposed that Reggie would be exultant over his failure.

"Is Connie all right? My God, Dev, you look like you need a drink."

The Marquess gave a bark of laughter. "That would be just the thing."

"Come in then," Reggie said, opening the library door a little wider. "What is it to be — Madeira? Or is this a job for brandy?"

"Definitely brandy. The Devil take all women, brother, for I swear I cannot understand them at all. What sort of woman would turn down a Marquess, eh?"

Reggie paused, decanter in mid-air, and looked at him in astonishment. "She turned you down? Good God! But why?"

"That is the worst of it, I have not the least idea. I thought she liked me well enough, but she got all hoity-toity, and shouted at me, if you please, and I have no idea what has got into her."

Reggie poured two generous portions of brandy, then, after a moment's thought, poured some more. "Here, get that inside you. It will help."

The Marquess took a large gulp, and then, almost at once, another. Settling in a worn leather wing chair, one long leg over the arm, he said, "You have two minutes to gloat. I will allow you that."

"By God, Dev, what sort of a brother do you take me for? Whatever has gone wrong, I am sorry for it, for your sake. I know how much you love her."

"I *do*, it is very true. She is the sweetest little thing, and she warms my heart whenever I am with her. I had almost despaired after that last business, but Connie has quite restored my faith in womankind. I had so much looked forward to— And I thought she wanted me, too. Well, there is no use repining. She will not have me, and there is an end to it."

"But what did she say?"

"She said no. The rest of it hardly signifies."

Reggie was silent for a minute, sipping his brandy and frowning. "Hate to disagree with you, brother, but I think it *does* signify. Because *I* thought she wanted you, too. The way she looked at you, sometimes, and the charming way she became a little conscious when she talked to you. She was never like that with *me*, and when she fell against me last night— yes, yes, I know, but hear me out — she fell against me, I say, and I pulled her close by instinct, you know, as anyone would, and she was quite angry with me. She thought I was making love to her, I expect."

"Well, that is exactly what it looked like to me, too," the Marquess said testily. "But we will not go over old ground."

"Good, for I should not like to repeat that argument," Reggie said, ruefully stroking his bruised face. "Point is, it seems to me that you had Connie in your hand and you scared her away, somehow. Perhaps if you think over what you said and what she said, you might work out what you did wrong."

"It hardly matters now," the Marquess said gloomily. "I can scarcely run round after her like a lovelorn goatherd. The Marquess of Carrbridge has a position to maintain. I have to consider my dignity."

Reggie was silent for a long moment, twirling the brandy in its glass. At length he nodded. "Well, if that is how you feel, you will not mind if I try to win her, will you?"

~~~~~

Connie had not thought to bring an umbrella. As a result, her pelisse was soaked and in all likelihood her bonnet was ruined. Annie had forgotten her gloves, too, but she had not cared to wait any longer. Now she felt quite improperly attired, as if everyone must be staring at her. She could not see them, fortunately, for tears blurred her vision.

Twice she made a wrong turning, but Annie called her back and steered her in the right direction. Brook Street was so close, and yet how easy it would be to lose herself in the multitude of identical streets in London. But at last she arrived and ran up the steps to ring the bell. As soon as the maid opened the door, Connie ran past her into the hall.

"Is Mrs Ambleside at home? Or Mrs Burford?"

"No, madam. Only Mr Ambleside."

"Oh, pray take me to him at once."

She could not wait a moment, following the maid up the stairs, with Annie trailing behind. She was shown into a small library, and there he was, jumping to his feet in alarm at her bedraggled appearance and tears.

"Good God, Miss Allamont, whatever has happened? Come, sit here. Peggy, some brandy at once." He knelt at her feet, chafing her hands. "You are so cold."

"So sorry…" was all she could manage through her sobs. "So very sorry to burst in like this."

"Nonsense. Here, drink a little of this. Careful! Let me hold the glass for you. There! That will do you good. Peggy, send the boy for the physician—"

"No, no! Just… just want to see Amy and Belle."

"Of course you do! Peggy, send the boy at once to Mrs Cavendish's house — do you know the direction? Good. Mrs Ambleside and Mr and Mrs Burford must return home at once, for Miss Allamont is taken ill."

"Oh, do not alarm them so! I am quite well, only—"

"Of course," he said. "Say only that Miss Allamont is arrived unexpectedly and wishes to talk to them at once. There, Miss Allamont, they will be here directly. Have a little more brandy."

"Thank you. You are so kind."

She sipped the brandy, with his steadying hand on the glass. He asked her no questions, but held her hand and talked constantly in a soothing monotone, and gradually his calm good sense brought some abatement in her sobs. Indeed, his behaviour was in such marked contrast to that of the Marquess, that she was moved to say, "*You* may call me Connie. We are good enough friends, surely."

"I should be very honoured... Connie. And if you wish, you may call me Will, for no one uses my full name, you know."

"Wilberforce," she said, smiling through her tears.

"Indeed. I cannot imagine what my parents were thinking, and Mama always used the name in its dreadful entirety."

In this comfortable way, a quarter of an hour passed, and then the door burst open and Amy and Belle rushed in, with Burford behind them. That started the tears all over again, and it was some time before she could speak a word.

"Dearest, can you tell us what happened?" Belle said. She had taken over Ambleside's spot at Connie's feet holding one hand, while Amy sat beside her on the sofa holding the other.

"Marquess..." she managed. "Proposed... but... so *obnoxious*. Could not marry such a man." And gradually, as Amy and Belle gasped and murmured "Oh no!" and "How dreadful!", she told the story.

"Well, that was indeed very bad of him," Belle said at length. "To presume in that way... no, that is not at all right. And although you had some thought of marrying him at one time, there is at least this consolation, sister, that your affections are not engaged. You are not in love with him, after all."

"But I *am*!" she wailed. "I *do* love him, I do! He is of all things the right man for me, but *not* when he is so… so high-handed and arrogant. I wish he were not," she added in a small voice. "For I should very much like to marry him, but I do not think he loves me at all."

17: Morning Callers

Connie was not ill, but her sisters treated her as though she were an invalid all the same. She was given a tiny room to herself, and tenderly undressed and helped to bed. Trays were brought at intervals, offering weak tea and cake, or beef broth, or bread and cheese, whatever might tempt her appetite. Amy and Belle stayed with her all evening, taking their own supper on trays, too, and chatting easily about all that they had seen and done in London, so that she had no need to talk. And then, as it finally grew dark, she was given a hot posset and left to sleep.

"But the boy will sit outside your door all night, dear," Amy said. "If you need anything, anything at all, you have only to call and he will fetch one or other of us."

"Try to sleep a little," Belle said, kissing her forehead. "Goodnight, sister."

At first she thought she would never be able to sleep for the disordered thoughts running around in her head like mice in an attic. Every time she closed her eyes, visions of the Marquess rose up before her — his handsome face, the elegance of his dress, the graceful way his hands moved as he talked. She felt she could look at him for ever. Her heart performed a little dance every time she saw him, and when he smiled at her, that lazy, intimate smile that made her feel she was the only woman in the world he cared for, then she loved him with every bone in her body, a love more intense, more consuming than anything she had ever felt before. She had tried to put him out of her thoughts when she had believed him betrothed to Jess, but now that she knew the truth, she could admit to the full depth of her attachment to him.

Yet he was lost to her. His words, his manner, the presumptuous way her had treated her! She could not remember everything he had said, but a few phrases floated into her mind... about judging her character, and making sure she would do, as if she were a horse. He was insufferable! And how badly he had treated Jess, to let everyone think they were on the point of betrothal, when all the time his intentions were quite otherwise.

But her anger drove away the regret that she might otherwise have felt. She could not possibly marry a man who spoke so to her, no matter how much she loved him. She had freed herself from her betrothal from Mr Ambleside because of his managing attitude, and the Marquess was a hundred times worse! Perhaps in time she would be overcome with grief for what she had lost, but for now, all she could feel was gratitude that she was free of him, and that she was safe with her sisters.

Exhaustion overtook her quite soon, and to her surprise she slept deeply and woke refreshed. The awkwardness of her position now struck her forcibly. She had come to London as the soon-to-be-betrothed of Lord Reginald, living in Marford House, and now she had left without a word to him, or to Viscountess Moorfield, or Lady Harriet. She did not regret her action, for staying another moment under the same roof as the Marquess would have been insupportable, but she felt the rudeness of it. And now what was to become of her?

As soon as Amy and Belle woke and came through to see how she did, she burst out, "What should I do now? I must go home, but I do not know how."

"You will stay here with us, of course," Amy said. "We have another month in town, so you need not rush away. You can hide here at the house, or, if you wish, we will take you with us when we go about, for there is no danger of meeting the Marquess, you know. We move in very different circles. Of course, if you wish to go straight home—"

"Oh no! I should like of all things to stay here with you, with my own family. The Marfords have been very kind to me, but they are quite different from everything I am used to, and I do *not* like all the racketing around that they do, to be seen here, and be seen there. I should like London much better if there were fewer grand balls and more quiet card parties."

"Well, perhaps it is all for the best, then," said Belle. "It does not sound as if you would have been very comfortable as the Marchioness of Carrbridge."

"I suppose I would have got used to it, in time," Connie said doubtfully. "But it will be pleasant not to be junketing about every evening."

"You must stay in bed this morning..." Amy began.

"No, no," Connie said. "I should like to be up and about, and trying to do normal things. I am not ill, Amy dear, and now that I have had my little cry, I am quite calm, for I am absolutely sure of the rightness of my decision. Besides, I had better write to Lady Moorfield, and Lady Harriet, and Mama. And what about Lord Reginald? I ought to give him some explanation, but we were not truly betrothed, so I do not feel I can. Besides, he deceived me just as much as Lord Carrbridge. So much pretence..."

"But you were pretending, too," Belle said gently. "Although I believe your motives were more honourable than theirs."

"Of course Connie's motives were honourable," Amy said, shocked. "She wanted only to see if the Marquess might turn to her when he realised how unsuitable Jess Drummond was."

"And to have a season in London," Connie said wistfully. "That was selfish of me, but it seemed so providential at the time. And by then I had quite given up on the idea of making the Marquess in love with me, so there was no entrapment, or anything in the least underhand about it. Whereas *they*..." She could not go on, her trembling voice betraying the emotions not far below the surface, despite her declaration of calmness.

"There, there, dearest," Amy said. "What they did was most reprehensible. To deceive you in that way! It is of all things the most dishonourable."

"Dishonourable?" Connie said in a whisper.

"Dishonourable," Amy said firmly. "A gentleman can never be too open and honest in his dealings, in my view."

Connie said nothing, remembering that even that most upright of gentlemen, Mr Ambleside himself, had deceived her when they had been betrothed, and he had wished to extricate himself to marry Amy. He had confessed his deceit in the end, but it had convinced her that she could never marry a man who was so overbearing. A little firmness was understandable, but a true gentleman should always respect a lady and take her wishes into account, and that applied just as much to a Marquess as anyone else.

~~~~~

They were all at breakfast, and Connie was toying with some devilled kidneys, when Lady Harriet and Jess were shown in. Connie was surprised to see Jess looking calm, and almost complaisant.

"My dear Connie, how dreadful this is!" Lady Harriet said, sitting down beside her and taking her hand. "Forgive us for calling so early, but we could not wait a second longer to be sure that you are not completely overcome by all this foolishness of Dev's. I am entirely out of patience with the silly boy. What a mull he has made of it! But you are not to worry about a thing. We made excuses for you at the Duchess's ball, so you may come straight home with us now and no one will be any the wiser. Everything will be as it was, you will see."

"You are very kind, my lady. I do not know what the Marquess may have told you, but there is no possibility of my returning to Marford House."

She sat abruptly back in her chair. "What? Why ever not? Whatever misguided things he may have said to you, he did not mean any of it, you know. Men are hopeless at such things, and I speak with some authority on the matter, for I have had a number of offers over the years, and not one of them elegantly phrased. I do not understand why it should be, but gentlemen do seem to get tongue-tied on such occasions."

"Not all men," Connie said, throwing a quick glance at Ambleside. "*Some* men know how to treat a lady with the proper respect."

"Oh. He *does* respect you, that goes without saying, but being a Marquess, he naturally feels some superiority."

"Then he should not!" Connie cried. "His rank may be superior, but his manners are not."

"I see," she said, thoughtfully. "So may I give him no cause to hope? If he were to approach you with greater humility, perhaps?"

"It is not just his manner," Connie said. "It is the deception that distresses me more. He was not honest with me, and that is dishonourable in a gentleman."

"I see," Lady Harriet said again. "That does seem rather final. I am sorry for it, for it always seemed to me that you would deal well together. However, I trust that *I* may still count you a friend?"

"Oh, that would be wonderful, my lady, and I cannot thank you enough for all you have done for me. Please tell Lady Moorfield that I shall be writing to her to express my gratitude."

"You may express your gratitude in person, for she plans to call on you later this morning," Lady Harriet said with a smile.

"Well, you are not as distraught as I had envisaged, so I daresay you will go on very well. And you have enjoyed your little season—"

"Indeed I have, very much!"

"—and it has been good for Jess, too."

"How so?" Connie said. "She has been used very ill, and is left with nothing, I fancy."

"Not at all," Jess said with a smile. "My arrangement with the Marquess was that I should have my season, and the clothes, and so forth, and he has paid for a cook for Alex while I am away, also. He has been very generous. But the best of it is that not everyone believes in this rumoured betrothal." She laughed throatily. "It is just possible that I shall leave town betrothed in truth. So you see, I shall do very well out of all this. You need not worry about me."

~~~~~

Lady Moorfield arrived several hours later, accompanied by three of her stout daughters and Mrs March, so that the servants were put to a great deal of bustle to find extra chairs, and the Brook Street drawing room, so small after the capacious rooms of Marford House, felt uncomfortably crowded.

Connie quaked at the thunderous expression on Lady Moorfield's face. But she had Amy on one side of her and Belle on the other, and standing behind, for there were not sufficient chairs, Mr Ambleside and Mr Burford loomed protectively.

"I am excessively displeased, Constance," Lady Moorfield began. "After all my efforts on your behalf, to be refusing a perfectly good offer and scampering off in the middle of a rainstorm like a hoyden, it is not good enough. I am most disappointed in you, and you need not expect anyone to take you up again, you know. You have had your chance, and have wilfully thrown it away. Such ingratitude, after all I have done for you, is beyond any bearing."

"Indeed I am not ungrateful—" Connie began, but there was no stopping the flow of disapprobation.

"We made some excuse for you last night, in the hope that you could be prevailed upon to see sense, but apparently you will not listen to advice from your betters. You young girls these days, you *will* have your own way, and there is no convincing you to do anything you have no mind for, even when it must surely be for your own good. It is a foolish kind of conceit, and I never tolerated it in my own girls, and look what good marriages they all made as a result."

Connie looked at the three of them in their fine gowns and stylish bonnets, their round faces empty and emotionless, and was thankful that Lady Moorfield was not her own mother. Mama perhaps took too little interest in her daughters' welfare, but that was surely preferable to constant overbearing scrutiny.

"I am very sorry to upset you, my lady, but I could not stay."

"Nonsense! Of course you could have done so. I daresay Francis did not make love to you quite as you hoped, for I know how you girls have your romantic fancies and like to be flattered, but you should not have thrown him over, for you will not get a second chance. You cannot expect a Marquess to grovel, you know. Now, I suppose, you will be an old maid and a pitiable sight, but *I* shall have no sympathy for you, you may be sure."

Connie could not stem the tears in the face of this onslaught. Silently Amy took one hand and Belle the other. Burford coughed discreetly.

"You approve, then, of this trickery perpetrated on my sister-in-law, Lady Moorfield?" he said.

"Trickery? A strong word, Mr... erm, Burton. A tiny pretence, no more than that, in everybody's best interests."

"Dishonesty is never in anyone's best interests. *'Bread of deceit is sweet to a man, but afterwards his mouth shall be filled with gravel.'* Proverbs, my lady."

There was a long silence. Lady Moorfield grew red with rage, her lips set in a thin line, but she could hardly argue with the Bible. Her daughters looked at her, blank-faced, and Mrs March huddled in a corner, head down, clutching her reticule so tightly that her knuckles were white. Connie held her breath.

Without a word, Lady Moorfield rose, her daughters scrambling to their feet in a flurry of rustling skirts and waving hat feathers. Then they swept out of the room, heads high.

Mrs March paused before she followed them, and looked at Connie. "Goodbye, dear. I am so sorry. I do not suppose we will meet again." Ambleside rushed to hold the door open for her as she trotted after the others.

"Well!" Ambleside said, closing the door quietly. "That was unpleasant. But well done, John. There is nothing like a clergyman in the family for producing the very best set downs."

~~~~~

Finally, very late, at an hour when Connie was beginning to wonder what she might wear for dinner, since her boxes had not yet been sent round, Lord Reginald arrived, bearing a huge sheaf of flowers and an apologetic expression. Belle, Burford and Ambleside had gone to the circulating library, so only Amy was in the room with Connie.

After the formalities, he said quietly, "You are very kind to see me, for you must wish all of us at Jericho, I am sure, Miss Allamont. I will not impose on you and Mrs Ambleside for long, but I wanted to assure myself that you are being well looked after, which I am very happy to see is the case. I can only apologise for my part in Dev's trickery. I hope in time that you may find it in your heart to forgive a deception which was conceived with the best of motives. For myself, I can see now that our schemes were quite wrong, and deeply injurious to your peace of mind."

"Thank you, my lord," Connie said.

"Perhaps it is wrong of me, but I regard our pretend betrothal as one of the pleasantest times of my life." He paused, as if hoping for an answer from her, but she could not find any words, and merely hung her head. After a moment, he went on, "Will you return to Allamont Hall now?"

"No, my sisters are in town for another month, and I am invited to stay with them."

He brightened. "Oh — that is excellent news! I am exceedingly glad to hear you say so. Perhaps you would be so good as to allow me to call upon you occasionally?"

"Your brother will permit that?" Connie said, before she could prevent herself.

His face darkened. "Dev does not *own* me!" he spat back. But then he stopped and took a deep breath, controlling his sudden anger. When he spoke again, his voice was its usual even tone."I am my own master, I hope, Miss Allamont. I may have my own friends, without reference to my brother. We *are* friends, I trust?"

He was the second member of the family to claim friendship with her, despite the rift with the Marquess, and Connie wondered at it. She and her sisters were marvellously united, but perhaps the Marfords were different, and familial loyalty was of little consequence to them. Just one more aspect of her recent dealings with them to puzzle over.

"I... believe so, yes," she answered, and found herself colouring in response to the sudden fire in his eyes. She had seen *that* look before, when she had been pressed against him in the saloon, his arm firmly around her waist. She grew hot with embarrassment at the very thought of it.

He gave no sign of noticing. "I am gratified to hear it," he said smoothly. Then he was on his feet, making his farewells, and within moments he was gone.

"That was interesting," murmured Amy.

"But what can he mean by it?" Connie cried. "Why would he talk so after all that has happened?"

Amy laughed. "Oh, Connie dear, I think he very much hopes to turn his pretended betrothal into a real one."

18: The House With The Blue Door

Connie soon settled into life at Brook Street. She could not forget the distressing end to her stay at Marford House, and in quiet moments she would grow tearful again, her misery overwhelming her, but if at any time she felt particularly unhappy at the loss of the Marquess, she had only to recall his arrogant words and the superciliousness of his manner, and she would be quite restored to acceptance of the situation.

She could not feel quite easy in her own part in the deception. Even though she herself had been deceived by the Marquess, with the connivance of Lord Reginald, Lady Harriet and Jess, Connie could not deny that she too had willingly allowed assumptions to be made about herself and Lord Reginald. She remembered her initial discomfort with the proposal, and now wished she had listened to her conscience and refused to comply. The Marfords had dazzled her, and drawn her in with the prospect of a London season. How foolish she had been, allowing herself to be beguiled by their glib talk! From now on she would trust her own judgement.

Her sisters and their husbands were her greatest comfort. There was an ease and familiarity subsisting amongst the five of them which was a welcome relief from the protocol of Marford House, and their unfailing kindness supported her through even the darkest hours. Their routine was a gentle one, for they received no invitations to grand balls, but most evenings brought a dinner engagement or a card party with one of Mr Burford's extensive range of distant relatives, or Mr Ambleside's friends from school or university. None of them moved in the first circles, but they were friendly and unstuffy, and Connie felt entirely at home with them.

Each day when the weather was fine they drove out in the barouche, sometimes visiting the shops but mostly exploring London's finest streets and squares and parks. One day they were driving through Hyde Park when Amy said,

"May we get down and walk for a while? There is an interesting little shrubbery over there. I should like to examine the flowers more closely."

Ambleside laughed. "Is there a shrubbery in the world that you do not find interesting? By all means let us walk."

It was very pleasant to stroll about on the paths, while the barouche waited for them. The hour was early, so there were few people about, but there was one whom Connie recognised. Lady Hartshill was approaching at a fast pace, head down. Connie dropped into a deep curtsy as she passed by, having no expectation of any acknowledgement, for her acquaintance with Lady Hartsill was of the slightest kind, and solely through the Marfords. But to her surprise, Lady Hartshill, stopped, turned and smiled at her.

"Miss Allamont, is it not?"

"It is, Lady Hartshill."

"We were told you had left town."

"Your information was mistaken, my lady. I am staying with my sisters."

"Your sisters, eh? The two ladies standing over there? They have a house in town?"

"They have taken a house in Brook Street for the season, my lady."

"Hmm. I should like to meet them. Will you introduce me?"

"It would be an honour, my lady."

The introductions were made, some commonplace remarks were exchanged and Lady Hartshill made her farewells.

"She is very amiable, Connie," Amy said. "That was exceedingly gracious of her, do you not think? For she is quite high-flown, I believe you said."

"Very," Connie said. "Yet her card parties are the most delightful occasions, not stuffy or formal in the least. I was only invited to one, but I enjoyed it better than all the grand balls. Ah well, that is all over now." And she laughed, not at all cast down.

But it was not all over. Later that day, a note was delivered to Brook Street by Lady Hartshill's footman, inviting all five of them to a card party that very evening. The others found that Connie was quite right in her opinion of them.

When she thanked her hostess at the end of the evening, Connie added impulsively, "I like your card parties better than anything else in London."

Lady Hartshill laughed, and said, "And that is why I invited you, my dear, and your family. Unlike most of society, you are not trying to impress me. How long are you in town? You must come again."

It was a cheering moment after the misery of her departure from Marford House.

~~~~~

"I am sorry we have no dancing to offer you, Connie," Belle said one morning over breakfast. "You must think us sadly flat after all the excitement you have become used to, and it is your first real season, after all. There ought to be balls for you to meet young men, for that is the point of a London season, after all, but we know no one grand enough to hold one."

"I am weary of such affairs, to tell the truth," Connie said. "So much effort and expense, solely to impress people determined not to be impressed. But how did you manage to meet people when you had your come-out season?

"We only had a month, in the end, not a full season," Belle said. "It was supposed to be three months, but nothing was settled upon and so it was all done in a rush. If you want my considered opinion, I believe Mama and Papa quarrelled over it. They each thought the other was arranging matters, but neither of them did, until Amy got upset about it one day, and then Aunt Lucy came down from Liverpool to see to everything. We stayed with a friend of hers who had a daughter coming out that year, so it was excessively kind of her to take us under her wing, for Amy was much prettier than Rachel."

"But you went to dances?"

"Yes, but it was all very odd, for we received invitations from any number of people that Aunt Lucy and her friend had never been acquainted with. Not to Carlton House or anything as grand as that, but several times we went to parties hosted by Earls or Viscounts, and a Duchess, once."

"Invitations from strangers?" Ambleside said. "That is indeed odd."

"We just assumed they were friends of Mama's," Belle said. "She knows a great many people, and the Heatheringtons move in the uppermost levels of society. But we were never formally introduced to those who sent invitations, and sometimes the hostess was quite cold with us as we made our bows, so we could not understand why we were invited at all."

"Probably your Mama asked them for the favour, but they did not quite like it, for some reason," Ambleside said.

"I think there is something not quite proper in Mama's past," Connie said. "Lady Melthwaite hinted as such, anyway."

"That would account for why she has avoided society all these years," Belle said. "But she is so utterly respectable now, that one would imagine any rift from years ago would be healed after all this time."

"The Melthwaites do not seem like forgiving people," Connie said sadly.

"Have you seen much of the Melthwaites since you came to town, Connie?" Burford asked.

"Nothing at all. I left my card, but they did not call and I have not encountered them at any of our engagements."

"Are they not going into society at all, then?" Ambleside said.

"Oh, I am quite certain they are, but some of these grand occasions are vast," Connie said with a smile. "At one ball, there were a thousand guests, I was told. People come and go, and in all the crush, there is no hope of finding anyone in particular. I am surprised they did not call, however. Tambray Hall borders Drummoor, so the two families know each other well. It is disappointing not to see them at all."

"You can do nothing more there," Ambleside said. "They may call on you if they choose, but the approach must come from the higher rank. Belle, are there any other relatives we might call on to help introduce Connie into a wider society than we enjoy at present? It would be a shame not to take full advantage of our time in London."

"There is only Aunt Tilly," Belle said doubtfully. "I wrote when we first arrived, but I have had no response."

"Such a disconnected family," Burford said with a wry smile. "But there would be nothing improper in calling on her, surely? Not when we know that Lady Sara has stayed with her recently."

"It is awkward, when there has been no prior contact," Ambleside said. "But perhaps the Lady Matilda lives quietly in reduced circumstances, and is ashamed of her poverty. I believe we may venture to drive to the address and see what manner of dwelling it is, and then we shall make a decision as to whether it would be proper to make a direct approach. Once Amy is dressed, if she feels well enough for an outing, we will order the barouche brought round."

No more than two hours later, they set off in the barouche. The day was fine, and might be warm later when the sun broke through the clouds, but Ambleside was not prepared to risk his wife's health with a chill. There were hot bricks, and several thick rugs to keep the slightest untoward breeze at bay.

It was an unfashionably early hour to be abroad, so the streets were not as crowded as they had been in the early morning bustle of delivery carts or as they would be at five o'clock, when all those with pretensions to fashion ventured forth to see and be seen. They soon arrived at their destination, which turned out to be a large, attractive house in a fashionable square, with well-tended gardens in the centre.

"This is an expensive district, I should surmise," Burford said. "No sign of genteel poverty here."

"Such a pretty little square," Amy said. "I should have liked to stay somewhere like this, with trees about, and a pleasant view from the windows, and not so much smoke everywhere."

"We looked into one or two such, but we thought them too expensive, my dear," Ambleside said. "Perhaps next year we will reconsider, if you like the idea."

"Too large for just the four of us, also," Burford said. "Much larger than we needed. Which is Aunt Tilly's?"

"Number eight," Belle said. "The one with the blue door, I believe."

They drew up outside, and looked at each other. Such a prosperous residence was not what any of them had expected.

"Perhaps this is a mistake," Amy said nervously. "After all, Mama was quite adamant that none of us should ever visit Aunt Tilly."

"And Lady Melthwaite fainted away when she heard Mama had stayed here," Connie added. "There must be *something* peculiar about Aunt Tilly's situation."

"Nonsense," Belle said briskly. "We are here now. What is the harm in knocking on the door and asking if she is at home? She is our aunt, after all. If she does not wish to receive us, we shall leave our cards and go away again."

"I do not think—" Amy began.

"You should stay here, well wrapped up, Amy dear," Belle said. "There is no need for all of us to get down from the carriage. Give me your card, and Connie, too, and I will go and hand them in at the door."

"I do not like you to go alone," Connie said. "I will come with you."

"Shall I accompany you?" Burford asked. "You will not be more than ten paces away, but even so..."

"There is no need," Belle said with a smile. "I believe we can manage to call on a middle-aged lady without your assistance. If she is friendly, and willing to receive us, we shall summon you to join us."

Connie followed Belle out of the barouche and up the steps to the front door. The street was silent, the only sound the blowing of the horses and a rustling from the trees in the centre of the square. No one else was about, not so much as a maid scrubbing steps, or a single person walking along the wide pavement. Yet it was a respectable neighbourhood, and Connie felt no apprehension as Belle pulled sharply on the bell-rope. Distantly, the bell jangled.

Connie had expected either a butler or footman to answer the door, or perhaps a housekeeper if Lady Matilda preferred to keep an entirely female household, as some ladies did. Instead, the door was opened by a young woman wearing the most fetching morning dress, in quite the latest style. To Connie's surprise, she scarcely looked at them.

"Come in, quick!" she said, holding the door wide for them. "You should have gone round the back, you know. Do not stand on the step like that, get inside."

Exchanging glances, the two sisters stepped over the threshold, to find themselves in an airy, high-ceilinged hall with a tiled floor and marble-topped console. Elegant curved stairs led to the upper floors.

The young woman pointed to a door. "Wait in there. Do *not* wander about."

Then, without another word, she dashed away and vanished into some fastness behind the stairs.

"Well, that is strange," Belle said. "Perhaps she is a companion of some kind?"

"What shall we do?" Connie said.

"Why, we shall wait in here, as we have been directed, and we shall *not* wander about," Belle said, with a twinkle in her eye. "This room looks out to the street, so we can assure ourselves that the barouche still waits for us. Oh — the library!"

It was indeed a book room of sorts, although there were not many shelves of books. There were snuff jars, and heavy leather chairs, and decanters of Madeira and brandy set out, and paintings of nymphs and angels and the like, rather scantily clad, as nymphs tended to be. Connie thought it was very much a gentleman's room, for the dark furniture and smoky atmosphere reminded her of Cousin Henry's book room at Willowbye.

Belle walked around the room peering at the books. "I cannot read the lettering on the covers at all," she said, reaching for one. "I wonder what kind of reading Aunt Tilly likes — oh!"

With a squeak of alarm, she snapped the book shut.

"Whatever is it, dearest?" Connie said. "Is something wrong?"

"Oh — well, not exactly, but... oh dear!"

"You have gone quite red, Belle. Are you all right? Is it the book? May I see?"

"No! Let me put it away at once. Do you know, I am not at all certain that this is Aunt Tilly's house at all. Perhaps she has moved lately, and some other family altogether now lives here? For this is not a ladies' room, I am sure of *that*."

"Perhaps we should go?" Connie said, but before Belle could answer. Steps were heard tapping rapidly across the hall outside, and a middle-aged woman appeared at the door, also very stylishly attired, although in the greys of a widow.

"Well, now, what have we here?" she said without any greeting or civility. "Nicely dressed, yes, and *one* very pretty. The other... hmm, although the cap is a nice touch. Turn around, will you?"

"How dare you!" Connie burst out. "You are very rude to talk about my sister and me in that way."

But the woman laughed. "You must expect that now, my dear. But sisters... that has possibilities."

Belle broke into this exchange in her calm way. "I do not know what you are about, madam, but we are here to call upon the Lady Matilda Heatherington. Is she at home?"

The woman laughed even more at that. "Oh, my mistake! Are you *customers*?"

"Customers? I have no idea what you mean," Belle said coldly. "Is the Lady Matilda at home or not? For we are her nieces."

For the first time, the woman's composure failed her. She gasped, covering her hands with her mouth. Then, to the sisters' consternation, she ran out of the room.

"That was... very peculiar," Belle said. "I think perhaps you are right, dear, and we should leave. There is something not *proper* about this house. It is not a normal establishment, by any means and I do not think we should have come here."

"Oh, yes, by all means let us leave at once!" Connie said. "I should dearly like to meet Aunt Tilly, but I do not even know whether she still lives here. Perhaps something dreadful has happened to her?"

"Perhaps," Belle said doubtfully. She opened the door and peered into the hall. "There is no one about. We should slip quietly away, I think. The sooner we leave this place the better."

From somewhere upstairs, a burst of girlish laughter drifted down, making the building seem, just for a moment, like a normal family house or perhaps a school. But Connie knew it could not be so. It was unsettling, to hear such innocent sounds in a place which, in some way she did not quite understand, was not innocent at all.

They crossed the hall to the front door, but it was large and heavy, fitted with several latches and chains, so that it took some manoeuvring before Belle, with a soft exclamation of triumph, pulled it open. They were almost out when they heard footsteps behind them, and a voice calling peremptorily.

"What are you doing here?"

It was their mother's voice, the tone of maternal authority so familiar that they had spun round and dropped into their curtsies before looking up to see—

Not Mama, but someone so like her that they could only be twins.

"Oh," Connie breathed. "Aunt Tilly!"

"Yes, but you must go at once! What were you thinking? Did Sara not tell you to keep well away from me?"

"But Mama stayed here in this house!" Connie cried before she could stop herself.

"She is right, we must go," Belle said. "Come, Connie." She whisked out of the door and down the steps.

"Oh," Connie said, disappointed. "I had so hoped to talk to you. We have so few family members, and even fewer who want anything to do with us, and I thought perhaps you..." She trailed off miserably.

Aunt Tilly tipped her head to one side, in a gesture that reminded Connie forcibly of her mother, except that Mama never looked quite so mischievous. "Do you really want to know me better? I am quite disreputable, you know. Positively ramshackle."

"What does that matter! You are *family*."

Aunt Tilly laughed. "Well now, let me see... Do you know Hamilton's umbrella shop?"

"Yes, but—"

"Be there tomorrow at noon. Just you and your abigail. Do not tell the others, for they will try to dissuade you, I daresay. Now go with your sister. Go on! Shoo!"

Connie went. They drove home in complete silence, but Connie barely noticed, so full of happy anticipation was she. Finally, she would get to know Aunt Tilly.

19: Hamilton's Umbrella Shop

It was not, in the end, difficult to escape from the others. Amy was still abed, and Belle, Mr Burford and Mr Ambleside wished to explore a new bookshop they had discovered. As if they had not enough books already! There was an entire library at Willowbye, and Staynlaw House boasted a well-stocked book room, too. Connie could not quite understand why they needed more books. However, it made the task of escaping by herself all the easier.

"I shall take Annie and visit one or two shops," she said. "I might go to Hamilton's — the umbrella shop, do you remember? We passed it twice yesterday, and I should like to examine the wares."

"That would be a useful purchase," Belle said. "Have you enough money?"

"Oh, yes. I have hardly broached the purse Mama gave me."

"Very well, but do not stay out too long," Belle said.

"Shall you find the way by yourself?" Mr Burford said, ever practical, and then proceeded to write explicit instructions on the correct route to take.

In fact, Connie was quite glad to have it all written down clearly, for there were one or two points where she might otherwise have become confused. In the end, it took her no more than twenty minutes to find her way there, and she was early enough to have a thorough look about the shop, with a helpful assistant opening and closing any item she wished to look at more closely.

The bells of a nearby church alerted her to the hour. "Oh — is it noon already? I must go." She remembered Lady Harriet and Lady Moorfield insisting on examining half the goods in a shop, and then leaving without making a purchase. Turning to the assistant, she said, "I am so sorry. I have put you to a great deal of trouble. I shall return another day to make my choice and buy one of your lovely umbrellas."

"It is no trouble at all, madam, I assure you," the assistant said. "If you will forgive my saying so, madam, but I think that young lady knows you."

Connie turned, and saw someone waving to her from the door, someone young and fashionably dressed. Did she know her? Then she remembered — it was the girl who had opened the door to them yesterday.

"Oh, yes," she said happily, skipping across to where the girl waited.

"Miss Allamont, how delightful to find you here," the girl said with a sweet smile, as if she were indeed an acquaintance. "Will you come? My *aunt* is waiting for me and she would be most happy to see you again."

"Oh. Oh, I see. Yes, indeed."

Connie followed the girl out of the shop and a little way along the street, Annie walking a pace or two behind. They turned under an arch and into the courtyard of what must once have been a large coaching inn. Now it was a secluded hotel, the entrance guarded by a pair of bewigged and uniformed doormen. They bowed to the three women, however, and opened the doors wide to admit them.

Inside, all was polished wood and deep rugs in vibrant colours. Apart from another pair of servants waiting near the stairs, the entrance hall was empty. The girl led them unhesitatingly across the rugs, past the bowing servants and up the stairs, opening a door to one side of the landing. With that same sweet smile, she ushered Connie and Annie inside.

And there was Aunt Tilly, rising with a smile, kissing Connie on each cheek, then, as if she could not quite let her go yet, hugging her very tightly.

"Come, sit here. You did not give me your name, but you must be Connie, I think." She turned to the maid. "Now, what is *your* name? Annie, good. I am going to have a little chat with your mistress. If you will go with Deirdre, she will take you downstairs to the servants' quarters for some refreshments. And you will say nothing of this to anyone else, do you understand?"

"Oh no, mi'lady." She curtsied twice to emphasise the point.

"Good girl. Off you go then."

The room was small, a private parlour, Connie surmised. A square table dominated the centre of the room, laid with a lace cloth, tea and cakes conveniently to hand. Around the walls were spare chairs, a small baize-topped table for cards and a sideboard with decanters and vases of sweet-smelling flowers. A small fire hissed fitfully, although the day was warm enough not to need it.

"Will she keep her mouth closed? Annie, I mean?"

"I... am not sure. Here, perhaps, where the servants are strangers, but at home..."

"Well, it matters less there," Aunt Tilly said. "You must be sure not to mention me in company, however, and above all things, you must not be seen with me." Aunt Tilly sat opposite Connie at the table. "Tea? Some cake? The walnut cake is excellent here. Or there is fruit, but I prefer cake, myself. Now, let us talk. Or rather, you may ask and I shall talk, for I suspect I know a great deal more about you than you know about me."

"I know almost nothing of you," Connie said. Now that her aunt was seated and pouring the tea, the likeness to Mama was extraordinary, so that she felt quite at ease, with everything familiar. Yet her aunt was a stranger.

"Exactly. So ask me whatever you wish. I shall answer you honestly, but you should be aware that there are some parts of my life which it is better you do not know of. You are an innocent, a respectably brought up young lady, and so there are topics that are not fit for your ears. But if I can answer, I will."

"Thank you!" Connie said, leaning forward eagerly towards the face that seemed so well-known. "May I ask — why did Mama not tell us that you and she are twins?"

Aunt Tilly laughed and raised her hands in mock surrender. "And immediately you have hit upon a question to which I have no answer. Only Sara can tell you her reasons, Connie."

"Oh. Of course." She could not keep the disappointment from her voice. "Can you tell me why you are disreputable? Or is that something I may not know?"

"I am sure you can guess at the most likely reasons why a lady of impeccable station might lose her reputation."

"You are a fallen woman?" Connie hazarded. "Mr Endercott mentions such people often in his sermons."

"Does he, indeed?" Aunt Tilly said, eyes twinkling.

"He does. He is very lyrical on the subject of sin. And the Dowager Marchioness of Carrbridge said... oh, but perhaps I should not repeat gossip about you?"

"Gossip cannot harm me, my dear, and I daresay most of it is true. I would know what the Dowager had to say of me, for I had not imagined any lady of rank to remember my name after all this time."

"Oh, indeed she did, although she said that she had not heard anything of you for a long time."

"Ah, that is good," Aunt Tilly said, nodding her head in satisfaction. "I have tried my very best to keep out of sight. It is pleasing to know that my efforts are not quite in vain. What else?"

"That there was a viscount once, she thought. And there was mention of a prince."

Aunt Tilly laughed merrily at that. "Mention of a prince? Oh, there was more than a mention, *far* more. That was an interesting time in my career. He once took me to Brighton for the day in his curricle..."

They talked for an hour, and Connie had not enjoyed herself so much for months. Her aunt had a seemingly unlimited fund of amusing stories of her gentlemen acquaintance — always gentlemen, never ladies — and although she said nothing about what went on at her house in its secluded square, so respectable from the outside, Connie could make some guesses.

But that made her mother even more of a puzzle. "But why was it perfectly acceptable for Mama to stay with you?" she burst out. "My sister and I may not enter it, or be seen with you, but Mama may visit with impunity."

"Perhaps not with impunity," Aunt Tilly said thoughtfully. "But your Mama is a widow now, and may decide for herself how to go on. We were close as girls, as twins often are, but we took different paths a long time ago. Well... perhaps not so different, for we both turned our backs on the highest levels of society, she in her country retreat and I here. But now, perhaps, she may choose another path for herself, who knows? She is entitled to a little happiness, after all this time."

She seemed to be talking more to herself than to Connie, lost in reminiscences, so Connie diplomatically kept silent. She had no desire to quarrel with her newly-discovered aunt, and she was perfectly well aware that Mama had been kept in subjection by Papa just as her daughters had, so a little happiness was long overdue. However, Connie would not begrudge her mother her amusements if she were a little more helpful towards her daughters. Both Amy and Belle had found their husbands without any assistance from their mama, and refusing Connie her chance to go to London was perverse. None of this pretend betrothal business need have happened if she had been able to stay with Amy and Belle from the start. But it was not proper to find fault with one's mama, so Connie kept her thoughts to herself.

The time flew by, and it was Aunt Tilly who reminded her gently that she should not stay too long. "For it would never do if your sisters sent to the umbrella shop, and found you gone."

"May I see you again? Please? I should so much like to."

Aunt Tilly smiled ruefully. "And so should I, but it is better not to, I believe. I made my choice in life a long time ago, and it is too late to change my mind now. But you may write to me, if you will. I may even write back to you, who knows?" She laughed merrily.

"I shall," Connie said. "Do you have any message for Mama?"

"Only the same one I have given her these twenty five years or more — that she should tell you the truth about her life. But she has kept it to herself all these years, so I doubt that will change. She made *her* choice, just as I did, and since we are both of us excessively stubborn, she will no more give way than I will."

~~~~~

Connie returned to Brook Street just as the others were beginning to grow alarmed by her absence, but she intimated that she had become confused about the correct route, which was true enough, and although she was teased about losing her way, no awkward questions were asked.

Nothing more was said about Aunt Tilly. Connie asked Belle once when they were alone what she had told Amy and the gentlemen. Belle expressed surprise at the question.

"Why, nothing at all, except that Aunt Tilly does not wish to make our acquaintance."

And that was true enough, Connie conceded. Anything of her circumstances beyond that was pure conjecture. It was disappointing, almost as if they were pretending that Aunt Tilly did not exist. Yet within two days of their visit to her house, they had very real evidence, not merely of her existence, but of her connections within the web of society, for invitations began to arrive from people that none of them had ever met.

"Who is Lady Cunningham?" Belle said as they sat at the breakfast table. "For we are all invited to a ball at Clarence Street on— Oh! It is this very evening! I do not know her at all. Is she an acquaintance of yours, Connie?"

"I have never been introduced to her, but she is very well known. She is connected to half the dukes of England, and distantly to the throne. Exceedingly good *ton*. We are all invited? How interesting."

"Should you like to go?" Belle said. "I confess, it would please me greatly to accept, for I have had little enough dancing since we came to town, and now that I do not have to wait for a partner, I like a ball of all things. But if you feel you might meet anyone who would distress you, then of course we will not think of going."

It was delicately phrased, but Connie could not misunderstand her. She coloured, but answered very composedly. "If you mean the Marfords, I am not in the least bit afraid to meet with any of them."

"I am relieved to hear you say so, sister. You have had such an unpleasant time of it, that no one could think the worse of you if you had wished to avoid their company, although they must have a dozen invitations every night, so I daresay we shall see nothing of any of them."

But Belle was wrong about that. Almost as soon as they entered the ballroom at Clarence Street, Connie saw the Marquess and his brother lounging against a wall not far away. The Marquess had his head lowered, as if staring at his shoes, while Lord Reginald was watching the dancing, looking bored. Connie's heart skipped about for a while, but neither of them looked in her direction and after a few moments she was able to compose herself.

The ballroom was nothing more than three modestly-sized saloons with the doors between them thrown wide, so, having steered their party to the other side of the room, away from the brothers, Connie was able to find a quiet corner behind one of the dividing walls, out of sight. They found a seat for Amy, and then stood watching the dancing until the sets broke up, and Belle and Mr Burford walked out to join the new sets forming.

Connie had no expectation of dancing herself, unless Mr Ambleside was inclined to invite her, but she discovered that she was not quite well enough hidden, for an acquaintance found her almost at once.

"Miss Allamont! What a delight! We quite thought you had left town, and yet here you are! I could not be more pleased, for there is not such a crush about you here and I may perhaps have better fortune in soliciting your hand. Will you do me the honour?"

"Thank you, Mr Tennant, I should be delighted," she said, with her most gracious smile, for he was an excellent dancer and very stylishly dressed, as well as being charmingly attentive to her. He was also exceedingly rich, and were this all that could be said of him, he might perhaps have been a serious marriage prospect. It was unfortunate, to say the least, that he also had teeth as prominent as a rabbit, and eyes that stared like a frog, so that Connie could never look at him without suppressing a mortifying temptation to laugh.

She loved to dance, but there was one disadvantage to it in a ballroom so confined as this one was, in that she could not pass unnoticed. She and her partner had not progressed very far down the set when she saw the Marquess watching her intently. She could not read his expression, and she could not look at him for long for fear of catching his eye. Was he pleased to see her? Mortified? Or did he not care at all? It was impossible for her to judge.

When Mr Tennant returned her to Amy, she found Lord Reginald was there before her, deep in conversation with the Amblesides, with the smiles of genuine friendship on all their faces. As soon as he saw her, almost before her partner had made his bows and departed, Lord Reginald leapt to his feet, his face alight with eagerness, the words tumbling out.

"Miss Allamont, I had no thought to see you here. This is an unexpected pleasure. You are well, I trust? Are you enjoying the ball? And may I claim you for the next? If you would so honour me?"

She took his arm and allowed him to lead her to the very head of the set. There would be no escaping notice now, and she caught the little flashes as the dowagers raised their lorgnettes to examine her. She was unconcerned, experienced enough now in the workings of society not to be nervous or discomposed by the attention. Why should they not look? Her gown was quite the latest fashion, she knew the steps of the dance well and she was sure no fault could be found in her deportment. Why should she not lead the dance?

So she smiled and danced and talked comfortably to Lord Reginald in the pauses, and was rewarded by the unmistakable ardour in his eyes. From time to time she glanced at the Marquess, standing silent and immobile at the side of the room, his gaze never leaving her.

After Lord Reginald, she danced twice more, but during the second dance the Marquess disappeared. She discovered the reason when she returned to Amy's side, for there were both the brothers, and Lady Harriet and Jess, too, sitting in a cluster around the Amblesides and Burfords.

Lady Harriet claimed Connie at once, tossing questions at her without waiting for the answers, and then laughing at herself for doing so. "I am so glad to see you back in society," she said, for about the fifth time. "I had no notion that you and your sisters were acquainted with Lady Cunningham."

"We are not," Connie said. "None of us has been introduced to her, yet she sent us an invitation this morning." The bewildered expression on Lady Harriet's face was entertaining, but Connie had no intention of explaining the situation, or mentioning Aunt Tilly.

"How extraordinary!" Lady Harriet said. "I daresay it is because of your connection to us. Indeed, I am quite convinced of it, and I am glad of it, for your sake. But now we must be going. We have a rout to attend next. Dev, Reggie, we are leaving now."

"I shall stay here," Lord Reginald said.

The Marquess said nothing but made no move to rise from his seat.

Lady Harriet looked from one to the other, and then at Connie. "Well, in that case, I shall see you both tomorrow. Jess? Come along."

With that, the two left.

The Marquess rose languidly to his feet. "Miss Allamont." He bowed gracefully.

"Lord Carrbridge." Connie rose, too, and made him a deep curtsy. Inwardly she was quaking, and she knew her cheeks must be on fire.

"I am happy to see you again." But he did not look happy. His expression was sombre, with a look of sorrow in his eyes, and she could hardly bear to look at him, so distressing was it to see him in such low spirits.

"Thank you, my lord." It was all she could manage, but it brought the hint of a smile to his lips, which faded almost instantly.

"I do not dance myself tonight," he said. "Therefore, I shall leave you to my brother. He will take the greatest care of you. Good evening, Miss Allamont."

He bowed again, and strode away without a backward glance, leaving her bemused. The gentleness of his manner after the violence of their last encounter was such that Connie was quite undone. The rest of the evening was a blur of faces and snatches of conversation, for she could attend to none of it. Her head was full of the Marquess, and even though she only caught glimpses of him here and there as she danced or went in to supper, she could think of no one but him.

20: An Offer

At the ball, Lord Reginald had invited Connie for a drive in the barouche.

"You may name the hour that pleases you the most, Miss Allamont, and I shall bring Mrs March, so everything will be right."

He grimaced when she told him that she preferred noon.

"Well, I am not accustomed to such an early start to the day, but your company will more than recompense me for the exertion, Miss Allamont. Noon it shall be."

At the appointed hour, the barouche appeared in Brook Street, with Mrs March sitting beside Lord Reginald. Connie wondered if she, too, found it an exertion to be up and about so early, for Lady Moorfield rarely ventured forth before three or four o'clock. But Mrs March smiled, as always.

"Miss Allamont! How delightful! And how kind of Lord Reginald to invite me. I shall sit here, then you may sit beside his lordship, for the best views. No, I insist. There! How pretty your bonnet is! Did you trim it yourself? Such clever fingers you have! And now I shall be quite silent, for I know you will want to talk only to Lord Reginald. You may pretend I am not here at all."

To Connie's amusement, Mrs March turned her head and stared fixedly at the passing scenery, the very model of a discreet chaperon.

Lord Reginald had not thought to provide the ladies with rugs, so it was fortunate that the day was warm. He had, however, brought flowers for Connie, and a hamper of food, complete with a bottle of champagne, so they went on their way very merrily. They started in Hyde Park, stopping to sample the devilled eggs and chicken legs, and then they drove on to Green Park. Lord Reginald was charming company, attentive and witty, keeping the ladies very well entertained.

Connie found herself very drawn to him, and his intentions towards her were becoming more obvious with every day that passed. Perhaps she need not mourn the loss of the Marquess for long. And yet, she could not quite forget those piercing eyes, and the smile that so agitated her. Lord Reginald might be her destiny, but he would always be her second choice.

They were almost out of the park, and Connie was thinking about returning to Brook Street, when she caught sight of a familiar pelisse and bonnet.

"Oh, look!" she cried, without thinking. "There is Jess! But—"

She stopped, and wished with all her heart that she had not spoken, for Jess was standing amongst shrubbery, almost out of sight, talking animatedly with a man, and no chaperon to be seen. As they watched, Jess turned and half ran away from the man, and even from a distance, Connie could see tears on her cheeks.

"Stop the carriage!" she called out, and almost before the horses had stopped moving, she scrambled to the ground and tore across the grass towards Jess, calling her name. Jess stopped, looking at Connie with bewilderment.

"Whatever is the matter?" Connie said, a little out of breath. "Do you need assistance? What may I do for you?"

"Oh! Oh, Connie, I did not expect... but I see you are with Lord Reginald. You must not keep him waiting."

"Never mind Lord Reginald! Whatever is the trouble?"

"I have been very foolish!" Jess burst out, between sobs. "I thought... I thought he would *marry* me, but... but..."

"That man you were with? How horrid! But where is your maid?"

"I had no time to find her. Oh, Connie, what am I to do?"

It roused all Connie's indignation to see Jess, who had always been so composed and sure in her dealings with the world, reduced to such a level of distress. That it had been a man who brought her so low did not surprise Connie in the slightest. Her recent experience of the male sex was not such as to inspire the slightest confidence in their behaviour.

"What are you to do?" Connie said. "Why, for now you must come back with me to Brook Street, of course, and when you are feeling more yourself, you may decide what you wish to do. But you must not walk through the park by yourself. Come."

Reluctantly, protesting at the imposition, Jess allowed herself to be led towards the barouche. Lord Reginald himself descended and graciously added his invitation to Connie's, so Jess was helped into the barouche and they drove by the shortest route back to Brook Street. Connie was bustling Jess into the house when she realised she had rushed away rather abruptly, and went back down the steps to the barouche.

"I beg your pardon," she said to Lord Reginald, who was languidly propped against a wheel, smiling. "In my hurry, I had quite forgot my manners. Thank you so much for my drive today, my lord. I enjoyed it very much." She dipped him a formal curtsy.

"Your care for Miss Drummond is charming, Miss Allamont. I shall call on you tomorrow, if I may, to ensure you have taken no chill from your outing."

She blushed, and with a hasty farewell to Mrs March, skipped up the steps after Jess. She found that the others were all out, so she settled Jess in the drawing room, sent for Madeira and cake, and prepared to listen.

"You will think me very foolish, I daresay," Jess said, as soon as the servants had withdrawn. "I have made such a mess of everything, but I was desperate. You know my situation, Connie. All my father's money is gone, my oldest brother inherited nothing but debts and was forced to retrench, and Alex took the position of schoolmaster at Lower Brinford in order to be no additional burden on Donald. My chance of a dowry was lost, so I came with Alex, to act as housekeeper and cook. Our only hope was for me to marry a rich husband, who would drag us out of poverty. But we very soon realised that Lower Brinford offers very confined society, with few prospects for me. We could not afford even the assemblies at Brinchester from our own pockets. Kind friends have aided us so far, but we cannot live on charity indefinitely."

Connie nodded but said nothing, unwilling to disrupt the flow of confidences.

"Lord Carrbridge seemed the perfect solution," Jess went on. "Surely I could win his interest? But not so — it seemed his thoughts were elsewhere. Even so, he offered me a way out of my predicament, which you know about. In your eyes, I was believed to be secretly betrothed, but to others I could reveal the truth, that there was no betrothal, not even an understanding. My object was nothing less than to attract a rich man willing to marry me. You will blame me, perhaps, but I was quite dispassionate about the business. It mattered not to me whether the man was noble or not, young or not, handsome or not — so long as he could keep me in comfort, and perhaps Alex too, and, if he were truly generous, there might be some help for the rest of the family. That was my only aim. Was that wrong of me?"

"Indeed not," Connie said. "Not when your difficulties were so great. No one could blame you for seeking such a way out of your troubles. Many marriages begin on such terms, and often end happily enough. It is an honourable solution."

"Honourable," Jess said, with a wry smile. "Indeed! And yet—! But I am running ahead too fast. I had several suitors, and a number of offers, but I made a fatal mistake — I fell in love. How foolish of me! His name is Middleton — do you remember him?"

"I do. There was an older brother, very fat, and married to a Lady something-or-other, but the younger one — Mr Jeffrey Middleton, was it not? — he was very handsome."

"Oh, he was — he *is*," Jess sighed. "Young and handsome and amiable. He has only a modest income at present, for his father left his manufactories to the elder brother, but there is a large fortune waiting for him from his aunt, who brought him up. Trade, of course, but I do not regard *that*. I thought he was in love with me, too, and he had no wife, so naturally I expected... I declined my other offers, and one of them a viscount, too, but it was taking such a long time to get him to the point. I began to worry that he had changed his mind. Also, and this is not at all your fault so you must not think that I blame you in the slightest, but the atmosphere at Marford House has been... difficult, let us say. Now that the true situation is known, I am quite out of favour and Lady Moorfield would have me sent straight home, if she had her way. Lord Carrbridge and Lady Harriet have been excessively kind to me, but still, I felt uncomfortable there, and all my hopes began to dwindle."

She paused, sipping the wine thoughtfully. "Then today I received an urgent message from him to meet at Green Park. He was called away by his aunt, and wished to speak to me before he left for Derbyshire. I had only an hour's notice, and I could not find my maid, or anyone I could take with me, so I went alone, for I felt sure that this was the moment I had been waiting for — he would make his offer, and all would be well."

Connie could say nothing, but she guessed the next part of the story.

Jess set her glass down on the table at her elbow, and heaved a sigh. "So he offered, but it was not a wife he wanted, but... something less formal. A little apartment in Manchester, where he often has business, and he would take care of Alex and even settle some money on me so that I would not be destitute... afterwards. For there would be an afterwards, would there not? Eventually, he would tire of me and that would be the end of it." A tear trickled down one cheek. When she spoke again, her voice was low. "I could not answer him, not then. I am to send a letter to his club, and they will forward it to him. But I shall have to agree to it."

"What? Are you mad?" Connie cried. "Of course you must not! He is despicable even to suggest such a thing."

"Oh, do not say so, for it is quite the usual thing in his set, apparently, and his aunt wishes him to marry well, and who can blame her for that? Besides, what else can I do?" Jess said despairingly. "If I go back to Lower Brinford unwed, there will be no more opportunities. Alex will have to marry a farmer's daughter, and I shall be an old maid, and I do *not* want to die a spinster, Connie, truly I do not. I never wanted anything in my life but a husband and a house of my own and children to raise, and all the respectability of being a wife. I was never ambitious."

"Even if you *never* marry, it will be better than this!" Connie said with some heat. "Once you take this step, you can never go back. You will be cast out of all good society for ever." The vision of Aunt Tilly rose in her mind, who was so disreputable that her own niece could not be seen with her.

"There is nothing wrong with being a spinster. Look at Miss Endercott, who is the very image of respectability, and loved by everyone."

"Indeed she is," Jess said. "She is content to keep house for her brother, I daresay, and they can afford a cook and a maid or two. Anyone may be contentedly respectable with servants. But we have just one maid-of-all-work, and I have to do the cooking and look after the chickens, and Alex digs the garden and grows vegetables, and it is *hard*, Connie, when I have been used to doing nothing but decide whether to ride my horse or drive out in my own phaeton, and which new bonnet to wear. It is very hard."

Connie had no answer to that, except to stroke Jess's hand, feeling quite helpless.

When the rest of the family returned and heard the sad tale, they repeated Connie's advice, and in such strong terms that, even through her tears, Jess could not ignore them.

"I know you are right," she sobbed. "But I cannot go back to Marford House and face Lady Moorfield without some arrangement made for my future."

"Then you must stay here, of course," Amy said. "Connie will not mind sharing for a few days, and you may travel with us when we go home. Then we shall see what can be done to make your life more comfortable."

"You are not without friends," Burford said gently. "I met your brother on my very first day at school, when he was very kind to me. He is quite my oldest and dearest friend. I would not have either of you sink into abject poverty or despair."

"We are grateful to you for recommending Alex for the post of schoolmaster, but we do not want charity," Jess said with dignity.

"Not charity, but perhaps a helping hand until you get back on your feet?" Burford said.

"Not money," she said firmly. "We still have our pride. A cut of beef occasionally would be very welcome, for we cannot afford to buy it."

"Beef it shall be, then," Burford said with a smile.

But Connie's heart was wrung by Jess's bravery.

21: A Little Advice

Connie's time in London was drawing to a close. The season was far from over, but Amy was anxious to be at home, and for all of them the excitement of town had begun to pall. They were not destined to sit quietly at home, however. Jess was too low in spirits after her encounter in the park to go into company, but Connie and her sisters were caught up in a final whirl of evening engagements from Aunt Tilly's connections.

Another invitation to Lady Hartshill's brought Connie's first meeting in town with the Melthwaites. Having studiously ignored her for weeks, now Lady Melthwaite was all polite smiles and civilities. She did not, however, ask to be introduced to Amy, Belle and their husbands, even though she must have guessed who they were, and Connie felt justified in responding with nothing more than cool courtesy before moving away. The Melthwaites were the epitome of respectability, but Connie far preferred the disreputable company of Aunt Tilly.

One event that Connie missed, however, was the ball at Marford House which she had helped to plan. She read the reports in the newspapers, and heard it mentioned once or twice in company, but she had no regrets about not attending it. It fell into the category of elaborately ostentatious affairs, and while it was undoubtedly wildly successful and much talked of, she far preferred the smaller, more intimate engagements that were now her lot.

Connie wondered how the Marfords had explained the disappearance of two guests from under their roof. Had they invented some crisis calling them home? Or sudden illness, perhaps. But then she recalled that they were officially there as Lady Harriet's provincial friends, and taken notice of only through courtesy. It was quite likely that no one remembered them at all.

Eventually the day came when they set off for home. The addition of Connie and Jess, Connie's maid Annie and the extra boxes meant that a second chaise had to be found to accommodate their larger party. The inns they stayed at were not quite as salubrious as those used by the Marfords, but Connie minded no inconvenience, so glad was she to be going home at last. There was much that she had enjoyed about her season, but there were unpleasant memories too, and she was relieved to put them behind her.

Jess was less buoyant about her return to normal life, but for her the contrast between partying with the upper echelons of the *ton* and her role as unpaid cook for her brother was dispiritingly large.

"We both return home as failures," she said glumly to Connie as they prepared for bed one night in a room tucked under the eaves. "You failed to catch the Marquess, and I failed to catch anyone at all."

"I did not set out to *catch* the Marquess," Connie said quietly. "I believed him to be in love with you, and it was never my intention to steal him away. That would have been quite wrong. But Lord Reginald thought his brother might lose interest in you..." She paced restlessly up and down the tiny room. "That was all a sham, of course, and the Marquess was never in love with you."

"Not in the least," Jess said. "His attachment was always to you."

"If he ever had the slightest attachment to me, he never showed it," Connie said with heat. "He ignored me for weeks, and then told me I am to marry him! Dreadful man!"

Jess smiled sadly. "He managed the business very ill, I will admit that, but I truly believe he loved you sincerely. He talked of you all the time he was with me, you know. I did think, at first, that being so much thrown together I might turn him away from you, but not a bit of it. I can scarce believe you turned him down — a marquess! How brave you are! I should never have dared to refuse him."

"His title is of no interest to me," Connie said in surprise. "How should I care about that? It is the man who matters, not the rank he holds. I want a marriage of love and respect, and a man who cares for my well-being above his own. I cannot marry for less, no matter how high his rank might be."

"That is exactly as it should be!" Jess said. "If only I could afford such scruples, but I have wasted my one chance to attract such a paragon."

"There will be plenty more opportunities," Connie said. "With your looks and lively manners, you will not be single for long, I warrant. There will be another assembly at Brinchester quite soon, and you were very popular there."

"I do not think we can afford to go again," Jess said. "Quite apart from the tickets, the cost of an hotel for the night is prohibitive. We had a little money to spare when we first arrived, but we must be prudent now and only spend as much as our income allows. I hope we will still be invited to one or two private balls, however. Do you think there are bugs in this bed? The inn looks very ill-kept to me. I am glad we thought to bring our own sheets."

~~~~~

With the Amblesides and Burfords disappearing to their respective houses, and Jess dropped off at the schoolhouse in

Lower Brinford, the chaise bore Connie and Annie in stately solitude the short remaining distance to Allamont Hall. As soon as they rounded the last corner of the drive, the front door opened and out poured Dulcie, Grace and Hope, bouncing with excitement, and hurling questions at Connie so fast that her head was spinning.

"Wait, wait," Connie cried, as they danced around her. "Let me get into the house and take off this wretched bonnet, for the chaise was so hot and stuffy, I am sure I am melting like a candle."

"Come on, come *on*!" cried Grace. "Tell us everything!"

"I will but there is little new to tell since my last letter."

That hardly mattered to the three sisters left behind, for they wanted to hear it all again — the balls, the fashions, the name of every gentleman Connie had stood up with and for which dance. No detail was too small to be gone over again and again. But one subject kept recurring.

"And so it was all a sham with Lord Reginald?" Grace said. "It was the Marquess who offered for you in the end? But you turned him down?"

"I could not marry a man who behaved so abominably," Connie said stoutly.

"Of course," they said. "We quite understand."

"But it is very provoking of the Marquess," Hope said plaintively. "Dulcie cannot marry until *you* do, Connie dear, and Grace cannot marry until Dulcie is wed and at this rate I shall *never* marry! Whatever is to become of us?"

It was a question that had been vexing Connie, too, but she had reached no conclusions.

However, she received a possible answer two days later in the shape of Lord Reginald, who arrived unexpectedly bearing a huge bunch of hothouse flowers for Connie. She blushed and blushed again at the eagerness in his face, which there could be no misunderstanding. And when Grace, in her tactless way, asked him why he had left London when the season was not yet over, he had smiled and looked directly at Connie.

"The charms of the country far outweigh the attractions of London, Miss Grace."

There could be no doubting his intentions, for he called every day, bringing flowers or fruit from his great-aunt's glass-houses, or a journal newly arrived from London, and it was only a matter of time before he paid his addresses in proper form. It was a good match for her, she knew that. He was personable and she liked him a great deal. Even though he did not make her heart sing as the Marquess did, Connie began to feel that, for her sisters' sake, she must consider the prospect seriously.

If only she knew how the Marquess felt! Their parting at Marford House had been steeped in bitterness, but his manner at Lady Cunningham's ball had been gentleness itself, and he could almost inspire pity in her. What was in his mind? Jess believed him truly in love with her, and perhaps at one time it had been so. Did he feel any residual affection for her, or was that all over? But he was still in London, according to Lord Reginald, and there was no way for her to find out.

~~~~~

The Marquess was miserable. The first engagement he attended after Reggie had left town was a masked ball, something he usually enjoyed enormously. With all the guests' faces hidden away, there was far less stuffy formality than attended a regular ball and a great deal more fun. He thought wistfully how much Connie would have enjoyed it, for she had disliked the rigidity of high society protocol, too. It would have been the greatest pleasure to have her on his arm for such an occasion, trying to guess the identities behind the bejewelled masks — and she was so clever at remembering names, and who was related to whom, so she would have been far better at guessing than he was. And then her sweet face rose up in his mind and he was overwhelmed with sorrow again.

What had gone wrong? He had been so sure of her, so confident that she was eagerly expecting his addresses, that he had never thought what he would say to her. And there was all that business with Reggie clutching her as if she were quite his own and they were really betrothed instead of pretending. It had put Dev so much out of countenance that he had determined to settle the matter at once, so he had rushed in and startled Connie, and she had shied like a horse.

And somehow, he was not quite sure how, Reggie had then stepped in and taken the initiative, and Dev could not interfere with that. He himself had failed and lost his chance, so now he had to support Reggie's efforts to win her. That was what brothers did for each other, after all, although it was very hard when his heart was quite broken. Reggie was doing all the right things, it seemed, with drives in the park and flowers and such like. Did ladies like to be courted and flattered and given presents? Probably they did, and that was where he had made his mistake with Connie. His suit would have gone better if he had been able to buy her little gifts, like that fan she had so liked, that Reggie had bought for her in the end.

Sunk in gloom, he milled about on the fringes of the masked ball, snarling at anyone who approached him. Then they went on to a regular ball, and finally some kind of a rout, by which time he was heartily sick of London and society and his own family, and wanted nothing more than to escape. He told himself he would follow Reggie purely to support his suit. He would stay in the background, and watch how he went on. Then, if he were ever again so fortunate as to meet a young lady who inspired in him such deep affection, he would know how to woo her.

So he sent for his curricle at the extraordinarily early hour of ten in the morning, distressed his valet by giving him only half an hour to pack, and set off for Lower Brinford at a fast pace.

The whole journey was consumed by thoughts of Connie, and wondering how many hours it might be until he could see her again. It was only when he reached his great-aunt's house that it occurred to him that Reggie might be put out by his appearance.

Great-aunt Augusta took one look at him, and said, "Oh, Francis, you silly boy!"

At such times, he wished Mama were still alive. She had been confined to her room for years, and latterly to her bed, but she had always listened to his troubles and given him advice that cleared his head and made everything straightforward. Whereas Grandmama and the great-aunts all terrified him, and made him feel like a naughty child. Worst of all, they confused him by telling him what he ought to do, and yet somehow it was exactly the opposite of what he wanted to do.

As Great-aunt Augusta did at once. "What are you doing here, Francis? Can you not let go of this girl so that Reginald may have his chance with her?"

There was no possible answer that would not make matters worse, so he chose to say nothing. Then, of course, he was berated for that. It was what they did best, the great-aunts, berating. He asked himself sometimes if they trained women in the art of berating their younger male relatives, or if it came naturally.

He mooched about the house for a while, wondering when Reggie would come back from Allamont Hall, and whether he was proposing to Connie at that very moment, but then callers began to arrive, and good manners dictated that he take his place in the drawing room. Besides, it would be a distraction, and anything that turned his thoughts into more productive channels was a blessing.

He found himself sitting next to Miss Endercott, the sister of the Lower Brinford clergyman. For a few minutes they spoke of generalities — the weather, the prospects for the harvest, the roads from London — but then she said, "Lord Carrbridge, I find it quite close in here. I wonder if you would be so good as to show me around the garden for a few minutes, so that I might take the air?"

It was not until they were some way from the house that she came to what he supposed was the point of her little manoeuvre and said, "I must congratulate you, Lord Carrbridge. I was entirely taken in by your little stratagem with Miss Drummond, and I am not easily fooled. I should never have supposed that your interests lay elsewhere. Such a pity that it was all for nought in the end."

He hardly knew how to answer her, so he said nothing.

"I daresay not much can be done about Jess," Miss Endercott said. "You, on the other hand, control your own destiny, my lord. You will have to move quickly, however, for your brother is pulling ahead of you, I fancy."

"It is not a race, Miss Endercott," he said gruffly, for he found it a difficult subject to talk about.

"Is it not? And yet you could still win her."

"How?" he burst out. "Miss Allamont made her feelings on the matter very plain. She will not have me."

"Nonsense!" she said briskly. "You have all the attributes to charm a lady, if you set your mind to the endeavour. Your brother woos her with gifts, but in my experience young ladies prefer a gentleman who makes a grand romantic gesture."

"Grand romantic gesture," he repeated, bemused. "What would that be?"

"Do something to enhance her comfort. Take an interest in those subjects which are important to her. Attend to her wishes. I am sure you know her well enough by now to think of something that will draw her away from your brother."

"But that I cannot do, Miss Endercott. I had my chance with Miss Allamont, and failed. Now Reggie wishes to try his luck, and I must not interfere. What kind of brother would I be if I tried to snatch Miss Allamont away from him? It would be dishonourable in me."

"Ah. I see. Then you must hope she turns him down."

"Why should she?" he said gloomily. "He is a personable enough fellow, and would make her an admirable husband. He is tolerably certain of her attachment to him."

"We shall see," she said. "But even if she accepts him, she has been known to change her mind before. Did you know that she was betrothed to Mr Ambleside for a while last year?"

"Good God, I did not! What happened?"

"Oh, she wisely thought better of it, and gave him over to Amy. A much better match! So do not give up all hope, my lord. And remember — a grand romantic gesture. I believe I have had enough air for the moment. Shall we go back inside?"

Dev returned to the house in a far happier frame of mind than he had left it. To be sure, there was not much to encourage him, for his prospects had only lifted from *'no hope'* to *'the tiniest sliver of hope'*. But it was better than nothing, and he had something to think about — what kind of grand romantic gesture might please his lovely Connie? He set himself to reconsider every conversation with her, however trivial, for some clue to her wishes.

22: *An Assembly*

Her sisters' excitement at Connie's return from town lasted for days, and they listened avidly to every tiny detail over and over. Their former governess, Miss Bellows, who now acted as companion and chaperon, sat quietly in a corner of whatever room they were in with her needlework, listening just as keenly. Now that she had seen a little more of the world, Connie's heart went out to poor Miss Bellows, making her own way in the world, with no prospect of ever having her own establishment, a spinster dependent on the whims of her employers. She had no place in the world, being neither family nor servant. Yet she seemed contented enough with her vaguely-defined role, and had no wish to leave.

Only one person displayed no interest in her tales of grand society and that was Mama. But one morning Connie was summoned to Lady Sara's sitting room, where she found her mother trying on new caps at her dressing table.

"Well, Connie, I am a trifle confused about your situation, for your letters were not entirely clear. You left this house betrothed to Lord Reginald Marford, but that was all false. Then Lord Carrbridge offered for you, but you turned him down. And now it appears that Lord Reginald wishes to marry you in earnest. Do I have that right?"

"That is correct, Mama."

"You turned down a marquess in the hope of securing the second son?"

"It was not quite—"

"You are not falling into *romantic* nonsense, I trust?"

"If you mean loving the man I marry, and expecting him to love me, then indeed I am, Mama. I cannot bear the idea of a marriage without love. It would be unendurable to me."

"Love," Lady Sara said contemptuously. "Respect, certainly. Admiration, perhaps. But love? Love is a transient emotion, strongly felt but soon over. It is no foundation for a lifetime commitment, and no man deserves a woman's love."

"Just because *you* are bitter at the choice you made does not mean I should not hope for something better," Connie cried, before she could stop herself.

Her mother set down the lacy confection she held and half turned, one arm resting on the back of the chair, to face her daughter. "What would you know of my choice?"

Connie wished the words unsaid, but since they *had* been said, she was unwilling to draw back now. If only her mother would be open with her, would talk to her as one woman to another. If only they could be friends. But perhaps this was an opportunity to pierce the barrier of coldness her mother had raised.

So she said composedly, "Very little, except what Aunt Tilly told me."

There was a long, long silence. Her mother stared at her, but there was neither anger nor dismay on her face. Eventually she said, "You know, Connie, I took no interest in any of you girls. You were your father's children, in looks and in ways. He took Amy from my arms when she was a baby, my first child, taken away from me to be raised according to his own precepts, so why should I take the slightest interest in you? And you were all such silly girls, I had no time for any of you. But since you have been free of his malign influence, you have grown up. I see differences in you now, and more than once you have surprised me. I did not think you had it in you to step outside the rules your father set. But you have courage, Connie, I will grant you that. To turn away a marquess, and then to meet Tilly... What did you think of my sister?"

"It was such a shock — like meeting *you*, only a different you. So strange! But I liked her very much indeed! She is quite delightful, and she seems... contented with her life now. Whatever it is. She did not explain the details."

Her mother laughed. "Quite right too. There is no need for you to know what goes on there. But when I say that love is not the answer, I speak from experience — my own, and Tilly's too. We were so wild when we were young, both of us, and stepped quite beyond the bounds of propriety, but we were in love, we were swept up in the delights of love. It could not last. The man I loved rejected me, and Tilly's was already married, so there was no hope there. Papa offered to find husbands for us, but we had to accept his choice — men who would provide the regularity so lacking in our disordered lives. I chose marriage, and here I am, a respected member of society, even if I choose not to move in the first circles. Tilly chose love, but that lasted a mere three years. Oh, she has made a life for herself since then, and she is comfortably off, but it has been a miserable time for her. We have *both* been miserable."

"Yet you would have me marry a man I do not love, and perhaps be miserable too."

"When you marry, child, you put yourself into the power of a man. He will have complete domination over you, and order your life however he sees fit. Whoever he is, peer of the realm or commoner, he will rule you, and it will be as much as you can manage to keep a part of yourself alive inside you, and not surrender your true self entirely. And when you discover that, as you surely will, being in love with him will make it a thousand times worse."

"Some marriages are happy," Connie said lifting her chin. "Amy and Belle are happy."

"For now. Who knows how long that will last? You are better by far to take the first man to offer, if he is wealthy enough to support you, and I say that not in bitterness but in the hope that you can avoid the mistakes that Tilly and I made. Do not be dazzled by love!"

It was the most revealing conversation Connie had ever had with her mama, and the intent was clear. "You think I should accept Lord Reginald, then, if he offers?"

"Certainly, if you cannot get the Marquess. Lord Reginald may be a second son, but he has some money from his mama, and presumably his brother will support him from the estate when he is married, if his expenses exceed the income from your dowry. Or he might take a commission in the army."

"Is the estate worth much? For I heard it was en... encum... short of money."

"Encumbered?" Lady Sara laughed. "True enough, but not from debts or mismanagement. The present Marquess's grandfather was a true eccentric, and he liked the idea of ladies living in independence. He bestowed a number of smaller estates on the family's dowagers and spinsters and widows for their lifetimes, whereupon they immediately set out to live to be a hundred. And I seem to recall there were huge French estates at one time, which are all gone now. So the family itself is very rich, but a great deal of its income is keeping these elderly ladies in fine style, while Drummoor and its pleasure grounds go to ruination. So your dowry will be a strong inducement to either of the brothers. But do try for the Marquess if there is any chance of getting him to the point again, for to be a marchioness would be quite a triumph for you."

Connie no longer cared about being a marchioness, having seen how the upper ranks behaved, but she thought wistfully of a certain handsome face, and that glorious smile, and wished with all her heart that she could foresee the day when she would gaze at it every day over breakfast. But there was not the smallest chance of the Marquess offering again. She knew he was staying with his great-aunt, having arrived the day after his brother, but he had not once come to see her. His feelings towards her were very plain. It was Lord Reginald or no one.

There was just one tiny shred of hope left to her — the next assembly at Brinchester. She knew Lord Reginald planned to attend, so surely the Marquess would accompany him? And then at least she could see the expression on his face, and determine once and for all if there were any affection left in him, or if she had offended him too deeply. And even if that were so, it would be some comfort to her to gaze at him.

But when she walked into the Assembly Room, the first person she saw was Lord Reginald, loitering at the bottom of the entry stair, and he was alone. She had barely registered her disappointment at this discovery, when she saw another familiar face, and this one far less welcome. Mr Jack Barnett was grinning insolently at her, from the midst of a crowd of gentlemen of worthy townsfolk. She recognised Mr Martin from the bank, and the two brothers who owned the White Rose Hotel, and some aldermen.

"What is *he* doing here?" she hissed to Lord Reginald, before he even had time to make his bow.

"Ignore him," Lord Reginald said. "Do not let him distress you. Come now, Miss Allamont, remember that you are a daughter of Allamont Hall. You need not concern yourself with the likes of Barnett. Take my arm and we will walk past very slowly, our heads turned to admire the dancing, so we will not see him at all. There! That was not so bad, was it? And now we are conveniently placed for the next dance. May I have the honour?"

The evening was a strange one. When she was with Lord Reginald, Connie felt entirely at ease with him, as if nothing could trouble her. He was an excellent conversationalist and kept her well entertained, the flow of wit only faltering when they danced the quadrille and he had to concentrate on his steps. "What next?" he would say in an urgent undertone, and she would try to explain, but even so, he would go wrong more often than not.

"Well, we brushed through it tolerably well," he said afterwards, making Connie giggle. "However, perhaps we should reserve ourselves for the country dances in the future."

"But I like the quadrille," Connie said. "It is very elegant, when correctly executed."

However, there were distressing moments, too, when she caught sight of Barnett. "Oh! He is dancing now! And his sister! I cannot bear to watch them. Oh!" She spun round to put her back to him. "Do you see how he grins at me! I cannot bear to look at him."

Lord Reginald looked about at the dancers forming up, to see the object of her exclamations. "Ah, Barnett and Miss Barnett. It does appear as if they are beginning to be accepted in Brinchester society. And he has acquired a superior tailor, I observe. That coat is almost acceptable."

"I... I do not wish them any harm, for their parentage is not their fault, but I should be happier if I never saw them again," she said.

"And perhaps, before too long, you may not need to," he said smoothly.

She coloured and said no more, for his meaning was plain. Before very many days had passed, he would seek a private audience with her and make his proposal formally, and she must accept him. There was no question of refusal, for she would not get a better offer. She was mindful, too, of her mother's advice about men. It was rather lowering but she knew herself that there was some truth in it, for had she not rejected Ambleside in the end because of his overbearing character? All men were like that, to a greater or lesser extent, so it made no difference which particular man she married, did it? Lord Reginald was personable and kind, and she could not expect more.

And she liked him, she told herself. She liked him very well, and that was close to love, was it not? She was almost certain that it was.

~~~~~

"You danced the quadrille with her? Good God, Reggie, what were you thinking? I imagine you made a great mull of it."

"I did rather, but she did not seem to mind a bit. Connie is such a sweet, good-natured little thing, she said not a word of reproach."

Dev and his brother were alone at the breakfast table the following morning, Reggie having that moment stepped out of the carriage after driving home from Brinchester. Dev made no answer. He had no disagreement with Reggie's assessment of Miss Allamont, but somehow his throat was tight and he could not form the words.

"It was an excellent evening, all round. You should have come with me, instead of sulking here like a schoolboy," Reggie said.

That was too much to endure. "Sulking, indeed! I have been walking about the neighbourhood, being agreeable to the locals." That sounded better than wandering aimlessly in the woods, and being miserable. "Paid a call on the Drummonds, too, just to make sure Miss Drummond is going on all right." She had put a good face on it, but he thought her cheerful demeanour rather forced, and she was unnaturally pale. It was worrying. "Then I took twenty pounds off Great-aunt at the card table, which I regard as something of a triumph, for she is as sharp as a needle when there is money to be made. So I have been far better employed than I should have been watching you pay court to Miss Allamont, I assure you." He paused, then said as casually as he could, "Going well, is it?"

"Very well indeed. She is all amiability, and very encouraging, I must say. Mind you," Reggie went on, "she did get in a tizzy about that Barnett fellow, and I am very much of her mind about it. Parading himself all over in that forward way, and he is getting very cosy with some of the bigwigs of the town. He is even a member of that club that we were invited to join when we first stayed here. What was it called?"

"Lewis's," Dev said shortly. "These provincial clubs let anyone in. Was Miss Allamont greatly upset?"

"She was. In quite a taking over the boy. I must say, I blame the late Mr Allamont for leaving his by-blow so much money that he can afford to pass himself off as a gentleman. It never *does*, that sort of thing."

"My understanding is that the bulk of Barnett's fortune has come from Mr Burford, who paid the fellow off to ensure he would not pursue any claim against the Hall."

"Well, *that* was a mistake. So he takes a tidy sum from a benevolent patron, and then sets himself up to cause the most distress to his benefactors, people who have never done him the least harm."

"That is about the long and the short of it."

"No wonder poor Connie was so distraught. She said she wished she might never see any of them again."

"Miss Allamont," Dev said.

"I beg your pardon?"

"Her name is Miss Allamont. You do not have the right to call her anything else. Not yet," he added in lower tones.

"True." Reggie chewed his lip. "Dev, you will not interfere, will you, or cut me out? You will leave her to me?"

"Have I not said so? Good God, whatever makes you imagine that I *could* cut you out. She will not have me, Reggie, and there is an end to it. I shall keep well out of your way."

"Thank you! You are the best of brothers! Although if you are keeping out of the way, I am not sure what you are even *doing* here. You could have stayed in town until the end of the season, and looked about you for someone else."

This was so out of line with his wishes that Dev jumped up, and paced across the room. "I do not have to account for my movements to you or anyone else," he said testily. "But perhaps I *can* be useful, now that I am here. Enhance her comfort, that sort of thing. If Barnett upsets Miss Allamont, then Barnett must be dealt with."

"Dev, what bee have you got in your bonnet now?"

The Marquess chuckled. "A good game, I assure you. But we shall need Humphrey and his crowd of disreputable Oxford cronies. They will not mind coming down for a few days, and I am sure the college will not miss them. Quick, let us find pen and paper and ink."

23: *Games Of Chance*

Lewis's club for gentlemen was not as exclusive as some of the London clubs, but it was quiet and discreet, and pleasingly deferential towards its newest members, the Marquess and his brothers. Dev and Reggie sat in a secluded corner, hidden behind newspapers, waiting. Across the room, Lord Humphrey Marford sprawled in a wing chair, twirling a glass of claret and making himself conspicuous. He was as unlike his two older brothers as could be imagined. Where they were slim and dark-haired, Humphrey was splendidly broad-chested, with bright blue eyes and a mop of unruly blond curls. He fancied himself rather as a Corinthian, so his attire was stylishly flamboyant. Amongst the dark coats of the burghers of Brinchester, he stood out like a peacock amongst hens.

Thanks to the willingness of one of the club's stewards to accept a sovereign or two in exchange for information, the brothers had not long to wait. Mr Jack Barnett strolled into the room as if he owned it, smirking at the stewards and nodding in an over-familiar way to one or two of his acquaintance. He stared at Humphrey as he passed him by, and Humphrey raised a hand and said, "Good evening to you, sir!" in a jovial way, that one who did not know him well might suspect to have been affected somewhat by drink.

Barnett murmured a greeting in return and settled himself in his usual chair. Stewards rushed forward with his regular glass of claret and a newspaper. For a few minutes, the room lapsed back into its customary quietude. Then Humphrey's voice, loud in the stillness.

"More of your excellent wine, steward, if you please."

When the decanter was brought, there was a murmur of conversation between Humphrey and the steward, after which the steward led him across to Barnett and made the introductions.

This was the dangerous moment. There was no hiding Humphrey's identity, and if Barnett were at all astute socially, he would remember the name Marford, and immediately connect Lord Humphrey Marford with Allamont Hall. And if he made no demur at that, there was still the matter of Humphrey's very flimsy excuse for requesting an introduction. Dev shuddered at the thought of it — a Corinthian like Humphrey, fitted out by the finest tailors in London, pretending to admire the coat of a provincial like Barnett.

But it seemed to have worked, for Barnett moved to a small writing desk and wrote a note — presumably the direction of his tailor. Even from across the room, Dev could see the laborious way Barnett formed his letters. Clearly his father had not bothered to pay for a decent education for his natural son.

The two stood chatting for a while, and then, in the friendliest manner, went into the dining room together.

"There," Reggie said, with a relieved sigh. "That is the worst of it over. Humphrey has everything well in hand. The boy can always be relied upon, I will say that for him. Are you sure you do not want to go round to our little place of business tonight? It would be the greatest fun."

"We will keep to the plan," Dev said curtly. "And I would not agree with you that the worst is over. Tonight may be fun for Humphrey and his friends, but tomorrow will be a challenge for everyone."

"So long as it is a challenge for Barnett most of all," Reggie said. "Very well, then, brother, back to the hotel we shall go."

~~~~~

The following night, there was no need to go to the club at all. A note from Humphrey had revealed that everything had gone well the previous night, and all was set for the final spring of the trap. Dev and Reggie dined quietly at the Royal Oak, and then sat in their room until the appointed hour.

It was almost dark when they set off, and the moon was not yet risen, so the streets were appropriately shadowy for the clandestine nature of their mission. The house they had chosen was supplied by a sister of the so-helpful steward, and a great deal more than a couple of sovereigns had been expended to secure it. But it was perfect, Dev had to admit — an ordinary house on an ordinary street, all extremely respectable and not in the least suspicious.

They knocked and were admitted by a nervous looking man. "Upstairs at the back," he whispered, although there was no one else about to hear.

"Thank you. You may disappear now."

"Yes, sir. Thank you very much, sir." He scuttled off into the nether reaches of the house.

The two brothers left hats and gloves and canes in the hall with the many others collected there, and then trod up the stairs. The furnishings were plain, everything a little shabby and worn. Dev would have preferred something more ostentatious, but perhaps these nonthreatening surroundings would keep Barnett off his guard.

There was no question as to which room to enter, for male laughter spilt out even through the closed door.

Dev knocked, and an abrupt silence fell. Then footsteps, and Humphrey's face, a picture of mingled nervousness and innocence which was perfectly convincing.

"Dev!" he burst out. "And Reggie! By God, I thought you were the constables and we were sunk. Come in, come in. Shut the door. There! But what are you doing here? I thought you were with Great-aunt Augusta still."

It was wonderfully believable. Dev knew that Humphrey had done a little amateur acting, but clearly the boy had talent. He made his prepared speech about Humphrey being secretive, and coming to find out what games he was up to.

"And here I find you with a little gambling going on," Dev said. "It is too bad of you to try to keep us out of it, you know."

"Only found out about it myself a couple of days ago. Would have brought you in on it in time, old fellow. Glad you are here now. Come and meet our friends."

Four of them were, indeed, friends of Humphrey's, although he stumbled convincingly over their names as though he had only recently met them. "And this is Mr Jack Barnton."

"Barnett."

"Beg your pardon. So muddling, all these names. And these disreputable fellows are my brothers. The one with the Roman nose is Dev. Well, the Marquess of Carrbridge, formally. And the one with the baby face is Reggie — Lord Reginald Marford, you know. The best of fellows. Do you have any objection if they join the game?"

Nobody had. Chairs were brought, brandy was poured, coins were tossed onto the table, the cards were dealt and the play began. Dev could see at once that Barnett was more interested in his illustrious opponents than the play. He kept looking round at the three brothers, as if to memorise their faces. He could hardly believe his luck, no doubt, getting friendly with a genuine lord like Humphrey, and now an actual peer of the realm — a Marquess, no less! He was savouring the moment, storing up memories to boast about later.

Dev could almost feel sorry for him.

For an hour, they played cards, gradually increasing the stakes but allowing Barnett to win just enough to keep him enthusiastic. Dev liked how Humphrey's friends played their parts — one noisy and appearing slightly drunk, one serious and intense, one making a joke of everything, and one cheerfully losing every point. It was very clever. When Barnett made a big win, Dev moved in for the kill.

"This is amusing enough, but tame, very tame," he drawled, in his most languid manner. "What do you say to dice? And shall we make it more exciting? A hundred a game?"

The others jumped on it, and Barnett, with his heap of notes and coins in front of him, smiled and nodded too.

"Does everyone have dice?" Humphrey said. "I have spare sets."

Barnett shook his head. "I don't have mine with me."

"Here. Have these," Humphrey said, fishing a small box from a pocket. "The usual, Dev?"

They had agreed on the game beforehand. One of Humphrey's friends pretended not to know it, and Humphrey explained the rules. Barnett nodded wisely, as if he had known it all along.

They began. This was the heart of the deception, and if Barnett had had an ounce of common sense, he would have been wary at this point, for the stakes were high and large sums were being won and lost on a single throw of the dice. He could not know that the dice were loaded, and his so-called friends were switching his set about to ensure that he won a little, then lost a lot, then won a little and lost a lot more. A joke or a melodramatic gesture or some business with the brandy to distract him, and one pair would be replaced with another. And as he began to lose heavily, Barnett smiled and seemed to take it as a great joke.

One of Humphrey's friends ran out of funds very quickly, but paper was found to write IOU notes, and the play continued. One by one they dropped out, until it was only Dev and Barnett, and the pile of IOU notes was growing large.

"I believe I am out of the game," Barnett said, after a spectacular loss, trying to smile. "You have the better of me, my lord."

"Nonsense," Dev said. "You have had a run of ill-luck, but that makes it highly likely that the next throw will be in your favour."

"I am not sure…"

"Well, now, Mr Barnett, I am a fair man, and a gambler to my core, so let us have one more throw, eh? You put in — oh, shall we say a thousand? And I will wager everything on the table. Winner takes all. How does that sound?"

"A thousand? I am not sure… I may have over-extended myself already."

"Not quite the thing, old fellow," Humphrey said severely. "Not proper for a man of any standing in society to refuse an offer like that. Very generous, if you ask me. Dev could just take his winnings, you know."

"Perhaps I should do just that," Dev said. "I have had an extraordinary streak of good fortune which cannot hold. I begin to think—"

"Just one more throw," Barnett said eagerly. "A thousand, you said?"

"Well…"

"Two thousand, then."

"I am still not sure. I stand to lose a great deal."

"Five thousand!"

"What a capital fellow!" Humphrey said. "Such spirit! I commend you, Barnett. I wish I had half your courage. Dev, you cannot refuse."

Dev pulled a face in what he hoped was a convincingly dismayed manner. "Very well, although I am certain this is a mistake. Barnett, your IOU?"

The note was written, the dice were rattled, the atmosphere was genuinely tense. If this went wrong…

Barnett threw first. A four and a five. In any normal game, that would be a good throw, hard to beat. He smiled, but his hands were shaking.

Dev made a great show of rattling the dice, of nervousness, of hesitation.

"Get on with it, old fellow," Humphrey said.

He threw. A pair of sixes. Shouts of jubilation from the watchers, and a barely audible groan from Barnett. His face was ashen. But he knew what was expected.

"How much is it?" he croaked.

Dev rifled through the notes. "Fourteen thousand six hundred," he said cheerfully.

"Fourteen thousand!"

"And six hundred."

"I… I shall go to my bank first thing tomorrow, my lord. You are staying at the White Rose?"

Dev said nothing, scooping up coins, bank notes and IOU notes in one sweeping motion.

"My lord?" Barnett said, an edge of panic in his voice.

With a flick of his head, Dev dismissed Humphrey's friends, who slipped quietly out of the room, leaving only the three Marford brothers and Barnett.

Barnett jumped up, his chair falling with a crash, and made a dart towards the door. Humphrey was there before him, his intimidating bulk blocking the way.

"Do sit down, Barnett," Dev said. "I mean you no harm, I assure you. All I want is to talk to you. Your fortune is quite safe."

Barnett sat, his expression bewildered, as Reggie pushed a glass of brandy towards him. "My lord? I do not quite understand."

"Let us talk plainly," Dev said. "You cannot help the circumstances of your birth, any more than I can help being a Marquess. That is just the way the dice have fallen for each of us. All we can control is the manner of our passage through this brief mortal life allotted to us. We can tread the path quietly, in humility, with a care for our fellow humans, or we can be brash and noisy and as troublesome as possible. You, Mr Barnett, have chosen the latter course."

"What gives you the right to lecture me?" Barnett said hotly.

Dev waved the notes he still held.

"I owe you money — so what? I can pay you, and I shan't be ruined, either. I shall come about."

"Maybe so, and maybe not. You will find your new friends fading away once your circumstances are reduced."

"And if I tell them how you bamboozled me? I've been foolish to let myself be led on, but you've tricked me, my lord, and I could go straight to the constables and tell them what you've done."

Dev sighed. "Do not compound your foolishness, Barnett. How do you think *that* would turn out? The word of a Marquess against the word of—" He paused, and all that could be heard was Barnett's ragged breathing. "Well, let us not get into that. You are nobody, Mr Barnett, and not a soul will stand up for you against me. I say that not to cow you, but as a simple statement of fact. That is the way of the world."

"What do you *want*?" Barnett snapped.

"I want you to go away. I want you never again to trouble a young lady who is very dear to me. If you do this — if you leave Brinchester and move far away — then these notes of yours need never be repaid. I do not want your money."

"Go away? I was born and raised here. Where am I supposed to go?"

"Anywhere you like, except Brinchester, London or anywhere near my estate at Drummoor. And take your mother and sister with you. Any more of you at home?"

"Another sister." He chewed his lip, anger giving way to calculation. "If I go, I need not pay you what I owe? I have your word on that?"

"You do." Dev suppressed his annoyance at the intimation that he might not be trustworthy. "I shall keep your notes, of course, as a guarantee of your compliance, and if ever you turn up where you are not wanted, I shall destroy you, you have my word on *that*, too."

"My mother has family in Liverpool," Barnett said.

"Liverpool! Perfect," Dev said. "You will find you can cut quite a dash in Liverpool, should you care to, and no one will know anything of your origins there. A fresh start for you. Are we agreed?"

He held out his hand, and after only the slightest hesitation, Barnett took it. Humphrey opened the door for him, and Barnett, without looking back, walked through it.

"You let him off lightly," Reggie said. "I should have left him a bruise or two as a reminder."

"And you would have him swearing vengeance on you," Dev said. "So long as we have seen the last of him, I shall be content. And Miss Allamont need never be plagued by him again."

"She must be quite a lady, to inspire you to such trouble on her behalf," Humphrey said.

Dev smiled. "Indeed she is. Delightful."

"She is the sweetest little creature imaginable," Reggie said.

"Very rum, though, to have the two of you chasing after her," Humphrey said. "I have a mind to meet the lady for myself, and cut both of you out."

"That would be very bad form," Dev said.

"Yes, you stay well away from her," Reggie said. "Dev is keeping out of my way, and it would be too bad if *you* start interfering."

Humphrey raised his hands in mock surrender. "All right, all right. But I do not understand why she would want *you,* Reggie, when she could have Dev. He is far better looking than you, *and* he has the title, you know. Much better deal for any young lady."

"Who knows?" Reggie said, laughing. "*I* thought she liked Dev better, too, but she turned him down."

"She turned him down?" Humphrey said, startled.

"She did. He botched it, she turned him down and that allowed me to try my luck. I must say, Connie has been very encouraging to me. Quite waiting for me to speak, I fancy. Now that all this business is done with, I might as well go and tie things up with her."

"And Dev is letting you do it?" Humphrey looked from one to the other. "Not my business, of course, but I wonder you do not *both* go to her, and let her choose, you know. Because it may be that she regrets throwing Dev over, and would like a second chance. Her happiness is paramount, surely."

"You see, this is exactly what I was afraid of," Reggie said hotly. "Humph, you must not interfere, there is a good fellow. Just keep out of it."

"Brothers cannot fight, and certainly not over a lady," Dev said firmly. "I had my chance, and I have lost Miss Allamont's good opinion. I wish…" For a moment the words stuck in his throat, but he forced them out. "I wish her every happiness with Reggie. She deserves it."

"Thank you, Dev! You are too good. Tomorrow will see me the happiest of men."

24: Sonnets And Flowers

Connie was determined to be cheerful. Any day now, she would be betrothed to Lord Reginald, and this time the engagement would be a real one, with a notice in the Gazette, and wedding clothes, and banns, and all the happiness of marriage and her own establishment and the prospect of children. She should be joyful, smiling through the day and dreaming of her future husband at night, and although Lord Reginald never disturbed her dreams, at least she managed to display a sunny countenance in company.

She was troubled, though, by darker thoughts. Often, her reflections centred on Jess. Connie's heart ached for her friend, caught in the most difficult of dilemmas. Whenever they met, Jess was uncharacteristically subdued, all her merriment dissipated by one faithless man who had stolen her heart and then treated her abominably.

Connie was haunted, too, by Jess's opinion of the Marquess. *'I truly believe he loved you sincerely. He talked of you all the time...'* So she had said. If only Connie had ever heard him speak of it! If only he had approached her with respect and talked of love when he made his addresses. In that one conversation — no more than ten minutes of her life — Connie had thrown away her best, perhaps her only, chance of happiness. Regret was such a corrosive force, eating her from the inside out, and making her doubt her own mind.

Then there was Dulcie. It had shocked Connie beyond measure to discover that Dulcie had told the Marquess all her childish little schemes. She had never intended to trap him into marriage, only to put him in a romantic frame of mind so that perhaps he might fall in love with her. Even that innocent endeavour had given way when she had learned of his betrothal to Jess. There was no harm in any of it, and surely Dulcie had wanted her to succeed as much as anyone? Was Dulcie not her best friend and strongest ally, the one person who could always be relied upon?

Yet when she had remonstrated with her, Dulcie had only laughed a little shame-facedly. "Well, of course I wanted him to marry you, silly! I thought if he knew what you were about, he would take notice of you and that might start him on the way to love, do you see?"

"But then he naturally supposed that I was quite in love with him and made no effort to court me. He was so unromantic and cold and overbearing, Dulcie, and then I had to turn him down, and it is all your fault!"

"I was only trying to help," Dulcie said huffily. "I am sure he would never have paid you the least attention if I had not. Besides, I never for a moment expected that he *would* offer for you. Who could have imagined such a thing? But I meant it for the best, sister."

"You always do," Connie said sadly. But this time she was not sure she could forgive Dulcie for her interference. It was painful to consider that her dearest friend had been instrumental in ruining her hopes of marrying the Marquess, and that she had done so deliberately was the cruelest discovery. Although the two sisters still shared a bedroom, all confidence was at an end between them.

And so Connie waited for Lord Reginald to pay his addresses. Each day that failed to produce such an outcome brought a brief burst of relief, only to be succeeded the following morning by the familiar knot in her stomach which ought to be happy anticipation, yet felt suspiciously like dread.

Eventually, he came. There were no flowers this time, as if signalling that the courtship was now moving into the next, less frivolous, phase. It did not surprise Connie when he suggested a walk in the garden, nor when he dallied to admire a flower so that they were left behind by her sisters.

"The others are going down to the lake, but I know that path well," he said. "Shall we go this way instead? I should like to explore a different part of the grounds."

Meekly she went, head bowed to her fate, and it was not long before he began his speech. He spoke well, of admiration and love, of respect and honour, of how his life would be incomplete without her. He was articulate and persuasive, saying all that was proper. Still she kept her head lowered.

"Connie?" he said gently. "Will you not look at me? I would see your lovely face."

When she could not, or perhaps would not, for she was not sure herself which it was, he lifted her chin with his hand. Even then, she averted her eyes.

"Ah," he said, and there was disappointment in his tone. "This is not how it should be."

"My lord?" she said, and for the first time she looked directly at him.

His expression was rueful. "You are not excited, Connie. This is not what you want."

She was too confused to answer him.

"There is an arbour in the wall over there," he said. "Let us sit."

Dutifully, she let him lead her to the bench. She sat and he sat beside her, gazing at her face, still holding her hand. Again, her eyes dropped.

"You must forgive me," he began. "I have quite mistaken you. I thought you were waiting, hoping for my declaration. I flattered myself that you were in love with me. But now I see the situation very clearly."

Connie's head was spinning at this sudden change, but she grasped at a possible meaning. "Are you withdrawing your offer, my lord?"

"Not at all," he said. "If you truly wish it, I will marry you gladly, and cherish you for ever. But I do not want you to marry me from duty, Connie. That would be a dreadful thing."

"But I must marry!" she burst out. "I have three younger sisters depending on it."

"That is the worst reason in the world!" he cried. "What sort of life would that be, to have you always moping about with your head down like this. I want you to love me, Connie. I want you to look at me with fire in your eyes, the way you look at—" He stopped himself with a click of the tongue.

She said nothing.

He released her hand abruptly. "I can hardly credit this, but I believe that Humphrey, of all people, had it right."

"Humphrey? Your brother?" She put a hand to her forehead, bemused. "I cannot understand you, my lord. What does your brother have to do with this?"

"Everything!" he said, with a bark of laughter. "And perhaps nothing. Lord, but this is humiliating. I thought I had one over on Dev for once, but now I find he has had the better of me all along." Another burst of laughter.

Connie jumped to her feet, anger rising inside her. "If it were not so early in the day, my lord, I might suspect you of being in your cups," she said coldly. "Did you offer for me to spite the Marquess?"

"Nothing of the sort," he said, rising to stand beside her, but making no effort to take her hand again. "My feelings, my wishes are genuine, although putting Dev's nose out of joint added a little spice, I will not deny. However, Humphrey was right and your wishes are what is important. I must not, *cannot* be so selfish as to conceal the truth from you. Miss Allamont, you should know that Dev most sincerely loves you, and would do anything to win you back. He has already taken steps to remove Jack Barnett from the county, only so that you might not be troubled by him. Nothing but his loyalty towards me prevents him from pressing his suit. We *both* love you, Miss Allamont, and... and you may choose between us, if you will."

She was too astonished to speak. He made some civil farewells, saying something about leaving her to think over all that he had said. Then he bowed and went away to send for his horse. She was very near the main drive, and if she stayed where she was she could not help but see him ride past, and that she could not bear. There was a gate a little further along the wall, so she made her way there and escaped into the cool stillness of the woods, the canopy green over her head. Finding a side path, she half ran along it to be sure of undisturbed solitude. A fallen tree provided a seat, and for a few minutes she gave way to tears of distress and hope and joy, all mingled together.

He still loved her! Out of all the confusions of Lord Reginald's words, that was the message that echoed in her head. Despite all that had happened, the Marquess loved her and wanted her, and was only kept away by honour towards his brother.

She was too agitated to sit and compose herself, so she walked on, she hardly knew where, her tears giving way to exhilaration, so that laughter bubbled up inside her. What an end to her darkest fears! She had resigned herself to a betrothal with Lord Reginald, but now that unhappy prospect was replaced by a far more joyous possibility. The Marquess's handsome face rose up in her mind, smiling at her in the intimate way he had that made her dizzy.

She had begun to consider how long it might be before she would see him again when a bend in the path revealed the man himself, seated on a stile, his hat in his hands, head low, the very picture of dejection.

Her heart turned over, but she did not hesitate. "Lord Carrbridge?"

~~~~~

The Marquess had left his great-aunt's house not long after Reggie, too upset to sit around. If he had had a riding horse, he might have burned off his fidgets on a fast ride, but he only had his curricle and that was too slow in the village lanes to calm his restlessness. So he had set off on foot, although he had no idea where he was. And every step of the way, the same thought revolved in his head — is she lost to me yet? Followed rapidly by a second thought — how can I bear it?

Eventually, uncertain of where he was and filled with despair, he had found a convenient stile and cast himself down.

And then, the miracle had happened. There she was, her lovely face so concerned.

He jumped up, his treacherous heart leaping with joy. But then, bewilderment, for where was Reggie? Was she betrothed now? Or had she missed him altogether, and Reggie was even now riding home, his offer unmade?

"Miss Allamont?" Dev said tentatively. He hesitated, but he had to know. "Have you seen Reggie this morning?"

"Indeed I have!" she said with a smile of pure joy on her face.

"Oh," he said, his spirits dropping instantly. But then why was she here? A flicker of hope entered his breast.

"He very kindly made me an offer."

"Oh."

"I did not accept him." The smile widened even further, if that were possible.

"Oh." And then, because his brain was flapping about ineffectually, "Oh."

She laughed. "Does that surprise you?"

"It does. I thought…" He began to get his disjointed thoughts into some semblance of order. "Are you going into the village, Miss Allamont?"

"The village?" She gazed about her, as if surprised to find herself where she was, so close to the edge of the woods. "I had no notion I had walked so far. I must turn back."

"Then may I escort you home?"

She accepted with alacrity, taking his arm. They talked of nothing very much at first, but he felt such a jumble of conflicting emotions that it was quite a miracle that he was able to talk at all.

Then, a flash of white caught his eye. "Flowers! Wild flowers! Should you like some, Miss Allamont? For I know how you love such things."

When she assented, he dashed off into the undergrowth. "Oh, pray mind your trousers!" she called. "They will be so torn."

"I do not regard it, if the flowers please you," he said gallantly. "Here — they are very pretty, I think."

She smiled and blushed and agreed that they were indeed very pretty. She looked up at him with such a sweet smile on her face that he was quite overcome. His own words failing him, he said the first thing that came into his head.

"'Shall I compare thee to a summer's day? Thou art more lovely and more temperate'"

"Oh!" she breathed. "Are you reciting *poetry* to me, my lord?"

"I believe I am," he said. "You said you like such things, you know, so I learned a poem for you. I thought it might please you. Do you like it?"

"I do! Pray continue."

"Oh. Well, I have lost my place now, so I will have to start again from the beginning. Here I go. *'Shall I compare thee to a summer's day? Thou art more lovely and more temperate: Rough winds do shake the darling buds of May, And summer's lease hath... hath...'*"

" *'all too short a date'*," she said.

"You know it, then?" he said.

"Certainly. It is one that Papa made us all learn. He was very fond of Shakespeare's sonnets. Please go on. The next line is *'Sometime too hot the eye of heaven shines, And often is his gold complexion dimm'd'.*"

" *'...complexion dimm'd. And every fair from fair sometime declines, By chance or... or nature's changing course...something; But thy eternal summer shall not fade, Nor lose... nor lose...'*"

The words dried up. "Miss Allamont..." he began, although he hardly knew what he was saying.

"My lord?"

"Miss Allamont, you make the words fly out of my head when you look at me in that way. You are adorable, and delightful, and I have been the world's greatest fool. I treated you shamefully. I can scarcely bear to think about the dreadful things I said to you that day. Can you ever forgive me? And please, please tell me, can you give me any hope, however small, that you might one day look favourably on me?"

"Yes."

"Because I cannot bear to think that... Yes?"

"Yes, I forgive you, and yes, you may hope, my lord."

"Oh!" A long pause. "Oh!" Then, "Not Reggie?"

"Not Reggie. I like him very well, but I do not love him, and I am not very sure that he loves me, either, for I suspect he was driven by a wish to get the better of you. And that is not right, is it? A wife should love her husband, do you not agree? And he should love her."

"Not *love* her, no," he said firmly. "He should *adore* her. Oh, Miss Allamont!" Heedless of the mud, he dropped to his knees. "My dearest Miss Allamont, I *do* adore you! How can I live without you? Would you... could you possibly ever consider doing me the inestimable honour of becoming my wife?"

"Oh yes!"

"Because I would always... Yes? Yes! Oh, my darling Miss Allamont, you cannot imagine how happy this makes me."

"Indeed, but *do* get up, for your poor trousers will be quite ruined. Think what your valet will say!"

"I hardly think my trousers matter at such a moment," he said, but he rose and dusted himself down as best he could. "Oh, Miss Allamont, I shall spend the rest of my life ensuring that you are happy."

"I think you might call me Connie now, if you wish," she said, smiling shyly up at him.

"Connie," he murmured, one finger tracing the soft outline of her cheek. "My sweet, adorable Connie. Do you think you could call me Francis?"

"Perhaps I could, Francis. Do you know, these flowers have the most peculiar scent."

He sniffed them. "Oh dear. I believe I have presented you with a bunch of wild garlic flowers. I am so sorry."

She could not help laughing at the look of dejection on his face. "You must not be sorry, for it was such a romantic and lovely thing to do. And the poem — you memorised that for me?"

"I did, and very hard it was too, but I thought... I *hoped* it might please you."

"And you made Jack Barnett go away. How can I ever thank you enough?"

"My darling girl, your happiness is all the thanks I need. Whatever you want, you must have, you know. If you do not wish to racket around London, you need not, for I do not think you enjoyed your season very much."

"Indeed I did, only I should prefer not to attend quite so many engagements, you know. It was so fatiguing, and one never has an opportunity to become familiar with anyone."

"When you are the Marchioness of Carrbridge, you may do as you please in that regard. In fact, you may sit quietly at home, and allow the *ton* to fight for your approbation. You will be quite a leader of society, my love."

"That sounds amusing," she said, smiling up at him. "I believe I shall be very happy as a marchioness."

He took her hand and raised it to his cheek. "Ah, Connie, my sweet Connie! It shall be my life's work to make you happy, my angel. I would not have you miserable, not for one second. Everything shall be as you wish, so if you do not want to live at Drummoor or Marford House—"

"Oh, but I do! Whatever made you think I would not?"

"Great big barns, both of them. I thought you might like something less sprawling."

"Marford House only needs refurbishing, and Drummoor is perfect just as it is. We can make a very cosy little nest for ourselves in one wing."

"Oh — a cosy nest! That sounds quite wonderful, my sweet, and the dragons will not stay for ever, luckily."

"I do not mind if they do," she said. "Indeed, Lady Hester is too frail to live on her own. I should love to take care of her, and the others too, if they will let me. Now do not look so horrified, for they would have they own wing, and you would hardly see them, my love. And then you would have the income from their estates, you see, and you would not be in such want of funds."

"Good God, what a clever little thing you are! That is quite ingenious. Do you really like the dragons?"

"I do. It would be the most wonderful thing to have a huge family all around me. I have so many relatives that I have never seen," she said wistfully.

"Then it shall be as you wish, my darling. I wonder... your loveliness is driving me quite to distraction. Might I be permitted to kiss you?"

"Oh, yes. Yes, please."

He bent his head and gently brushed his lips against hers. Such sweetness, such softness, such warmth! "You taste of honey and... and all sorts of sweet things," he whispered.

"Why did you stop?" she whispered back, her lips quivering with merriment.

With a bubble of laughter, he leaned down to kiss her properly, the kiss of a lover at last, and to his astonishment and delight, she kissed him back with equal fervour. He thought his heart would burst with joy.

Thanks for reading!

If you have enjoyed reading this book, please consider writing a short review on Amazon. If you'd like to know more about the Allamont family and their friends, the next book in the series is **Dulcie: The Daughters of Allamont Hall Book 4**. You can read Chapter 1 at the end of this book

A note on historical accuracy: I have endeavoured to stay true to the spirit of Regency times, and have avoided taking too many liberties or imposing modern sensibilities on my characters. The book is not one of historical record, but I've tried to make it reasonably accurate. However, I'm not perfect! If you spot a historical error, I'd very much appreciate knowing about it so that I can correct it and learn from it. Thank you!

About the books

The Daughters of Allamont Hall is a series of six traditional Regency romances, featuring the unmarried daughters of Mr William and Lady Sara Allamont. When their father dies unexpectedly, his will includes generous dowries for the sisters, but only on condition that they marry in the proper order, the eldest first.

Book 1: Amy
Book 2: Belle
Book 3: Connie
Book 4: Dulcie
Book 4.5: Mary (a novella, free to mailing list subscribers)
Book 5: Grace
Book 6: Hope

About the author

I write traditional Regency romances under the pen name Mary Kingswood, and epic fantasy as Pauline M Ross. I live in the beautiful Highlands of Scotland with my husband. I like chocolate, whisky, my Kindle, massed pipe bands, long leisurely lunches, chocolate, going places in my campervan, eating pizza in Italy, summer nights that never get dark, wood fires in winter, chocolate, the view from the study window looking out over the Moray Firth and the Black Isle to the mountains beyond. And chocolate. I dislike driving on motorways, cooking, shopping, hospitals.

Any questions or comments about the series? I'd love to hear from you! Email me at mary@marykingswood.co.uk.

Acknowledgements

Thanks go to:

My grandparents, Henry and Hannah Austin, who named their four children Amy, Constance, Ernest and Frank, and thereby inadvertently inspired these books

My good friends at AC (you know who you are!) who provided me with advice, support, encouragement and kicks up the backside, hand-holding and hugs, laughs and tears, woo chickens, tacos and tubesteak

My beta readers: Mary Burnett, Clara Benson, Marina Finlayson

Last, but definitely not least, my first reader: Amy Ross

Sneak preview: Dulcie - Chapter 1: A Wager

Dulcie could scarcely believe her ears. "You want me to do *what*?"

Connie sighed. "I am not asking you to walk to Brinchester, sister, or trail through muddy fields. There is no need even to go into the village, for the schoolhouse is nearer than that. It is no distance through the woods, and you would be there and back in an hour, or not much above it."

"But I had planned to look through the journals you brought from London to decide on how to trim my new bonnet."

"And you will have the rest of the day to do so," Connie snapped. "I would go myself, but I must go to Brinchester with Mama and Hope if I am to have my clothes in time for the wedding."

"Why cannot Grace go to the schoolhouse?" Dulcie said.

"Because she has already agreed to go with Miss Bellows to High Brafton Farm to take some things for poor Mrs Tarpin. You would not have wanted *that* task, I know, for it is a long walk over the fields and through Brafton Woods. I am giving you the easiest commission, dear."

"I do not know why Jess Drummond thinks she is so important that we have to run round after her all the time," Dulcie said.

"Oh, Dulcie, have a little compassion," Connie said. "She is very sick, and although she has been bled and leeched repeatedly, nothing has answered. Mrs Cooper says that this broth of hers has never failed yet. It is her mother's receipt, it seems. Please, will you go? I should be happier knowing that Jess has this today, and the servants cannot be spared from their duties."

"Oh, very well, if I must. I suppose I can call in at Mr Wiseman's shop to make the journey worth my while."

"Thank you, dear," Connie said. "We should always show kindness to our neighbours in need."

"It is not for you to preach at me," Dulcie said sulkily.

"Perhaps not, but with Mama away, I must do my best to take her place."

"You may have charge of the household and give orders to the servants, but you have no right to give orders to *me*."

Connie sighed. "I give you no orders, dear, I merely make suggestions. But if I see you in error, I feel obliged, as both sister and closest friend, to give you a little hint. I sincerely wish that you would be kinder to those who need your help without so much argument, for it is very trying, I declare. Why can you not be more obliging?"

"I do not in the least mind being obliging," Dulcie cried, "but not to Jess Drummond, who has every advantage of beauty and wit, and enjoyed a splendid season in London, and instead of being grateful, she takes to her bed and sulks because she could not have the man she wanted."

"What a nasty, jealous thing to say!" Connie spat. "I despair of you, Dulcie. Such selfishness! If you want to make a good marriage, then you must strive to make yourself likable. Gentlemen do not like a waspish sort of wife."

"Just because you are betrothed to a marquess, you think you know everything about love and men and marriage," Dulcie said heatedly. "Well, I shall make a *very* good marriage, you may be sure of *that!*" And with those words, she stormed out.

~~~~~

Alex Drummond was tired. He had thought that being a village schoolmaster would be a quiet but rewarding life, with small faces gazing raptly up at him as he imparted the mysteries of numbers and the wonder of books to their innocent minds. Instead, he had six boisterous boarders, who shuffled restlessly on their benches, whispered behind their hands and raced each other to the door as soon as he released them. At least he was not required to feed and board them himself, for the cottage was too small. Instead, they stayed at the parsonage, which kept them out of the way, but also deprived him of a little extra money.

Apart from the boarders, there were a handful of farmers' and millers' children, who turned up unexpectedly for odd days, dirty and ragged, whenever their fathers could spare a coin or two, and disappeared for weeks on end to help with the harvest or lambing or painting the barn. It was dispiriting.

When he was not teaching, he was digging the small patch of ground behind the house, and watching his potatoes anxiously for signs of... he was not very sure what maladies might afflict potatoes, but if he saw a leaf disfigured with a brown or black patch, or a particularly noxious-looking beetle, he immediately fell into gloom that they would starve over the winter. And then there was the pig. Never had a beast caused him such worry before, except his horse once or twice, and that was understandable. The pig had seemed such a harmless creature when it first arrived, a little pink, bald thing scampering round its pen. But oh Lord, as it got bigger! Every time it lay down, he thought it was on the point of expiring, and it lay down a lot. His sister Jess was no help. She would just laugh, and say, "Can we eat it yet?" and then run away consumed by laughter..

He never imagined he would be quite so glad of the respite on the Sabbath. He had always previously found the prohibitions tiresome, but now he was heartily glad of a day when his only required activity was to walk to church and back twice. Mr Endercott, who held the living at Lower Brinford, was such a long-winded and soporific preacher that Alex even managed a nap during the sermons, with only Jess's kicks when he snored to disturb him.

He tried not to repine too much on the life he and Jess had left behind. Two years ago, he had had his own curricle and a magnificent hunter, and the promise of one of his father's subsidiary estates. It had made him one of the county's most eligible bachelors, and he had even begun to consider the prospect of marriage. That dream had died with his father, and the discovery of all his debts. The promised estate had been sold, and now he lived in poverty far from home, still moving on the fringes of society, but for how much longer? He could not go on patching and mending his good coats indefinitely, and he could certainly not afford to replace them yet.

Then there was Jess. It had seemed like such a good idea to let her go to London, pretending to be on the point of a betrothal to the Marquess of Carrbridge. She had had a real season in the very best circles, and, with her beauty and liveliness and accomplishments, had been a great success, if the reports were to be believed. Miss Endercott, the clergyman's sister who kept house for him, had brought Alex some of the notices in the London newspapers which had mentioned Jess along with the usual array of duchesses and viscountesses and the like. *'Miss Jessica Drummond of Wester Strathmorran in the county of Morranshire, Scotland'*, dancing with this or that earl or viscount. It had made him so proud of his sister. If only she had not met Mr Middleton, who had stolen away her heart and offered her nothing but—

Alex could not bear to think of that. Jess had refused Middleton, naturally, but she had returned home a shadow of her former lively self, and had gradually sunk into despondency and grief, and, inevitably, a physical decline to which there seemed to be no end.

When he had finished his meagre breakfast, and their maid Polly was clattering away in the scullery, he went into the kitchen and made some chocolate. Then he climbed the stairs to Jess's little room under the eaves. A quick knock on the door, and, after a moment of silence, he pushed it open and went in.

"Are you awake? I have brought you some chocolate, made just how you like it. Miss Connie Allamont was so kind as to bring some the other day, remember? Jess? Are you awake, dear?"

The covers on the bed writhed a little, and then a head of dark curls emerged. "Alex?" a muffled voice said.

"Indeed it is. I have brought you some chocolate to drink."

"You may leave it on the table. I will drink it in a little while."

"You said that last time, and then went back to sleep and forgot all about it. Can you sit up, if I help you? For I do think it would do you some good if you could drink just a little, you know."

With his help, she struggled to a half-sitting position, and managed three sips before she was exhausted. "Delicious," she said, her voice weak. As soon as she lay down again, she closed her eyes.

He straightened the blankets, so rough after the silken sheets they had grown up with, and quietly crept out of the room.

~~~~~

Dulcie was cross to begin with, after her spat with Connie, and became crosser still before she had even left the Hall grounds. The pot of broth was heavy in her basket, and her woollen cloak was too thick for summer wear and now she was hot. As if that were not enough, her old straw bonnet was scratching her ear. She should have gone upstairs to fetch her spencer and one of her pretty caps, but Connie was up there and she did not want to meet her again.

Once she and Connie had been like twins, doing everything together, sharing every thought, as close as two sisters could possibly be. But Connie had become so grand as soon as she had accepted the Marquess's proposal, and once she was a marchioness there would be no bearing her hauteur. Dulcie would have to address her as *'my lady'*, and curtsy to her, and give precedence everywhere. It was such a lowering thought. Dulcie had always secretly hoped that *she* would be the first of the sisters to catch a titled husband, and how was she to outrank Connie now? It would take a duke to do it, and there were only a few of those, most of them old or married.

What would become of her once Connie was married? There would only be Grace and Hope left, and they were just as close as Dulcie and Connie had ever been. There would be no room for Dulcie. She would be quite alone. Who could she chide and tease and quarrel with and lark about with? Who would help her trim bonnets and mend her gowns and tell her that she looked fetching in a new pelisse?

A worse thought — how was she ever to find a husband now? Under the terms of her father's will, the sisters had to marry in the proper order or forfeit the handsome dowry he had provided for them. Amy, Belle and Connie had all succeeded, and now it was Dulcie's turn. She *had* to find someone to marry or else she would be a spinster all her life, and her younger sisters with her.

She was practically an old maid already — three and twenty, and not a single offer to boast of. In a small corner of her mind was the thought that perhaps Connie was right, and Dulcie was just a horrid person that nobody liked, and that no man of standing in society would ever willingly marry her, even for her dowry of twenty thousand pounds. Apart from the cousins, of course, who stood to inherit Allamont Hall if they married one or other of the sisters, but James had a wife now and as for Mark and Hugo—! She shuddered, and hoped she was never that desperate for a husband.

By the time she reached the edge of the woods, the roofs of the village in sight, she was hot and miserable and not at all happy with her appointed role as benefactress to the poor and sick. To make matters worse, the brambles along the lane to the schoolhouse reached long, spiked fingers towards her, catching on her gown and tearing the delicate muslin, and scratching her face.

It was not surprising, therefore, that Dulcie was in something of a temper when she arrived at the little cottage that served as schoolhouse. It had been the gamekeeper's cottage once, in the days when the Allamont estate had boasted extensive shooting land. Most of that land had been sold off or leased out to neighbours, since Dulcie's father had never much cared for the sport. When the old gamekeeper had died a year or two ago, Grace had taken over the cottage for a school.

It was not much — just a schoolroom and parlour at the front, and a kitchen and scullery at the back, with some bedrooms tucked under the eaves. Behind the house were a few outhouses and a modest plot of land for chickens and a pig and some vegetables. Still, it looked neat and cared for. The window frames and doors had been repainted, there were flowers growing around the front door and the parlour had fresh curtains.

Polly, the maid of all work, was scrubbing the front step. She was a solidly-built woman of some thirty years, plain-faced, with round red cheeks that made her look like an apple. "Oh, Miss Allamont! Have you come to see Miss Jess?"

"I have brought some broth for her to try. Our cook thought it might help."

"That's right kind of you, so it is. Would you mind goin' in through the scullery door, 'cause I've just mopped the hall floor, and your feet's a bit dusty, like."

"What, like a servant? I hardly think so, Polly."

She pushed open the front door and strode into the hall.

A man's blond head appeared from the schoolroom door. "Polly? Oh, it is you, Miss Dulcie. I thought it must be a crisis, for Polly to walk over her clean floor."

Dulcie looked behind her at the trail of footprints. "Oh. She can mop it again, I daresay."

"Makin' extra work," Polly muttered, banging the bucket about.

"Well, never mind," Drummond said. "It will not take a moment to wipe over again." But Polly harrumphed, and disappeared round the outside of the house. Drummond sighed. "Do come inside, Miss Dulcie. It is kind in you to call." But his smile was strained.

"I have brought some broth for Jess. Our cook's mother always found it efficacious."

His face lightened. "Oh, how good you are to carry it all this way, and in this heat, too. It has been so hot that all my vegetables are wilting, and no doubt I shall be spending the evening watering again. Please, will you come through to the kitchen? I have no tea or coffee to offer you today, but the well water is cool and very refreshing."

He set down the books he was carrying and led the way to the kitchen at the back of the house. Polly was there before them, glaring reproachfully at Dulcie.

"What do we need to do with this broth?" Drummond said. "Just heat it on the fire?"

"How should I know?" Dulcie snapped. "I am not a cook."

"I can take care of it, Mr Drummond," Polly said, taking the pot from Dulcie. "Although I ain't a cook neither."

"Well, really!" Dulcie said. "Such impertinence! Just because I do *not* like to be sent round to the kitchen door like a servant."

Polly put her hands on her hips and was about to respond with equal vigour, but Alex Drummond waved his hands placatingly. "Thank you, Polly. Perhaps you could see to the goat now? If you would be so good."

She snorted, glared at Dulcie and then stamped away through the scullery.

"You must excuse Polly," Drummond said, running his hands through his hair. "We are all rather fraught at the moment, and so anxious for Jess."

"There is no improvement in her condition?"

"Far from it. Up until a day or so ago, she was able to get up and help a little — podding peas and so forth, chores that could be done while sitting. But now she keeps to her bed constantly and it is as much as she can do to drink a little water. Dr Torrington can find no cause for her malady, and no remedy to help."

"It is very likely a consequence of her stay in London," Dulcie said, not much interested in Jess's illness. "Too much gaiety is very debilitating."

"Hardly so," he said, his face darkening. "She may have been out enjoying herself every evening, but she slept late, ate the best food and had nothing at all to concern her. But she was completely taken in by this man she met there, this Jeffrey Middleton, who is *not* a gentleman, in my estimation. Her disappointment, combined with all the work she has to do here, is enough to account for her illness."

"Polly does most of the work, I imagine," Dulcie said. "What does Jess have to do, apart from a bit of cooking?"

"A bit of—!" He reddened and turned away from her, and when he turned back to her his words were clipped and angry. "I assure you, when she is well Jess works from first light until dusk. She takes care of the chickens, milks the goat and helps Polly with the laundry, for we cannot even afford to send it to Mrs Greenwood, and that is *not* what she is accustomed to. It is no wonder my poor sister has become exhausted and allowed this debilitation to overtake her. If only we could afford better food for her, and someone to take care of her. I fear for her life, truly I do, Miss Dulcie."

"I am sure she will recover soon enough," Dulcie said, not at all deterred. "We had a housemaid once who took to her bed like that, and could not be got to do the work she was paid to do. Papa beat her and she recovered quick enough after that."

"Are you suggesting that Jess is malingering?" There was no mistaking the anger in his voice now. "How dare you!"

Dulcie raised her chin defiantly. "I do not like your tone, Mr Drummond. It is my opinion that a lot of these vapours are mere figments of the imagination, and that with a sufficiently strong inducement, the person may discover themselves to be quite well after all."

"Quite well? Are you mad? I suggest that Jess is in mortal danger and the only sympathy you can offer is to suggest that her illness is all in her head?"

"That or laziness," she said with a shrug. "She has got very grand, after mingling with the cream of London society, and now she does not like the little bit of work she has to do."

"Jess works harder than anyone I know!" he answered hotly.

"Pfft! A little bit of cooking, and folding sheets once a week — that is nothing at all."

"I should like to see *you* do everything Jess does!"

"It would be easy! Anyone could do it."

"Very well, then, if you think it so easy, *you* come here and do all Jess's chores."

"Now you are being silly, and you are shouting at me, as well. I am leaving at once. You are very rude, Mr Drummond."

"Not as rude as you are, young lady, and at least I am not spoilt and ignorant, like you."

"I am *not* spoilt or ignorant. You just do not like to hear the truth!" she cried.

"Truth? You will have to demonstrate it. If you really believe that every task Jess carries out is easy, then prove it to me. Come here and do everything that Jess does — or did, when she was well enough."

"And what about *her*? She gets to sit about like a lady, I suppose, while I do her chores. A fine arrangement!"

"Well, why not? She *is* a lady, far more so than *you*. *She* should be the one at the Hall, wearing silk and diamonds, with servants to do her bidding and enough food to eat. She would not be ill if she were better looked after!"

"Oh, so she is to go to the Hall and play the grand lady while I scrub floors, is that the idea?"

His eyebrows lifted in surprise. "An excellent suggestion, Miss Allamont, I thank you. Indeed, that would be splendid."

"Nonsense! I did not mean—"

But he continued relentlessly. "You take over Jess's role here, while she goes to the Hall in your place to recruit her strength. Do that for a month, or until Jess is recovered, and I will believe all you say, but I wager you would not last a day."

"Of course I would!"

"Prove it!"

She was too angry to consider her words. Her chin lifted. "Very well, then, I will!"

END OF SAMPLE CHAPTER OF *DULCIE*